To:
Karla
Thank You.
Enjoy
and
Best Wishes

Vicki Eide

VICTORIA PLACE

BY VICKI EIDE

authorHOUSE®

AuthorHouse™
1663 Liberty Drive
Bloomington, IN 47403
www.authorhouse.com
Phone: 1-800-839-8640

First published by AuthorHouse 3/2/2011

ISBN: 978-1-4567-1211-2 (sc)
ISBN: 978-1-4567-1212-9 (e)
ISBN: 978-1-4567-1213-6 (dj)

Library of Congress Control Number: 2010917523

Printed in the United States of America

DEDICATION

To my husband Dave, my biggest fan and supporter

To my son Alan who provided legal information and
operations of a county sheriff's department

To my son Kevin who designed the cover

To all my family and friends who gave me encouragement to pursue

PART I

VICTORIA PLACE

CHAPTER 1

It was a warm breezy spring day as I strolled down the road in a silent methodical trance. The trees were so brilliant in colors of reds, pinks and white, and waved in the breeze as petals fell to the ground. Birds were singing in the trees as though they had their own choir, truly a unique sound.

I walked along reminiscing, chuckling to myself to some thoughts and shedding a tear at others. I was interrupted by children playing as they hurried home from school, if they only knew the trials and tribulations that were in store for them in the coming years.

They reminded me of some of my childhood days and soon I was lost, once again in tranquility. I came to a small clearing with a long driveway leading to a beautiful white colonial style house. The driveway was lined on both sides with various bright colors of all kinds of flowers. What a gorgeous bouquet of flowers these would make for the dining room table or better yet, a May basket to the elderly.

Then I remembered the May Day celebration we had in grade school, dancing around the May Pole to music and singing. May Day was a May 1st tradition originating in Great Britain by dancing and singing around a maypole, tied with colorful streamers. The children celebrated the day by moving back and forth holding the streamers and weaving them around the pole. We would make flower baskets and hang them on the doors of the elderly, knock on their door and then run so they wouldn't know who hung it there. This was a tradition that somewhere along the way got lost in the shuffle, what a shame; so many childhood traditions have been lost.

I saw a big flat rock across the road from the long driveway and sat to watch the sun slowly drop out of sight. What a beautiful sunset, the sky so bright red and yellow as if on fire and reflected the same through the windows of the Colonial style house. A sudden gust of wind reminded me of the cool late afternoons and I was wishing I had my jacket. How peacefully quiet it was. My trance was broken as dusk was shortening the day and making the idea of cuddling up in front of a roaring fire with a good book very enticing.

As I stood up to make my way back home, I stretched and took one last look at the beautiful home and perfectly manicured landscaping, something caught my eye. A fast movement in the front big bay window, I heard a shrill scream of a woman and bright flash then a pop sound that stopped me dead in my tracks.

CHAPTER 2

I took off on a sprint through the group of trees directly to the left of the driveway, ducking in and out of the trees keeping crouched low and hoping not to be spotted. At the back of the house I suddenly realized I did not have my glock, cell or my badge. What the Hell am I doing here? Then, he came running out of the house, dressed in black from his shoes to a hooded sweat shirt. He darted to the opposite end of the house from me and I heard the engine start. I ran just in time to see a bright yellow Hummer take off with such speed that the driver had very little control to keep the vehicle on the driveway and was swerving off and on the drive and into the lovely flowers I had been admiring.

I ran back to the house and through the open door calling out and listening for a voice or sound. Walking through the kitchen slowly, and then the formal dinning room I noticed the table was set for two. In the living room I saw a woman lying on the floor in a pool of blood. Kneeling down I checked for a pulse at the same time scanning the room for a phone. Her pulse was weak and when I spoke to her there was no response or reaction of any kind, not even a flicker of her eye lids.

I grabbed the phone and dialed 911. The emergency operator answered, "What is your emergency?"

"There has been a shooting, an elderly woman is bleeding and her pulse is very weak."

"What is your location?" the operator asked, and then it hit me – I don't even know where I am. I had been in such a trance; I had not paid any attention to my exact location or how far I had walked.

"Oh, My God! I don't know! I know I am on Victoria Place", I replied.

"What is your name, Ma'am?"

"I am Sergeant Brenda Lou Weathers."

"Sergeant?" she questioned, "Stay on the line, help is on way."

I know from experience 911 calls can be traced to an address from a telephone number. I stayed on the phone still holding the woman's hand, checking her pulse and talking to her. She was totally motionless and her pulse was getting weaker.

The operator asked me, "Sergeant Weathers, what are the woman's injuries?"

"I can't tell for sure, I don't know if she was hit in the head or the upper back, I have not moved her." I answered.

"Good, don't move her, just keep talking to her. Help will be there shortly."

I continued rubbing the woman's hand and talking, trying to get her name without success. What always seems like forever for emergency vehicles to arrive, I know is only a matter of minutes. However, minutes could be too late for this elderly woman. Sometimes it is hard to judge the age of some people and I felt this could be one of those times. She was very attractive, dressed complete with hose and heels, navy blue print dress and wearing pearls around her neck, hair impeccably done and her make up was typical of most elderly women, blue eye shadow and too much rouge. The jewelry she was wearing was enough to make anyone drool, a wedding set that I would bet had at least a four carat diamond with a lot of diamonds in the set, a ring on her right hand that had a huge emerald stone also circled with diamonds, a tennis bracelet and a pretty fancy watch with diamonds as well. It was very apparent to me that robbery was not the motive for the intruder.

CHAPTER 3

I could faintly hear the sirens in the distance as the 911 operator asked me if I could describe the surroundings and the house, which I did. I heard them coming closer and make the turn up the winding driveway. I tried to open the front door and found it had too many locks I couldn't figure out in my haste, I ran out the back door to the side of the house to wave them in.

As protocol, the fire truck was the first to arrive, followed by a police car and soon the ambulance. Three firemen got off the truck each grabbing an emergency bag, followed me into the house and immediately began to check the woman's vitals.

I saw the police car through the dining room window and recognized the first officer, Captain Neil Dawson. Crap, why couldn't he have just been one of the on duty patrol officers. I was not prepared for his interrogation. But then I never was. Having been with the San Diego County Sheriff's Department for ten years, I had worked my way up to Sergeant Detective. Captain Dawson was hired two years prior from Rancho Bernardo City Police Department and we seemed to have an immediate mutual understanding of dislike for one another. Dawson had the attitude that the woman's place was at home and in the kitchen and he was not the least bit shy about letting the other females in the department know exactly how he felt.

CHAPTER 4

It was about five years ago who my then partner, Sergeant Bob King and I had been working a case down on the water front. From out of nowhere a twelve year old kid with a twelve gauge sawed off shot gun shot Bob in the leg just at the top of the knee. The kid was later found and charged with a number of crimes from being a runaway, illegal possession of a firearm, attempted murder, possession and soliciting drugs, a full rap sheet. Considering his age he was tried as a juvenile and sentenced to a reform school for boys until he was eighteen years old. Last I had heard of the boy, he was imprisoned for murder less than six months after being discharged from the reform school. Unfortunately, Bob was in the hospital for twenty seven days, the doctors had to amputate his leg as he had several infections the doctors were fighting. I stopped by to see Bob periodically and he seemed to be doing fairly well, although his wife, Penny, told me he was in a constant battle with depression. Dawson has held that over my head making it very clear I was responsible for not covering Bob and being more cautious. I have tried to stay out of Dawson's way as much as possible and I knew this encounter wasn't going to be any more pleasant than any other time.

"Well, Well, Well, if it isn't Sergeant Brenda Lou in person", were the first words out of Dawson's mouth.

"Good afternoon Captain Dawson, it's good to see you too."

The Captain and I made a quick sweep through the house to be sure no one else was there. Each room was 'spit polished and shined' and didn't appear to have anything out of place.

When we returned to the EMT I asked how the woman was doing and his response was less than encouraging. She had been shot in the back to the left of her right shoulder blade, but he was more concerned about her irregular heart beat and extremely high blood pressure than the wound itself. He had been able to stop the bleeding and had a compression bandaged over the wound. The ambulance had arrived and the EMTs were bringing the gurney in to transport her to the hospital.

"Ma'am," the EMT said to me, "What is your mother's name, how old is she and I..............."

"Whoa, wait a minute, this woman is not my mother and I have no idea how old she is. I don't even know her name. I just sort of happened by."

"Would you look around, find something with her name on it; get her medications and anything else the hospital might need such as insurance cards and phone numbers?"

I looked for Dawson and found him outside talking with other officers that had been called to the scene. By this time there were three more patrol cars. They were getting ready to tape the place as a crime scene. I told him what I was going to do and needed one of his officers to accompany me in my search. He called out to Officer William (Willy) McClain, "Go with her and watch your back." Damn, he is such an ass.

CHAPTER 5

Willy and I walked back into the house the EMTs had the woman on the gurney, an oxygen mask over her face, IVs in her arm, a heart monitor attached and was bringing her out to the ambulance. One of the guys gave me his card and said they would be transporting her to Valley View Medical Center and to bring the information requested a.s.a.p.

"Willy, let's start in the kitchen for mail and a name", I said. Willy agreed and we started opening drawers. The first drawer was the polished silverware, the second was neatly folded and pressed cloth napkins, the third drawer was cocktail paper napkins of various colors in individual stacks and all kinds of colored toothpicks and miniature forks, cheese spread knives, etc. Each drawer was very neat and tidy and evident of a woman that did lots of entertaining.

We left the kitchen in search of an office that was the second door down the hall. There was a very neat pile of unopened mail and another of opened mail. I started going thru the envelopes and noticed a variety of names: Mrs. B.L. Compton, Mrs. Blake Compton, Ms. Eleanor Compton and one that was just addressed to Miss Ellie. I carefully went through the opened stack of mail and found two envelopes that were addressed to Mrs. Blake Compton and Mrs. Eleanor Compton and gave them to Willy.

We went upstairs to the master bedroom and in the master bath was a drawer with six prescription bottles neatly lined up on the right side, on the left side of the drawer were aspirin, gluecosimine, calcium and vitamin C and a tiny bottle of digitalis. I opened the door under the sink and as luck would have it there was a box of small garbage liners, I took one and put all the medications, including the vitamins, in it, and Willy added the two envelopes to the collection.

I wanted to find Mrs. Compton's purse to take to her. Besides, I was sure there would be insurance cards and hopefully an address book for names and phone numbers of family or someone to contact. I went to the night stand on the left side of the bed with a single lamp. In the drawer was a Bible and box of Kleenex. On the right night stand was a lamp, telephone and radio alarm clock, in the drawer a book, another tiny bottle of digitalis, and a pair of glasses and a flashlight. No purse. Willy and I quickly went through all the drawers and the closet; we found several purses that were empty. We took the bag of prescriptions and headed back to the living room. I looked in the entry closet and there it was hanging on a hook. Inside appeared to be the information the hospital would need and an address book. Then it occurred to me Mrs. Compton might have listed in the front of the phone book important contact numbers and there they were: doctors, names and phone numbers. The only name that made for sure sense from the list was a Daryl Compton, which could be her son. There were two numbers after Daryl's name, one I assumed to be a residence and the other a cell phone. I tore that page from the phone book and added it to the sack of collectables.

After a quick conversation with Captain Dawson it was concluded that Willy would take me home, deliver the sack to the hospital and return to the crime scene. I would go home, call my partner Sam Davis, gather my badge, cell phone, and weapon, make a quick change of clothes and go to the hospital.

As Willy and I started towards the patrol car, the Captain hollered to me, "Hey, B.L., meet me at the precinct as soon as you're finished at the hospital. And don't dilly dally".

CHAPTER 6

The first thing I did when I got home was call Sam. "Sam, I have just witnessed a shooting over on Victoria Place off Dunlap Road. I need to talk to you about it; can you meet me at Valley View Medical Center in forty five minutes."

"I'll come get you and we can talk on the way".

"No, because I have to meet Dawson at the precinct when I am done."

"Brenda, we have had this conversation before, if you are going to meet with Dawson, I will go with you. We agreed you don't have to meet him alone, Okay?"

"Okay, Okay, get here as quickly as you can, and Sam, thank you".

I got in the shower, did a fast blow dry on my hair, slightly damp I did a single braid wrapped around into a bun and pinned it in. Put on some blush, eye shadow and liner grabbed clean underwear, black slacks, red blouse and black jacket. In the drawer next to the sliding back door, I picked up my weapon, put my badge and cell phone in my pocket, cleaned my glasses and set my purse on the table. This took a total of seventeen minutes and Sam was at the door.

When we were in the car and heading towards the hospital Sam said, "Fill me in Brenda."

I explained, "I had gone for a walk and was sitting on a rock across the road admiring the Colonial style house and the beautiful flowers along the winding driveway, I saw a flash, heard the woman scream and then the shot. I ran through the trees to the back of the house as someone totally dressed in black ran out the back door and got into a yellow hummer. He drove so erratically that he tore up many of the flowers and left tire tracks all over. I went in the house and found the woman lying on the living room floor in a pool if blood. I called 911, got the emergency on the way and of course Captain Dawson was the first response officer. Damn, he is an arrogant S.O.B. Anyway, Dawson and I did the security check in the house and found no one else around. Dawson sent McClain and me to find out her name, get meds, etc. to take up to the hospital. Willy dropped me off at home and delivered the stuff to the hospital and was to report back to the house. Then I called you and that's pretty much it."

"Were you able to get a license number of the hummer?" Sam asked.

"Of course not, Sam, I didn't have my glasses on and you know I can't read anything more than two inches from face without them."

Sam smiled and said, "So what were you doing over there anyway, Bee?" Bee is his pet name for me when he is showing concern, compassion and endearment.

CHAPTER 7

Sam and I have had our moments, but I have tried to keep us at arms length and keep it as low keyed and professional as I could. Sam was married for fourteen years and lost his wife to cancer about five years ago. About the same time Bob was shot. Sam had taken a six month leave from the department to take care of Linda and their three children. Linda took a fast turn for the worst and was gone in less than thirty days. Sam was devastated as he really believed they were going to win the battle with cancer. Friends and family were there for him and the children, but he was going deeper into a depression. It wasn't long after that Sam's Mother and Dad moved in with him and tried to take over. The children: Sean - twelve, Sara - ten and Sandy was eight were starting to become real handfuls, especially Sean since he was the oldest and thought he could run the house and boss the girls. Everyone was complaining to everyone else, except to Sam who was holed up in the master suite upstairs and refused to come down stairs. Mrs. Davis gave up trying to convince Sam to join all of them for meals and would take a tray to him.

This lasted two months after Linda had died when Monica, Sam's sister made a surprise visit. Monica was about 5'3", 112 lbs., light auburn hair and the most beautiful shade of green eyes I have ever seen. She had the sweetest disposition and calmness about her until she was riled. Then 'Katie bar the doors', Monica was riled. She had listened to her Mother whine, and it was whining and crying because she wasn't strong enough to take a stand on any situation with Sam.

That Saturday when Aunt Monica arrived is a day they all remember, then with fear and today with laughter. She spent about fifteen minutes talking with her Mother, marched upstairs, knocked on Sam's door, didn't wait for a response, walked in and yanked the covers off the bed and told Sam to get up and get in the shower, they were going out. She started going thru drawers and got underwear, socks, shirt and jeans out of the closet, threw them at him and said he better be out of the shower and shaved in fifteen minutes, then stormed out.

Her next stop was in Sara's room where both girls were fighting over a game. After the brief hugs and kisses she asked the girls to follow her to Sean's room, repeated the hugs and kisses and then sat then down on the bed. They were to follow her instructions without an argument: take a shower, get dressed and clean their rooms, take all their dirty clothes to the laundry room and hang up the clean. She and Sam would be back later that afternoon and it all better be done. And that is pretty much how it went for the first week she was there. The second week she sent her parents back to their home in Seattle. Monica had convinced Sam to go to a therapist and/or group therapy and he reluctantly consented.

Monica stayed another week as life seemed to be getting back to some sort of a normal style for all of them and Sam was getting better.

"Bee, I asked you a question, what were you doing over there?"

"I told you I had gone for a walk, was just thinking, sat on the rock admiring the house, that's when it all happened."

"So what were you thinking about that took you so far from your house?"

"Oh, you know me, I just got into one of my trances, it was nothing, just thinking, that's all."

"Yes, I do know you and there is usually an intent or issue that takes you there."

"Nah, oh, we're here, let's go in and see how Mrs. Compton is."

"Great, we'll take this up later."

"Nothing to take up," and I got out of the car.

CHAPTER 8

Sam and I walked into the waiting area of the hospital and to the information desk and I asked, "I would like Mrs. Eleanor Compton's room number, please."

Without looking at the computer screen or registry she said, "Are you family?"

"No I am not family, but I witnessed Mrs. Compton being shot. I am Sergeant Weathers and this is my partner Detective Davis. I would like to talk with the Doctor if possible."

"Yes, Miss Ellie came in about an hour and a half ago and I believe she is still in surgery. Let me check the nurse's station on the surgical floor, excuse me just a moment."

When she hung up the phone she said, "Miss Ellie is just leaving the surgery room and going into ICU. You can go up to the fourth floor and tell the nurses who you are and that you want to speak to the doctor. She'll have you wait in the lounge where the doctors come out to speak with those waiting."

"Thank you so much," and we turned towards the elevator.

On the fourth floor we sat in the waiting area making small talk and looking at magazines. Suddenly, I felt hungry. I guess my slice of toast and small glass of orange juice for breakfast and a small strawberry yogurt for lunch wasn't enough to hold me till dinner. I looked at my watch and it was 7:45 p.m., no wonder I was hungry. Naturally every magazine I picked up had nothing but pictures of food and recipes. Sam seemed to be engrossed in a sports magazine, so I leaned my head against the wall and closed my eyes for just a few minuets.

Sam nudged my arm and I saw a tall middle aged man that was obviously a surgical doctor dressed in powder blue pants and shirt with a matching blue cap and booties over his shoes, walking towards us. He smiled and extended his hand to us and said, "I'm Doctor Cutter, you must be here for Mrs. Compton?"

"Yes, I am Sergeant Weathers and this is my partner Detective Davis. How is Mrs. Compton doing?"

"She's just barely holding her own. We got the bullet out and sent it over to ballistics, but it was a very tricky surgery. She is one lucky lady if she survives. The bullet went in through the right shoulder blade, crossed her body at an angle, missed the spine and lodged just below her heart and missed everything in between. My concern is that we have been treating her heart condition and battling high blood pressure for several months now. She was unconscious when she came in, that could be related to shock. She might stay this way for a couple days and this could be good, but much more than that, we have another set of problems. She didn't lose much blood and the path of the bullet was pretty clean. Miss Ellie, as we all call her at the office, is a pretty spry and tough ole gal and she is a fighter", and again he smiled.

"How old is Mrs. Compton?"

"I believe she is eighty eight or eighty nine. I know she's not yet ninety."

"Wow, she is one classy looking lady. What about her family, has anyone been called them?"

"They have two children, Daryl and Susanne. I believe Daryl is in Chicago and Susanne is in Florida. I don't know if they have been called yet, you can check the nurse's station," the Doctor replied.

"Can you tell us anything about Daryl and Susanne?" Sam asked.

"Not much, and I need to get back in and check on Miss Ellie. All I know is that Daryl has a law firm in Chicago and Susanne is married to some politician and living in Florida. I know Susanne has been estranged from her mother for a number of years. Please excuse me, I must go now." He extended his hand again to both of us then turned and walked away.

"Thank you so much doctor." I said and he gave a slight wave.

Sam and I sat down in the comfy waiting room chairs, looked

at each other and almost simultaneously said, "Let's check with the nurses."

At the nurses station Sam asked the only nurse there, "Excuse me, do you know if any of the family have been notified about Mrs. Compton?"

"Let me check." She turned to her computer, clicked a few keys and said, "It looks like the emergency room receptionist placed a call to Daryl Compton and Susanne Farrell about 5:30, right after she got here. You do realize there is a three hour difference in time to the East Coast."

"Yes, I realize that. Has anyone tried them again?" Sam asked.

"It doesn't appear so," she said.

I stepped a little more forward and said to the nurse, "One of our officers brought a plastic sack that had Mrs. Compton's purse, medications and a sheet I tore out of the phone book that has a list of names and numbers. Would you by chance have that list that I can have, actually a copy would be just fine?"

"I believe Mrs. Compton's purse is in the safe downstairs in the main office. You won't be able to get it until tomorrow morning, sorry," the nurse explained.

"May I have Daryl and Susanne's phone numbers and I'll get the others in the morning?" I asked.

She gave me a questioning look, I pulled my badge out of my pocket and held it up in front of her. She turned and grabbed a piece of paper and jotted the numbers down and handed it to me.

"Thank you very much," and I turned to Sam and said, "Shall we go now?"

CHAPTER 9

We were walking out of the hospital Sam and said, "Let's get you something to eat, I'm sure you haven't had enough food today to keep a bird alive and I am starving. What sounds good to you?"

"I'm really not hungry now, Sam, but we can stop and get you something."

"Okay, let's just get a couple sandwiches from Subway, and then we can go back to your place."

We were driving back to my place with the sandwiches when I suddenly remembered I was supposed to go by the precinct. "Sam, you need to drop me off at home, I need to go to the precinct and meet with the Captain."

Sam pulled off the side of the road, turned to me and said, "Do you have any idea what time it is and do you really think Dawson is still there? Bee it is 9:45."

"I know, but he told me to report in when I left the hospital. I don't need to give him anymore ammunition to hold against me."

Without a word Sam turned the car around and started back to the precinct. Sounding a bit irritated Sam said, "Call, see if he is still there."

I called the office, the dispatcher answered and informed me he was not in his office. I tried his cell phone and when his voice mail came on I left a message, "Captain, this is Sergeant Weathers, it is now almost ten, since you are not in the office, I am going home and will report in the morning. Have a good night."

Sam turned the car around and once again we were headed back to my place.

As we entered my house I put my weapon and badge in the drawer and cell phone on the top of the stand by the front door. Went to the kitchen and got a bottle of wine and two glasses, two plates and napkins and went into the living room and placed them on the coffee table in front of the sofa. Sam was standing in front of the window, just staring out.

"Dinner is served, would you like to join me?"

I flipped on the news to see if there was anything about Mrs. Compton. There was only a brief blurb that the incident was under investigation. We ate in silence and watched the rest of the news.

CHAPTER 10

I started to pick up the plates, Sam grabbed my arm, and he picked up the plates and took them into the kitchen. When he came back he sat at the end of the sofa facing me and said, "Okay Bee, what is going on in your head?"

"Sam, I had a pretty busy afternoon. I shouldn't have to explain this again."

"You know that is not what I am talking about. There is nothing we can do about the incident tonight, we'll deal with it in the morning. What I am talking about is about you and me. You have been getting more distant from me in the past couple months than ever before. What's going on.?

"Let's not get into this tonight. It is late and I am exhausted."

"Bee, I know it's late, but I need to know what is going on with you."

"Sam, we have had our moments, it was nice and I do not regret one second of it. But this can't continue. We are partners, you know the rules of the department and we have been real lucky so far this past year. This isn't where I intended us to go, I want to be best friends, and we are; I want us to be partners we can depend on and trust, and we have that. Sam, we can't cloud all that with a relationship and a love triangle." I pleaded.

"What do you mean by a 'love triangle'?

"I mean you and me and your children. They would be part of this equation."

"So is this about my children?" Sam questioned as he raised an eyebrow.

"Of course it's not entirely about your children. I adore them and I believe they are equally comfortable with me. They need more stability in their lives than two parents keeping all hours of the night and day in life threatening jobs. They need a mother like Linda was and I can't be that to them."

Sam scooted across the sofa and put his arms around me and said, "Oh Baby, you can't do this to us. You know how I have felt for a very long time and I have been patient. I thought I could control my feelings toward you and instead they just keep getting deeper. I am in love with you, Bee."

I started to pull away and Sam held me tighter and closer and said, "Please don't. We can work this all out. I know you have feelings for me even if you won't admit it. Don't pass up the potential of a good thing."

I was trying to hold back, but the tears were streaming down my face. Sam released his hold and I got up from the sofa and went to the kitchen to clean up. Sam came in, turned me to him, cupped my face in his hands, with a gentle kiss on the lips then the forehead he said, "Let me get this, you get into bed and I will let myself out." He took his thumbs and gently wiped my tears. With that big beautiful smile of his he whispered to me, "We can work this out, please don't walk away." And he let go.

I went to my bedroom and climbed into bed.

CHAPTER 11

I woke the next morning to the sound of my phone ringing. I grabbed my glasses and checked the caller I.D. and saw it was Dawson and automatically I glanced at the clock, six thirty. I groaned and lay back down. I chose not to answer the call and just let it ring, I would call him in a few minutes. I got up and went in to make coffee and heard the ring of the cell phone indicating a message. I listened and of course I knew it was going to be from my captain. I listened, "Detective Weathers, report to my office promptly at 0700." That gave me thirty minutes to shower, get dressed and drive into downtown San Diego. I couldn't do it. I would be late.

Captain Dawson has always picked on me. He seemed to find fault with my procedures, my tactics and if everything else failed he could find fault with my personal life, which was on the edge of harassment. And there he seemed to be able to the draw the line to protect him self.

I contemplated calling Sam, then gave second thought to it and decided I would face the music on my own. I knew Sam would be angry as we had the conversation many times that I should not meet with the Captain alone. He is arrogant, egotistical and has a unique way of putting people down, yet keeping in the realms of being legal.

I got in the shower and got ready as quickly as I could and headed into town. I chose not to call either the Captain or Sam. With my traveler of coffee and the radio turned up I tried to put my mind into the music. I reached into the glove box and grabbed a pack of cigarettes and lit one. I had quit several months ago, but it was times like this I relied on them. Stupid, I know, but that was my hidden crutch and secret.

I walked into the precinct and announced to the dispatcher that the Captain was expecting me. It was now seven fifteen and she told me to go in.

I knocked on his door and he said, "Come in."

I walked in with my traveler of coffee and he said, "I see you brought your own coffee, good idea, this stuff you couldn't cut with a butcher knife. Sit down." And he gestured to a chair in front of his desk. "So Sergeant Weathers, why not tell me of the events of yesterday."

I proceeded to tell him everything, of course with the exception of Sam's and my conversation. He asked the same question Sam did, "Were you able to get the license plate number of the Hummer?"

I replied, "No, I did not have my glasses on and he drove away to fast."

"Why did you not have your weapon, badge, cell phone and glasses, Sergeant?'

"Sir, I was on the last day of my vacation, I was off duty. I took an extra day of vacation; I had just returned Monday morning from visiting my parents in Boise and my little sister's wedding on Sunday. I had decided to take a walk while laundry was drying. I was still on vacation. The department should be pleased that I was there because I probably saved Mrs. Compton's life, if she lives."

"Kudos for you. And what is Mrs. Compton's condition?"

Gritting my teeth and ignoring his first remark I answered, "We talked with the doctor and he said she was holding her own. She is in I.C.U. and it could be touch and go for a few days. She has other issues besides the gun shot wound which is her heart and extremely high blood pressure. The doctor said, and I quote, 'she is a tough ole' bird'."

"So I am guessing, we, means you and Detective Davis?" He asked, with a smirk.

"Yes, Sir, it does."

"Let me remind you, Sergeant Weathers, of the department's policy about fraternizing with those within the department," he said as he stood up and crossed his arms in front of his upper body.

"What is that supposed to mean? I am completely aware of

department policies, Sir. Sam happens to be my partner. Is there anything else?"

"Well, you know how rumors can fly around the precinct. I will be giving this case to Detectives George Jones and Stan Johnson. I want your complete report on my desk by seventeen hundred hours today. That is all."

I stood up and looked him squarely in the eye and said to him, "You can't do this, I was first on the scene. I want this case and I deserve this case and Sam and I have already made our preliminary plans for this case."

He leaned across the desk with both hands on the desk and looked me square in the eye and said, "Don't you dare tell me what I can and cannot do. You have screwed up damn near every case you have been on and almost cost the life of one of our best Sergeants. So unless you have something else to say, you can let your sweet ass out of here. You are excused, Sergeant Weathers."

I am ordinarily a pretty easy going person, I don't like confrontation unless forced into it and I feel I have been a very good detective having been in police work for the past ten years. I was not about to take his crap now.

I got up from my chair and walked over to his desk and positioned myself in the same manor as the Captain. Hands on the desk and approximately eighteen inches from his nose, "You know I am a damned good detective, and have closed more cases than you know about. The only thing you are holding me accountable for is the incident with Sergeant King. You weren't even around here then. You know that was not my fault. Bob told you that all the police reports confirmed it was an unfortunate and unavoidable accident. And yes, I have regretted that day ever since and wished I could have done something different. But you and I both know there wasn't a thing that could have been changed. You have been Captain for two years and you have ridden my ass for one reason or another and I am done with them all. And yes, there is one more thing I have to say. I want this case. Don't force me to challenge your decision."

"Is that a threat, Sergeant?" he said with another one of his smart ass smirks.

"No, Captain that was a promise." And I turned and stormed out slamming the door. The door slammed with such velocity the dispatcher jumped as did the others in the office. I just kept walking and felt everyone's eyes follow me until I got on the elevator.

CHAPTER 12

When I got outside, I stepped around the corner and leaned up against the wall and closed my eyes for a second. Taking in some deep breaths, I was shaking and felt like I wanted to throw up. I can be tough in almost any situation, but I hate shit like this. I hate having my integrity being questioned and my morals being attacked. That was what he was trying to do and I let him.

I was reliving Dawson's conversation and the more I thought about it the angrier I got. My Dad had been a police officer for 40 years before he retired. He had covered almost every area of policing during his career. So this was a field I had grown up in.

"Are you okay, Brenda?" I opened my eyes and was staring into Sam's.

"Oh just lovely," I replied. "Dawson and I just exchanged some unpleasantries right after he told me he was giving the Compton case to Jones and Johnson. It became a screaming match and got ugly and I slammed the door leaving his office. This is as far as I got."

"He can't do that, this is your case and I am your partner, therefore it is our case. Besides Jones and Johnson are the worst in the department. What was his reason behind that decision?"

"Because he is an S.O.B., because he doesn't like me, because he still blames me for King's accident and because he can. Plain and simple."

"I wish you would listen to me once in awhile and had let me go with you to talk to him. I am going up and talk with Dawson right now," Sam said.

"Do what you want. I'm going to the hospital and check on Mrs. Compton, go over to Bob King's and then I am going home. I have some serious thinking to do." I turned and walked away.

I got in my car and drove to the hospital, then I took the elevator to the surgical floor on the fourth and over to the nurses station. "I'm

Sergeant Weathers and I would like to inquire about Mrs. Compton's condition." I took out my badge before she had the chance to ask if I was family. She looked at one of the other nurses and said, "Would you mind having a seat in the waiting area and I will check, I believe the doctor is in with Mrs. Compton. It could be a few minutes." She smiled and walked towards the ICU unit.

It wasn't long until Dr. Cutter came out and sat down next me. "Good morning, doctor, how is our patient doing?"

"There isn't a lot of change. She had a restless night but is resting comfortably now. When you found Miss Ellie, was she next to anything that she could have hit with her head when she went down?"

I tried to remember the layout of the room and the surroundings around her when I found her on the floor. "Gosh, I don't think so. I came in thru the kitchen, then the dining room which had a wood railing between that and the living room and one step down. There was a long table against the railing and to the right a chair and footstool. Maybe she hit her head on the footstool, but I can't remember if she was that close or not. I can go back out to the house and check all of that if you would like," I said.

"That might be helpful. We are going to take her to ex-ray and check her head. Her eyes are dilated that could indicate a head injury, but then shock and trauma will show the same results. She has certainly experienced both shock and trauma. We would appreciate any information regarding her fall," he replied, again with that gorgeous smile.

I stepped back over to the nurse's station and asked if she would check to see if there had been any contact with Mrs. Compton's son or daughter. She checked her computer and told me there had only been the one attempt. When I got downstairs to the main desk I asked the receptionist for the phone list from Mrs. Compton's purse, and again I flashed my badge. She smiled and nodded, "Sure, just a moment." When she returned she had the list.

As I drove to the Victoria Place house my thoughts wandered to

Sam and his meeting with Dawson. I could only imagine how that was going. Sam is a gentle and soft speaking man, but still has that firmness about him. I have never seen a temper displayed from Sam; however, he has a quiet controlling way. I had just turned onto the driveway and my cell phone rang. It was Sam, "Hello Sam, how did it go?"

"Where are you?"

"I am at the Compton house."

"Stay there, I'm on my way," and he hung up.

I got out of my car and went to the back door. There were two officers who had guarded the house during the night. I showed my badge, with their nod of approval I went in. I stood in the dining room looking into the living room and pool of blood on the carpet. The living room had been taped off with yellow crime scene tape and I saw no reason for me to cross it at this point. I could see all I needed too. The wooden foot stool with a beautiful tapestry cover was turned on its side next to the pool of blood. That was enough to confirm to me that Mrs. Compton had hit her head when she fell.

Back outside I called the hospital to talk to Dr. Cutter; he was unavailable although still in the hospital. I asked to speak to Mrs. Compton's nurse, and then left the message that it was my opinion Mrs. Compton had hit her head on the foot stool when she fell. I left my phone number and said to feel free to call if there was anything else I could do.

I found a swing chair in the back yard under a weeping willow tree and sat there waiting for Sam. I called Dad and told him about Dawson's and my conversation. He was furious, "Sis, Dawson has crossed the line of sexual harassment. You need to file a complaint to the Sheriff or DHR or both. I have a feeling he is just playing you, but this is totally unacceptable. And his 'sweet ass' remark just hung him out to dry. Don't let this drop, Baby. He needs to be called in for that. What did Sam say?"

"I haven't talked to Sam about it other than a brief moment when I was too steamed to talk. But when I left the precinct Sam was going to Dawson's office to confront him. I am waiting for Sam now; I just wanted to talk to you."

CHAPTER 13

Although, my parents have never met Sam, they have a sense of security and respect for him that he was taking care of and protecting me. And they were absolutely correct. Sam does his absolute best to care and protect me and wants much more than they are unaware of, so I thought.

I had made my home in different little suburbs of San Diego since moving back eleven years ago. Even though I visited my parents a couple times a year and they had come to visit me, I missed them terribly, especially times like this when Dad's opinions were so valuable.

When Dad had completed twenty years and retired we moved from San Diego to a small town out of Boise, Idaho, Sun Valley. Dad's parents lived in the area which prompted the move to Sun Valley. We loved it there. I was twelve years old when we moved and my little sister, Candy, was nine. Dad took almost a year off and then joined the City of Sun Valley Police Department where he became Chief of Police until he retired a year ago. Dad and I have always been very close and I certainly took advantage of his expertise. After high school I attended four years at Boise State and graduated in elementary education. Why I thought I wanted to be a teacher is beyond me. I taught one year of seventh grade kids and thought I would lose my mind before the year was over. That is the most unruly age of children and I immediately decided I wanted to move to kindergarten or first grade. During my first year of teaching I met Brian. Brian was a medical student and would be doing his internship at Boise Medical Center. We fell madly in love and were married that summer.

In the fall I started teaching first graders and loved it. At Easter that year Brian announced we would be moving to San Diego as he had been offered a position in a private practice. One of his fellow class mates, Keith, would be working in his father's clinic and would eventually take over the practice. Brian was excited, as was I. I would have followed Brian to the end of the earth. My parents were less than happy about the move, but they still had Candy at home, soon to be graduating from Boise State in accounting. Brian and I loaded all of our worldly possessions in the U-Haul truck. Brian was driving the truck and towing his car and I followed driving m car. We kept in touch via our cell phones and had a great time in the travel to San Diego. We rented a cute little house not too far from the clinic that Keith had found for us. I was unable to find a teaching job that fall and became bored rapidly. Brian was working long hours in the clinic, when he came home for dinner, he would often leave for the hospital to make rounds. Seemed he was always covering for Keith or Keith's Dad. I hardly saw Brian during the week and then he took up golf that occupied most of his Saturdays and sometimes into the evenings if there was an awards dinner or cocktails, etc.

I decided I would check the college for a Police Academy. They had a six week program that would be starting in January, so I signed up. One evening over dinner I told Brian what I had done and he blew up. That was the stupidest thing he had ever heard of and forbid me to go into the program. I was shocked at his attitude and had never seen that side of Brian. He finished half of his dinner and stormed out saying he was going to make rounds. Brian did not come home that night and I finally fell asleep on the couch waiting for him. When he came in the next morning he went straight to the bath room, showered, shaved and changed clothes. He came out and headed straight for the door. "Brian?" and he turned to me and said "There is nothing to discuss, Brenda." And out the door he went. The next two weeks were the worst of my entire life. Brian was home less than ever and when he was he wouldn't talk to me rationally at all. He finally came home one evening and told me he would be moving out on the week end, so decide what I wanted and what he could take. I was so blind sided by his statement I could hardly breathe. Brian moved out that week end and moved right in with his girlfriend. As it turned out the new girl friend was Keith's sister that had also gone to medical school and was one of the doctors at the clinic. I never saw it coming. All I lived for was to get through the next three months until the Police Academy started and I could move on from there. I signed up in a couple of local school districts to substitute teach and that helped some to keep my mind off Brian and occupy some of my time until January.

CHAPTER 14

I looked up to see Sam walking across the lawn towards me. I was anxious about his conversation with Dawson. When Sam got to me he noticed my tear streaked face, wiped my cheeks with his handkerchief, pulled me into his arms and said, "It's going to be okay."

"So what happened, what did Dawson say?" I asked.

"Not too much. I just went into his office and he started in with his usual arrogant defense, I held my hand up, told him to stop and hear me out and then he could make his decision. I said to him, 'You have been all over Brenda from the very beginning and it is time you stop it and now. Brenda is a damn good detective and you know it. You are on the verge of sexual harassment and I am sure you do not want to go there. This is Brenda's case, I am her partner, therefore our case and we are going to take it, and with your full cooperation, I might add. Now unless you have information that I am unaware of that should keep us off this case, I believe our conversation is over' and I started to walk out. Of course, he could not let it go, with his powerful voice ordered me to stop and said 'I believe you just threatened me and I will not stand for that'. I walked back towards his desk and merely told him I was not threatening him, he was wrong and he knew it and he needed to rethink his position before it bit him in the ass. I walked out of his office. So, Sergeant Weathers, let's get to work, we have lots to do."

"I called Dad and told him about all this and he says I need to go to the Sheriff and DHR and report Dawson. He said Dawson has crossed the line and needs to be reprimanded and put a stop to all this bull shit."

Sam replied, "You can and probably should, but I think he knows he is has wronged you and maybe with your threat and mine, he might do some behavioral rethinking. You do what you need to do and you

32

know I will support you. Think about it and in the meantime, let's just move forward with this case, okay?"

"But Sam, Dawson told me to have my report on his desk at five o'clock today, that he had already turned the case over to Jones and Johnson."

"I know what he said, but that was only a threat and his scare tactic. I do not believe he is going to act on it considering everything else. I am choosing to ignore it."

"Okay then, let's get to work. I have the list of phone numbers from the hospital; no one has made another attempt to contact Daryl or Susanne. I was going to stop by Bob's for a few minutes; guess I'll do that another time. Let's go to my place since its close and start making calls, okay?"

CHAPTER 15

It was getting close to noon as we left Compton's house. I figured Sam would be getting hungry so I made a quick stop by the store. Since I had been on vacation the prior week I knew there wasn't anything in the refrigerator.

When I got to my house Sam was sitting out on the patio, jacket draped over a chair, enjoying the sun. Sam came over to the car to help with groceries and my computer case that I carried everywhere. "What a beautiful spring day," he said.

"I know, I watched the weather while I was in Sun Valley. It was so cold there, I was wishing I was back home," I laughingly replied.

Sam set the computer on the table and I put the groceries on the counter. Before I had a chance to start putting them away, Sam turned me into him and planted one of his soft, gentle kisses on my lips. When we finally came up for air, Sam held me tight and said, "Bee, I missed you so much, I wished I could've gone with you."

"I know, I missed you, too. But you know we couldn't both be gone from the department at the same time," I said still in his arms.

I freed myself and started getting stuff ready to make sandwiches and put the rest of the groceries away. Sam leaned against the wall watching me, arms crossed and said, "Do you know how much I want to be with you, how much I want to spend the rest of my life with you and how much I am in love with you? Bee, I want you to be my........."

I cut him off putting my hands up, "Oh my God, Sam. Please don't say it, not now. We have too much at stake here, mainly our jobs. Sam, we can't."

"Bee, listen to me. I've been thinking. Let's finish this case, get married, sell our homes and move to another area. Then we can get jobs as partners in another department. That is done all the time."

"You are not even thinking rationally, what about your kids? You can't do that to them. A new home, new area, new school, no friends, new job and new wife? What are you thinking?" And I turned away from him to make sandwiches.

"They're kids, they'll adjust. We have time to work into this gradually, I'm not talking about right away. But it is a plan I want us to work on together."

"I think you are giving them too much credit. It is too much for me to deal with and adjust to and I am thirty six years old, not twelve, ten or eight. I am not going anywhere, Sam, but I can't make any decisions now. Please, let's not do this now, please do not pressure me. This thing right now with Dawson is pressing on me and I do not know what to do about it. You seem to think it is going to go away, I am not quite so sure. I can only deal with one thing at a time. My job could be on the line; it doesn't appear you have a problem with that. Please, eat your sandwich, make some calls and I will make my report to Dawson by five and see what happens. If he pursues the issue of turning the case over to Jones and Johnson, then I have no choice but to go to the Sheriff and DHR, okay?"

"Okay, Bee, but I am not letting you go, personally or otherwise. Got it?"

"I got it."

CHAPTER 16

We ate pretty much in silence. I don't know for sure what my issues are. I don't know if I am afraid of taking on Sam's children or if it is merely the experience of my last marriage. I had totally trusted and loved Brian; was I afraid to trust again or was I too comfortable being single and not wanting the responsibility of a relationship, especially someone with children. I do know I care about Sam and adore his kids, I also know I am not a good one under pressure and I was feeling Sam's pressure. I had to put that on the back burner for now.

We finished our sandwiches and I cleaned off the patio table and came back with two glasses of iced tea. "Do you want to call Daryl or Susanne? You call one and I'll call the other."

"I'll call Susanne, okay, you call Daryl?"

I dialed Daryl's office first and got the receptionist, "Good afternoon, Compton, Stanton and Associates, how may I direct you call?"

"This is Sergeant Weathers of San Diego County, San Diego, California. I would like to speak to Mr. Daryl Compton, please."

"I'm sorry, Mr. Compton is out of the office, may I take a message for him. He checks in quite frequently for messages."

"Actually, this is regarding his mother and I need to speak with him right away."

"Mr. Compton is out of state and won't be back in the office until next Monday. May I take a message or would you like to leave a message on his voice mail? He does check his messages with frequent regularity."

"Is there another number where I can reach Mr. Compton? It is imperative that I speak with him right away."

"Mr. Compton is in California at a conference and only wishes to be disturbed incase of an emergency," she said with a great deal of firmness and irritation in her voice.

"Miss, this is an emergency, it is regarding his mother. She is in the hospital and in a life threatening condition. The hospital tried to contact him, which was unsuccessful. Now if I may have another contact number I would certainly appreciate it," I responded with the same tone of irritation.

"All I can do is call him on his cell phone, leave a message and ask that he contact you. What was your name again, and a number that he may return your call?"

I gave her my name and cell number and asked, "I have a cell phone number, is this one correct?" I gave her the number and she confirmed it was correct.

I called the number and got Daryl's voice mail, "This is Daryl Compton, I am unable to take your call at this time, leave your name, number and brief message and I will return your call as soon as I can."

"Mr. Compton, this is Sgt. Weathers of the San Diego County Sheriff's Department. I am calling regarding your mother. She is in the hospital in very serious condition. Would you call me as soon as possible?'

Sam hadn't had any better luck with Susanne. He called the only number we had, "This is the Farrell residence," the lady said with a very broken dialect.

"Is Susanne Farrell there?" Sam asked.

"No, she not."

"This is Detective Davis with the San Diego County Sheriff's Department. Who am I speaking with."

"My name is Maria, I am the nanny, I take care of Mrs. Farrell's children."

"Do you know when Mrs. Farrell will be back?"

"I do not know."

"Is Mr. Farrell there,?"

"No he is out of country."

"Do you have a telephone number where Mrs. Farrell can be reached?"

"No, I not allowed giving out numbers."

"Look, it is very important that I speak with Mrs. Farrell. There has been an accident and her mother was seriously injured. She needs to come quickly. Would you please give me her number?"

"No, I can't. You give me name and number an I give to Mrs. Farrell. Sam gave her his information. He had no choice. Now he just had to wait for Mrs. Farrell to call. In the meantime Sam started making calls to find out what he could about Mr. Farrell. He still didn't have a first name for him.

CHAPTER 17

I got on the internet to do a search on Compton, Stanton &Associates in Chicago. I found it to be a law firm with twelve lawyers, located right in the heart of downtown on Wacker Blvd. It appeared as thought they were mostly trial lawyers, one was listed for divorces, one in corporate law and another an advocate for children. I went into the Illinois Bar web sight and did search on a few of the named attorneys. There didn't seem to be any complaints filed on the firm, but some of the names in the firm had minor complaints filed against them Then I clicked on Daryl Compton's name and there was a list as long as my arm of complaints.

The list on Daryl consisted mostly of logging too many hours, some of those he was ordered to adjust the accounts and reimburse the client. One complaint was misappropriate use of a retainer fee and was suspended for three months. Another he was accused of sleeping with his client's wife and was suspended for six months. The last suspension was a real dandy, tampering with evidence and was suspended for twelve months. Sounded like a real cool guy to me. NOT! I found this to be very fascinating.

My cell rang, "This is Daryl Compton; someone from this number called and left a message regarding my Mother. What's up?" he inquired.

"Mr. Compton, I am Sgt. Weathers in San Diego. Your mother was shot in her home last evening; she is in the hospital in very serious condition. The wound itself is not a threat, but your mother's heart and blood pressure and the shock of it all has her in a pretty grave condition. She has not regained consciousness since the incident. I believe it is very important that you go to your Mother as soon as possible."

"What the hell do you mean she was shot in her own home? That is ridiculous, my mother didn't have any enemies. Was it a robbery?" Daryl asked.

"It doesn't appear so. It doesn't look like anything was out of order or out of place, she still had on all her jewelry. We do not believe robbery was the intent," I said.

"Then what the hell was it Sergeant?"

"Sir, we don't know yet. It is under investigation. Mr. Compton, where are you now?" I asked.

"I am in Los Angels at a legal conference. It is going to be very difficult for me to leave until it is over which is Wednesday afternoon."

"Mr. Compton, your mother may not be alive on Wednesday. We have also been trying to locate your sister Susanne. Would you happen to have another number other than her home phone." I asked.

"Well, good luck there. I haven't seen or spoken to Susanne in over five years and it has been sometime longer than that since she has spoken to Mother. If you got a hold of her she wouldn't come anyway. You are just wasting your time," he retorted.

"That may very well be true. However, she has a right to know about her mother and make her own decisions, as do you. If you come to San Diego, Mr. Compton, I would like to meet with you. Please give me call, okay?"

"Ya, Ya, I'll see what I can do," and he hung up. I just sat there and stared at my phone for a moment.

"Well, that went very well. I have a feeling we will be dealing with two very spoiled and dysfunctional adult children. I can hardly wait till you talk with Susanne." And I laughed.

Sam looked up from his computer and said, "I was thinking he sounded rather charming."

"Have you got anything on Farrell yet?"

"Not much, I have a couple calls I am waiting on. I didn't find anything on the internet about him in the political sector. Maybe the nurse doesn't know what she is talking about. I'll find out soon."

I stood up and stretched, looked at my watch, "Oh, my God! It is four o'clock. I have an hour to get my report done and into Dawson."

"If you insist on making out the report, go ahead, I'll drop it off at the office on my way home. I need to go home and check on Sylvia and the kids. Why don't you come over later and have dinner with us, you can relax in the meantime?"

"Thank you, Sam, that sounds good, but why don't you spend the evening with your kids? You were with me last night until late, they might like you by themselves. Let's plan this for another evening, I think I would just like to stay in tonight, okay?"

"Alright, get your report done and I will drop it off for you."

There really wasn't much to put in the report, I summarized yesterdays event, my stop by the hospital and the Victoria Place house and the call attempts today. I reiterated my phone conversation with Daryl, but I did not included my internet findings. I would save that for another time if I was still on the case. If not, Jones and Johnson could get their own information.

I gave Sam the report; he gave me a gentle kiss goodnight and left.

CHAPTER 18

Sitting out on the patio, now in my sweats and cocktail on the side table, I leaned my head back against the chaise lounge chair and just stared into the sky. My thoughts went back to Sam's conversation earlier today. Man, I don't know what I want to do about this.

All of a sudden I was awakened by the nudge of a cold nose. I opened my eyes and was staring into the face of Spook, the neighbor's dog. Spook is a German Short Hair and the best mannered dog I have ever seen. He gave me his mild 'woof', which means I want a treat. I got up and went in the house to the cupboard that has the box of treats. It's about empty, so I open the drawer for the pad and pencil to make a list, and there, a partial pack of cigarettes. I grab them, matches, ashtray and a couple treats and went back out side.

Spook and I have our ritual for him and treats, he sits and then I point my fingers in a gun position and say 'bang', he lies down and plays dead until I tell him "good boy". I love this dog as if he were my own. I have my best conversations with Spook, he offers no opinions or arguments; just listens with a cocked head as though he truly understands. On several occasions Spook and I have curled up on the couch and watched T.V., but he has an eight o'clock curfew so I have to let him out by then.

My house is located on the outskirts of Rancho Bernardo. I bought the house eight years ago from an elderly couple that were moving into a retirement center and I got an excellent deal. It is an eighteen hundred sq. ft. ranch style home with four bedrooms, two baths, a huge great room and an unattached, oversized two car garage with a shop in the back. I made the smallest bedroom into an office, the next bedroom my hobby room, and the third a guest bedroom and then the master bedroom and bathroom. The house is on an oversized lot sitting back from the street in front. A manicured front yard and a big back yard that goes back to a wilderness group of trees that slopes down into a creek bed. The slope is just enough that I have an excellent view of the hills surrounding Rancho Bernardo. On one side of the house is a row of arborvitaes and the other side is a very overgrown laurel hedge. My privacy yard is pristine and I love it. I have been known to put on my string bikini and sunbathe, I wouldn't be caught dead in this bikini in public, but my back yard, is perfect. In the laurel hedge is a path that Spook has made over the years in perfect line of my patio from his house next door. On the right side of the patio is a rock fire pit, to the right and closer to the house is a gas barbeque. In the next couple of weeks I will have all my pots full of various kinds of flowers and the front yard will have the same. Last winter was colder than usual, even for Southern California and I lost many of the plants in the front yard.

I glanced at my watch, "Spook, you let me fall asleep and it is almost six o'clock. How could you do this to me?"

I took a drink of my cocktail, ice half melted, lit a cigarette and looked at Spook as he gave me a disapproving look. "Don't look at me like that, Spook, I only have one bad habit, other than these stupid cigarettes I am perfect."

The phone rang in the house, I groaned as I got out my chair and ran inside and missed the call. I checked caller ID, it was Sam. I walked back to my lawn chair and my cell rang, I answered, "Hi There."

"I thought maybe you'd changed your mind and was coming over after all when you didn't answer the house phone, or are you? Are you on your way over?"

"No, Spook and I are enjoying a cocktail."

"So what's for dinner?"

"Actually, I haven't had dinner; I fell asleep on the lounge out here in the back yard. Spook woke me up or I would probably still be asleep. It is really pleasant out here, starting to get a little chilly, but not too bad, yet."

"Why don't you jump in your car and have dinner with us and

then you can go home? Sylvia has made a wonderful pot roast with all the trimmings."

"Sam, I am all settled in for the evening," just then my cell beeped at me and I could see it was Dad calling. "I gotta go, Dad is calling, I'll call you back."

"Hi Dad, how's everything going?"

"Just fine, how'd it go today?"

"Okay, I guess. Sam had a less than pleasant conversation with Dawson and I haven't heard from him. I made out my report and Sam dropped it off at the office. Sam thinks we each made our point with Dawson and he'll just drop it."

"So, does this mean you are not going to report Dawson?"

"I think for right now I'm not going to. I'll see what happens in the next day or two. In the mean time, Sam and I are proceeding with this case until we hear otherwise from Dawson."

"Sis, I want you to do one thing, right now. I want you to document the conversation you had with Dawson this morning. And if you can remember any other times and dates or incidences with Dawson; get them down on paper. Unless Dawson is smarter than I think he is, he is going to have a repeat performance and you need to be prepared. Don't let this Bastard intimidate you. You are way too good for his likes and I think he is just using his power and he is so wrong. He would've never gotten by with his shit in my department. He'd have been looking for another job." Dad was so emphatic in his beliefs and I knew he was right.

"I know, and I will right start writing stuff down. I just hope this goes away and he rethinks his tactics and position in all of this. If not, I will proceed."

"We love you and know you will do the right thing. Well, I guess I better get off the phone, your Mother has just called me for dinner."

"Thank you Dad and I love you both, tell Mom hi and I will give her a call soon." I hung up and looked down at Spook who was sound asleep. I got up and went in the house to see what I could snack on for dinner.

CHAPTER 19

I was not up to cooking anything nor was I very hungry. The easiest was a bowl of cereal. I took it back outside and sat back in my lounge chair, just then Spook jumped up with his back hairs standing straight up and growling very low. Then he took off in a sprint to the left side of the house. I followed Spook and barely got a glimpse of a man running around the corner of the house and down the driveway. As I got to the street I could see a yellow Hummer screeching around the corner at the end of the block.

Damn! How can this be? How does this person know I was the one at the Victoria Place house and how did he get my address?

I ran back to the patio and picked up my cell and called the precinct. The dispatcher answered, "San Diego County Sheriff's office. How may I direct you call?"

"This is Sergeant Brenda Weathers. I need an officer sent to my house as soon as possible. I have had an intruder."

"Let me check and see who is in your area. Are you okay?"

"Yes, I'm not hurt or anything like that, I just need an officer here."

"One is on the way. You hang in there."

Spook was still by side, his hair still standing up and staring at the left side of the house.

I laid my cell phone down and it rang. "Bee, what the hell is going on over there? Are you okay? I am on my way." Sam screamed.

"Yes, I am okay. I'll tell you when you get here. I can hear the patrol siren now, so they'll be here in a second." Sam has a police scanner at home so I was not surprised when he called.

Two patrol cars screeched into my driveway and the officers jumped out of the car with weapons drawn. First officer out of his car was

Willy, he and I have worked together before and I was real relieved Dawson hadn't shown up.

I put my hands up to indicate there was no need for drawn weapons and yelled, "Its okay, I'm okay. Someone was here a few minutes ago and was sneaking around this side of the house," as I pointed to the left side.

We walked around the side of the house and I spotted foot prints in the flower bed, right next to the house. Willy and Officer Matt Scott took out the crime scene tape, put a couple stakes in the ground and taped it off.

I heard Sam's car coming up the driveway, passed the two police cars and parked at the front of the garage. He came running around to the side of the house and said, "What's going on."

I told him what had happened and Willy showed him the foot tracks. Willy sent Matt up the street to see if there were any tire marks as I had described the screeching around the corner. Matt came back and reported there was rubber on the edge of the curb. So that would be analyzed as well.

Spook was still by my side, just sitting there in his protective mode. "I think Spook saved my life. If he hadn't scared that guy off I'm not sure what would've happened."

"I don't think you should stay here tonight. Go pack a few things and you can stay at my place," Sam said.

"I'll be alright. I am going to call Karyn and ask if Spook can stay with me tonight."

"Sergeant, I think Sam is right. You should not stay here, at least not tonight. Did he get in your house?" Willy asked.

"I'm sure he wasn't in the house, the front door is locked and the only way in is here in the back."

"Let's check it out anyway." We walked through the house and the only window open was in my bedroom, which is at the back of the house. Willy was the first one in my bedroom and immediately found a dirt foot print under the window. My knees went weak and I thought I was going to throw up. I backed out of the bedroom and ran square into Sam. He could tell by the look on my face that was now pasty white, something was drastically wrong. Sam grabbed my arm and took me into the great room and sat me on the couch, "I'll be right back."

I sat there in a state of shock. I couldn't believe what was happening. How does this person know who I am and why does it matter? I was thinking back to yesterday afternoon when I ran to Mrs. Compton's house, he couldn't have seen me crouching through the trees and he never looked back when he ran out the back door. Besides, if he did see me running through the trees, I was too far away that he couldn't have identified me.

Sam came out of the bedroom and said, "Get a few things together; I am getting you out of here."

Willy came out and said, "Before you go I want you to retrace all of your steps this evening. From the time you first got home."

"When Sam and I left the Victoria Place house we were coming here to make calls. Since it was close to noon I stopped by the store and picked up sandwich stuff. Sam got here first and was sitting outside. We went in the house and I made sandwiches, we ate outside and made phone calls. Sam left about 4:30, I went in and changed clothes, fixed a drink and went back out side and lay back in the lounge chair. I had two phone calls, one from Dad and one from Sam. I apparently dosed off, because the next thing I knew Spook, the neighbor's dog, woke me up," and I reached down and petted Spook now sitting at my feet. "Then I went back in the house, fixed a bowl of cereal and brought it back outside to eat it. That's when Spook sensed someone on the side of the house and ran after him. I ran after Spook and when I got to the street I saw the back end of a yellow Hummer squeal around the corner. Then I called the office and here we are."

I stood up to go into the bathroom and put together my toiletries, I turned to Willy and Sam and asked, "Can I go into my bedroom to get some clothes?" They looked at each other and shook their heads, "Not right now, maybe in the morning." Willy answered.

"But these are the only clothes I have; my closet is just inside the door."

Willy gave me the okay and I grabbed a change of clothes for tomorrow, shoes and underwear, considering I was wearing none. I gathered my computer, badge, weapon and put my cell in my purse and set it all by the back door.

"I'm going to call in forensic and dust for fingerprints, get the shoe prints from the flower bed and bedroom floor. Check out the rest of the house. I really don't think we are going to find anything. I think when you went back in the house for cereal, you startled him and he ran." Willy said.

"Willy, are you saying you think he was in the house the whole time I was home?"

"No, I don't. I'm betin' when you went outside after changing clothes and laid down in your lounge he didn't see you. Didn't you say the dog didn't show up till later?"

"Yes, that's right."

"Brenda, your car is in the garage, your house is dark and I don't think he thought anyone was home. Now what he was here for, I have no idea. You did say when we were at Compton's house he didn't see you running through the trees, didn't you? Where was the Hummer parked at Compton's?"

"That's right. I don't think he could see me. The garage is at the back of the house, you can't see it from the road. The Hummer was parked at the end of the garage. Remember the driveway goes around the house and circles back towards the garage. He was parked heading out at the end of the garage and I didn't see it until he ran out of the house. He never looked back, so I don't think he even knew I was there."

I went outside to bring in the dishes off the patio table and take them back in the house. I put the cigarettes and matches in my pocket for later, this was not going to be a good night.

Willy said, "You may as well go now. Forensics will be here before long and there is no need for you to stick around. When they are done, I will lock everything up for you. Do you have a spare key?"

"Yes, of course. Are you sure I shouldn't stay for awhile?"

"No, now give me the key, go over to Sam's place and if I need you for anything I will call."

CHAPTER 20

I finished cleaning up the kitchen and noticed Spook was still beside me. He had not let me get more than twelve inches from him all evening. I looked at my watch and it was almost 9:30 and Spook had made no attempt to go home. I told Sam and Willy I was taking the dog home and would be right back.

Naturally, when I went over to Karyn's she wanted to know what was going on at my place. I told her about someone snooping around my house and Spook had chased him off, I did not tell her he had been inside as well. No need to alarm her anymore. I patted Spook on the head and leaned down to kiss him on the nose, "You are such a good boy; I might just have to hire you to be my guard dog." I looked up at Karyn and smiled, "You are so lucky to have him."

"Brenda, I have been meaning to talk to about Spook. Daniel got a transfer to the East coast and he doesn't want to take him with us. Daniel is afraid we are going to have to settle in an apartment before we buy a house, it would make it too hard on Spook. He has never been cooped up all day inside and I don't want to do that to him. Would you be willing to take him? He is so attached to you. You are his other home and we would feel much better about leaving him with you rather than strangers," Karyn said in a pleading manner.

"Oh Wow! When did Daniel get the transfer and when will you be leaving?"

"He got the transfer last week and needs to report by the fifteen of this month. Not much notice, huh? I of course will stay here until school is out and try and get it all packed and ready for sale. I gave my two weeks notice at work on Monday. I need time to get packed. If the house doesn't sell within a month, we will leave it empty for two and then put it on the rental market. We don't really want to rent it out, but might have to."

"Let me think about this, you know how much I love Spook, but you also know the kind of hours I keep. I really need to get going; they are not letting me stay at the house tonight, so I need to get ready to leave. I'll talk to you in a couple days." We gave each other a hug and I patted Spook on the head and left.

When I got back to the house, Sam had already put my stuff in his car. "Are you ready? Better make a quick check that you haven't forgotten anything."

"I'm good, if I forgot anything I can always come back."

As we started for Sam's car I asked, "Shouldn't I take my car?"

"No need, I will bring you back in the morning to get it."

As we drove away heading towards Sam's house, he reached over and put his arm around me and said, "You okay?"

"Of course I'm not okay. Someone was in my house and I didn't even know it. If it hadn't been for Spook there is no telling what would've happened. NO, I am not okay, Sam," I said angrily.

He pulled his arm back and stared ahead. I reached over and touched his arm, "Sam, I am so sorry. I shouldn't have snapped at you like that. I know you are concerned and care about me, I am just terribly shook up. You know this happens to other people and we deal with it everyday. I never expected it to happen to me. I am sorry." He touched the top of my hand on his arm and said, "Its okay, I know."

CHAPTER 21

When we got to Sam's and went in the house, he took my things upstairs. The kids were already in bed, they should be it was well after ten o'clock and Sylvia was in the family room watching T.V. I walked in and sat down to visit with her. I didn't mean too but I had startled her. She was watching The Nanny and when she saw me she said, "It is really a good thing I am not those children's nanny. They would be dead." She gave a little chuckle.

Sam came in the room and asked Sylvia, "Are there any leftovers to make a plate for Bee?"

"That's okay; don't go messing up her kitchen."

Sylvia started to get up and I put my hand on her arm and said, "Please, I can make a sandwich. That's all I need, actually, I don't even need that. A sandwich will be perfect, I can make it AND clean up after. I promise." She smiled and turned back to her program.

In the kitchen Sam made the sandwich and we talked about the day's event and the connection to Mrs. Compton. I was still shocked over it all and totally exhausted. I really wanted to just eat my sandwich and crawl into bed.

"I have a short list of things I need to do tomorrow. One is to check ballistics on the shell and I wanted to go by the hospital again and check on Mrs. Compton. Did you ever hear back from Susanne?"

"No, I am going to try again in the morning. I haven't heard back from my two contacts about Susanne's husband, either. I will take you home and we can check on your house, and then go together to the ballistics lab and the hospital if you want?"

I finished the sandwich and a glass of milk, "Let me clean things up and then I want to go outside for a bit and get some fresh air. Which bedroom did you put my things in?"

"My room," he took his position at the counter, crossed arms and looked at me.

"Sam, we can't, not in your house. The kids and Sylvia."

"Sylvia will be up long before anyone else and she won't know, her room is downstairs, we will be up before the kids anyway. I want you close to me, okay? I'll clean up here, you go outside and I'll come out when I'm done."

Outside on the big wrap around porch, I stared out in the yard with the moon's reflection through the trees and felt safe. I stepped off the porch and walked out in the yard and sat on the swing chair reaching for my cigarettes and lit one. It was so peaceful and quiet. Then I thought I saw movement in the trees, I looked closely and was about to run back to the house and realized it was only a small tree moving slightly in the breeze. "Okay, now you are becoming paranoid, relax, take some deep breaths." I said to myself.

"Who are you talking too, Bee?" Sam said.

He really startled me and I jumped out of the chair and turned to face him, "Don't do that! You scared the hell out of me!"

"Sorry, I just walked out here, didn't mean to scare you. Hey, I thought you gave those things up?" He said and pointed to my cigarette.

"I have, I think, I just felt the need for one tonight." I put the cigarette out and said, "I am really worn out, I would like to take a shower and go to bed."

Without saying a word, Sam put his arm around me and we walked in the house. I went on upstairs as Sam was closing up for the night. I found all my things on the end of Sam's bed. I grabbed the hanging clothes and put them over a chair in the corner, my overnight bag on the floor and took my cosmetic bag to the bathroom. The shower felt so good, I turned the hot water up and just stood there letting it penetrate and pulsate my neck and shoulders. I got out of the shower, toweled off, put on a sleeping shirt and slipped into bed. I was almost asleep when Sam turned the light off and slid in beside me. He put his arm under my head and held me; I snuggled in with the feeling of comfort and safety and fell fast asleep.

I woke the next morning with the smell of coffee and looking into the eyes of Sam with his great big smile. "Good morning sleepy head."

"Good morning, what time is it?" I asked, stretched and propped myself up against the headboard.

"It's only seven o'clock, did you sleep well?"

"I did. Seven o'clock? I need to get up and get going." I started to get up and realized I needed a bathrobe.

Sam smiled and handed his robe to me. "There is no hurry; Sylvia has breakfast cooking for us. Come on down and have breakfast then you can get ready for the day."

"Like this?"

"Not to worry; Sylvia is cool, she won't ask and she won't tell."

We left Sam's house at eight thirty and headed to my house. Sam had called forensics; they hadn't found anything else other than what they had already found in my bedroom. Whoever this person was must have worn gloves because there were no finger prints, only the foot prints. The officer that had come with Willy had scrapped some of the rubber marks off the curb from the Hummer. The only thing this would confirm is the make of the tire; in the event the Hummer was found.

When we drove in the driveway to my house I got a little sick feeling in my stomach. As we walked around the back of the house I was surprised to be greeted by Spook. He never came over to the house during the day. "Spook, are you guarding my house?" and I petted him on the head. Inside everything looked the same as we left it; a little fingerprint dust on some of the furniture, but that seemed to be all. The bedroom window was closed and locked.

"Let's set up computers and start to work," Sam said. "We may as well just start here with phone calls and our search for information on Daryl and Susanne."

I replied with an, "Okay." We worked straight through until one o'clock. My first call was to Captain Dawson; he of course already knew about the incident and requested my full report. There was no mention of yesterday's conversation or my report Sam had dropped off the prior evening.

Sam had two return calls that confirmed Susanne's husband was not a politician. His first name was Clinton and his profession was rather sketchy. It seems he was in the banking business, but hadn't stayed with any branch for more than three years at a time. It was going to take time to find out why he moved branches so often. Sam put in another call to Susanne and got the Nanny; only to find out Susanne had not returned home nor had she called home. We did not believe the Nanny was telling the truth.

We went to the hospital and checked on Mrs. Compton and found there hadn't been much of a change. Her nurse told us she seemed to be less restless; blood pressure had come down slightly, but she was still unconscious. I asked if her son had been in to see her, but she could only verify that no one had been in during her shift. She checked her chart and didn't see where anyone had requested to talk with the doctor.

Damn, it had now been three days since Mrs. Compton had been shot and the only contact with her children had been her son Daryl. He was about as concerned about his mother and cooperative as a post. This was just way too weird for me to comprehend.

Sam and I got in his car and just sat there for a moment each in our own thoughts. I finally broke the silence and suggested we go by the ballistics lab to see what there findings were on the weapon.

Inside the ballistics lab we got copies of the full report. The 32 caliber casing was from a small hand gun. This explained why the bullet had not gone through Mrs. Compton, instead had lodged at the bottom of her heart. It appeared to both of us that murder was not the intent or a more forceful weapon would have been used. So who was this intruder and what actually was his intention? And why was he at my house?

CHAPTER 22

Sam suggested we grab a quick something to eat and go back to my place and try our calls again. It was now almost three o'clock and I was beginning to feel a bit hungry. We did a drive through at Burger King, I ordered a Jr. Burger and Sam got a full Colossal Burger meal deal. We went to my house to sit out on the patio to eat and work while the weather was staying so nice.

We got out of the car and walked around the back and laying at my backdoor was Spook. "My goodness, Spook, have you decided this is home now?" He stood up yawned, stretched and wagged his tail all at the same time. "He looks like he is smiling at us." I laughingly said.

We sat down at the table on the patio, "How about a drink? I could sure use one."

Sam nodded as he had just taken a big bite from his burger, "The usual scotch and water with a twist?" Again he nodded. I fixed his drink and vodka water with a lime for me and went back out side.

"I've been asked to take in a room mate and I am giving it some serious consideration. This guy would not only be company but would also be kind of a watch dog. Right now, I think I would feel pretty good about having a room mate. What do you think, Sam?"

"When did this come up? You've never talked about having a room mate before."

"Karyn sort of mentioned it the other night when I took Spook home and I explained what had happened over here"

"So how do you know this guy and what do you know about him. How long have you known him? This totally blows me a way, Bee."

"Well, let's see, I've known him about eight years; I know he is a kind gentle guy and I know he would be a great protector. I think you will like him." I said as I took a sip of my drink sensing jealousy and complete disapproval. I wanted to laugh, but I wasn't ready to give up my fun quite yet.

"I really wish you had mentioned this before. I didn't know you were afraid to be here alone. You have really caught me off guard. When is this room mate thing supposed to start?" Sam said with irritation.

"I was thinking he could stay part time for a little while and kind of get used to the living arrangement here. Then he will probably move in permanently in a couple months. Not really sure, we haven't discussed a definite move in date. I'm not really afraid to stay alone, although after last night's ordeal I think I will feel better after this guy moves in."

"I see, sounds like you have everything already arranged. Doesn't appear as though you've given any consideration to me or the plan I was hoping for us to work on."

"This guy isn't going to interfere with us, so don't worry. I really think you'll like him, Sam." I said smiling.

"You seem to think there is humor in this, Brenda, and quite frankly I don't like it at all. Well, it's about time the kids are getting home from school, I better go. I'll talk to you tomorrow." He got up started for his car.

"WOW! That's rather abrupt. Wouldn't you like to know his name; might be someone you already know?"

"Don't think it matters if I do or not." And he continued walking.

"Sam, stop, you are acting like a jealous, spoiled brat. Come here and meet my room mate, Spook meet Sam."

Sam stopped, dropped his briefcase, threw his jacket on the ground, turned and started running towards me with a vengeful, mischievous look in his eyes.

"Oh, my God." I squealed, kicked off my shoes and started running. Sam caught up to me and tackled me and we both went to the ground. Good thing the grass made for a soft landing. The he started tickling me, saying "You are so bad, rotten to the core."

I broke away and ran into the house and tried to get the door shut and locked. Sam was way too fast and too strong; he got the slider open and rushed after me. I ran for the bedroom, bad idea, and tried to get that door shut; he pushed his way in, picked me up and threw me on the bed. "I am going to screw your brains out for being such a naughty little girl." Sitting on top of me he started unbuttoning my blouse, leaned down and kissed me. I wrapped my arms around his neck and pulled him even closer. I loved his kisses, they were so soft and gentle, but this time there was more passion that sent shocking sensations throughout my body and I lost control. We started removing each others clothes as Sam whispered, "Easy Baby, not so fast, let's make this last. I love you so much. I don't ever want to let you go."

Sam's hands found every sensuous spot on my body and played them with pleasure. His tongue searched for my breasts circling them, tantalizing my nipples and down my stomach and back up. Chills ran up and down my body. I clung to him and moaned with pleasure, arching upward to feel his body. Sam's hand was rubbing up and down my thighs, first one leg and then the other and found I was already warm and moist waiting for him. He entered in slow motion and without warning we were both thrusting to a climax. We laid there both breathing heavy and Sam whispered, "You are amazing, Baby, sorry it was so fast."

I whispered back, "You'll get another chance someday." I giggled and he swatted my behind. We curled up in each others arms and when I awoke it was dark outside. I tried to slip out of the bedroom when I heard Sam say, "You get back her little girl, I am not done with you yet."

"I am going to check on the time and use the powder room."

"Who cares about the time, I sure don't. Get in here."

I got back into bed and we had a repeat performance of earlier, however, it was more pleasurable and sensual and took much longer. When we were all done, for the moment anyway, I got up and took a quick shower and went to the kitchen to fix something to eat.

Sam came out from taking a shower with a towel wrapped around him. He walked over and put his arms around me and started kissing my neck. "Now, now, at least let me get some nourishment into you." I said giggling at him.

As I looked at the clock and saw it was seven, "You better call home and report in to Sylvia."

"So does that mean I have an invitation to stay the night?"

"I would like it if you did, I would feel much safer." I put my arms around him and gave him a kiss, turned back to the counter.

I fixed bacon, eggs and waffles; a night time breakfast and my all time favorite. As soon as we finished Sam said, "I better go get a change of clothes and check in. I won't be long, but you keep everything locked up tight, okay?"

"I'll be fine." Sam left; I cleaned up the kitchen, turned on the T.V. and curled up on the couch. I was surfing the channels and heard a scratching on my patio door followed by Spook's "woof". I got up and let him in and he jumped on the couch with me and settled right in. It was at that very moment that the decision was a positive yes that I was going to have a new room mate. I have always loved this dog, I just never knew how much.

CHAPTER 23

I fell asleep and was wakened by a knock on the slider and Spook standing at the door with back hairs bristled straight up. I heard Sam's voice, "Bee, it's me."

I let him in and Spook immediately went out the door and headed for home through his usual path in the Laurel hedge.

Sam sat down on the end of the couch and turned towards me and said, "I was thinking on my way back about a plan. We need to make another attempt to contact Daryl and Susanne in the morning. If we are unsuccessful, I am going to follow up with Clinton Farrell and where he works. I think we need to make a trip to Florida and have a chat with Mr. and Mrs. Farrell. I find it very hard to believe they have made no attempt to return phone calls, even if Susanne has been estranged from her mother. What do you think?"

"I think you are right. I am going to call Daryl again in the morning after we have checked in on Mrs. Compton and her doctor. And of course we are going to have to clear this with Captain Dawson. By the way, any more from him?"

"Not a word. I told you he is going to drop it. He has no choice. So, tomorrow is Thursday, if we haven't had any results from either of them, I think we should take the red eye flight to Florida on Friday night and spend a few days. Then go on up to Chicago and have a little chat with Daryl."

"Sounds like a plan to me. I need to get that report to Dawson about last night. I better finish it tonight and drop it off in the morning when we go in to get approval for our trip." I got up and walked to the counter where I had set up my lap top. I opened it up and started typing my report. It all came back so realistically; it made feel creepy again that someone had been in my house. It only took about thirty minutes to finish it. I wanted it done and out of my hair.

I remembered what Dad had told me about writing specifics down about Captain Dawson in case I would need it later. I made a new file and called it "Captain Neil Dawson" and I started typing what I could remember of incidence where the Captain had inappropriately behaved towards me. Even though I couldn't remember exact dates, I could remember cases and remarks he had made. It would be no problem to look up dates later. Dawson had only been Captain for two years, but he had certainly used his authority to push his weight around, so to speak. Unfortunately, I was not the only female in the department he was inappropriate with. I just didn't know if any of the others called him on it or reported him. I had a feeling no one had reported him or his behavior would have changed. At least one would have hoped so.

"I think I am ready for bed. We have a rather busy day tomorrow if we are going to leave Friday night. I have phone calls to make, see Mrs. Compton and I would really like to get over and see Bob. I haven't seen him since before I went to Sun Valley, it's been about three weeks." I yawned, stretched and did ten toe touches.

We went to bed and snuggled in tight and before our heads hit the pillow we were both sound asleep.

CHAPTER 24

I woke the next morning to the smell of coffee and big beautiful smile of Sam. I was beginning to like this concept. Okay, get that idea out of your head right now, I thought to myself. I sat up and said, "How long have you been up? Do I smell bacon, too?"

"You sure do and I have been up since six thirty. It's only seven now, but thought you would want to get up and get started."

"Ah, so perceptive of you." I swung my legs to the side of the bed, grabbed my robe and went into the kitchen.

We ate breakfast, Sam showered, I cleaned the kitchen and I got in the shower. Then we set computers up on the dining room table and started making calls. My first call was to Daryl Compton.

"Hello, this is Daryl." I was shocked to hear his voice after the first ring.

"Mr. Compton. This is Sergeant Weathers, how are you this morning? I was hoping you had been in to see your Mother."

"Actually, Sergeant Weathers, I am at the hospital now. I got in late last night and was unable to see Mother. I am waiting for the doctor as we speak."

"Great, I would like to come over and meet with you and also Doctor Cutter. I should be there in about thirty minutes, depending on traffic."

I turned to Sam and said, "Well, seems 'our too busy little son' has finally shown up at the hospital. I am going to make a fast run over there. Any luck on Susanne?"

"No, the line has been busy. So either Susanne is home and on the phone or they have a very chatty Nanny. I'll keep after it though and I need to call my contacts about her husband. Keep in touch." Sam got up and gave me a hug and a kiss. I grabbed all my usual stuff as I went out the door.

When I got to the hospital I went straight to the fourth floor and found Daryl sitting in the waiting area. I walked over and stretched my hand out, "I am Sergeant Brenda Weathers, and I assume you are Daryl Compton?"

"I am, it is nice to meet you. The doctor is in with Mother now, then they are going to take her out of ICU and move her to a private room."

"Has her condition improved?"

"Not really, she still hasn't regained consciousness. I believe she is recovering from her wounds, though. Can you fill me on what happened? This is all so shocking to me."

Oh, yes, so shocking that it has you so terribly worried that you just rushed right over to your mother's bed side, FOUR days later, I thought to myself. I filled him in with as much information that I felt was pertinent for him to know. I did leave out the incident at my house. I assured him we were working as hard as we could with as little information that we had. The yellow Hummer seemed to be the only lead at this time. He seemed to be satisfied with what I had told him, but then why wouldn't he.

"Did you try to get a hold of your sister, Susanne?"

"No, she wouldn't talk to me anyway. Have you talked to her?"

"I haven't, my partner has tried several times and he has only gotten the Nanny. What do you know about her husband?" Daryl was about to answer when Doctor. Cutter came out of ICU and was walking towards us.

We both stood up as Doctor Cutter extended his hand to me, "Good to see you again Doctor Cutter, this is Daryl Compton."

"Nice to meet you. Let's sit down for a minute and let me bring you up to date. Miss Ellie's condition is stable. By that I mean all her vitals are good, blood pressure is where it should be for her, her heart beat is back in rhythm, her breathing is steady and not labored so we have taken her off oxygen. She is getting plenty of liquids and nutrition through the IV. The trauma to her head when she fell was quite a jolt and has kept her in a semi coma. We have kept a very close watch and a monitor on her head and the brain waves are strong; so far there hasn't been any swelling, which is excellent. I have her on a very mild relaxant, she could still wake up under this medication. The reason I am moving her into another room and out of ICU is because we can start some physical therapy and try to keep her muscles from atrophying and with that it could also stimulate her to wake up. I believe she was so traumatized by the incident she subconsciously does not want to wake up and face it. I believe there is a chance she might even know who the intruder was. That is only my personal opinion at this time. Do either of you have any questions?"

I was the first to ask, "Doctor, if you think there is a chance she knew the intruder, wouldn't it be wise to put security officers at her door around the clock?"

"You can, however, I have put her in a room directly across from the nurse's station where they can still monitor her machines and watch her room."

"ICU is cut off from the general public, but if the nurses are all busy with patients and away from the desk, anyone could slip in and out of her room in a split second. I think I will order the security anyway, if that is okay with you?"

"That is your call, Sergeant, I certainly have no objections. How about you Mr. Compton, do you have any questions?"

Daryl shuffled his feet nervously and asked, "How long do you think Mother will be in the coma?"

"It is hard to say, like I said before, I am hoping the physical therapy will offer some stimulation to waking her up. I would like a few of her friends to come by and talk to her and of course you and your sister are the most important to talk to her. Does she have any sisters or brothers, grandchildren around here that can come in?" asked the Doctor.

"No, Mother only had a brother and he passed away a few years ago. I don't have children and my sister lives in Florida with her three kids. Mother hasn't seen Susanne's youngest one that I think is three or four years old, maybe five, hell, I don't know. I haven't talked with Susanne in over five years, she might even have another one by now." Daryl said laughingly.

"What about friends, church, the minister, anyone you can think of?" asked the Doctor.

"I know she always goes to church, or at least she used too. I don't know which one or the ministers name, you know they move around a lot, so who knows who he would be now. I don't know any of her friends, for all I know they could all be dead."

Doctor Cutter gave me a quick glance and said to Daryl, "Would there be a chance you could check out Miss Ellie's friends and the minister and see if some of them could stop by and see her. Even if she is still in a semi coma, familiar conversations could be very beneficial?"

"I don't know if I am going to have time, I have a one o'clock flight back to Chicago this afternoon. I might be able to come back in a week or so. I would like to go in and see Mother now if it would be alright." Daryl said as he got up.

Doctor Cutter explained, "It will be a little while since they were moving her to another room. You can check at the nurse's station on the third floor and they will let you know when she is settled in."

Daryl excused himself to the restroom and to make a couple calls.

The doctor and I exchanged confused looks and I smiled at him and said, "Well, that certainly went well from a very concerned son. I can hardly wait to see what the daughter's reaction to all of this is going to be, if we ever get a hold of her. So far we have had absolutely no luck. I'm sorry if I sound a bit on the negative side. It just amazes me the lack of concern these two have for their Mother."

"You would be surprised at some family reactions I get. Nothing much surprises me anymore. Let me know if there is anything you need from me regarding security for Miss Ellie." And he turned and walked away.

CHAPTER 25

I sat down and waited for Daryl to come out of the restroom. I wanted to get as much out of him as I could, I wanted to know about Susanne and her husband.

Daryl came out with his cell phone at his ear. I grabbed a magazine and tried to act like I was oblivious to his being, all the time listening intently. Occasionally his voice would raise and he would turn from me, he was one of those pacers as he talked on the phone so it was really hard to track on the conversation. When he finally hung up and walked over to me, he sat down and asked, "Have they moved Mother yet?"

"I don't know, I imagine they will use the patient elevator to take her down. Why don't we go down to the third floor, check in with the nurses and when they get her settled they will come and get you."

When we got to the waiting area, I sat down and patted the chair next to me for Daryl to sit. "I need to ask you some questions and talk to you about your sister. I need to know where you were on Monday, May 1st about 5:30 p.m.?"

Daryl stood up, hands on his hips and said, "You are kidding aren't you? You don't actually think I tried to kill my Mother do you? This is unbelievable. Just so you know, I arrived in Los Angeles at two for a Lawyer's Conference. We were at the Convention Center and I believe at five was the social hour, at seven was the banquet and after that I met friends in the bar at my hotel. Is there anything else you would like to know, Sergeant Weathers?"

"I'm sorry Daryl, but I will need verification. Receipt copies of your plane ticket, hotel registration—check in and check out—names of people you talked with during the social hour, who you sat with at the banquet and who you met in the bar at your hotel. This is procedure and nothing personal. I would like this information as soon as possible.

Here is my card, please fax all your information to me. Now may I ask you about your sister?"

"I don't know what you want to know. Susanne is ten years older than I and we have never gotten along, as kids and especially as adults. Susanne got all of the attention until I came along and she resented me and still does. Her perception is I got everything and she never got anything. As I remember, she seemed to be in trouble most of the time. Dad had bought her a sporty little car and when she didn't obey his rules, he would take the keys and she had to ride the school bus or depend on friends. Mother doted on us kids and never made us do any chores, she and Dad were in constant arguments over it. But we had a house keeper and she thought it was appropriate for us to just be kids. So when Dad was home he was constantly after Susanne to clean her room, help Mother with dinner or dishes, do the laundry or some damned thing. Dad didn't ever do that with me and it made her mad, so when our parents weren't around she would pick on me, hide my favorite toys and threaten if I ever told she would beat me up. When Susanne went away to college, Dad and I became real buddies, he would take me fishing and camping, he took me to Disneyland, Disneyworld, we went on a Safari and all kinds of trips. Dad bought a fifty two foot sail boat when I got into college. We used to go out on it for days in the summer. Of course we had three crewmen that did all the sailing and cooking and we just fished and when in dock we just partied. Dad made me go to a local college so I wouldn't be too far away and we could still do all of our fun stuff together and occasionally he would let me bring a friend or two along, but not very often. When Susanne was getting married she wanted a huge wedding with ten attendants. Dad said no, she could have four. What ever Susanne wanted, Dad would say no and give her only one alternative or nothing. Dad did not like Clinton at all; he believed him to be a scheming shyster and tried to talk Susanne out of the marriage. Mother had given up many years earlier ever arguing with Dad, he was the Master Mind of the family and she let him.

When Dad died Mom gave me all of Dad's guns, fishing gear, watch, a gold nugget necklace that he always wore and a bunch of his personal stuff and his Will stated $100 thousand to me and $100 thousand to Susanne. Susanne didn't think it was enough considering I got all of Dad's personal stuff, I don't know what she wanted. Maybe the watch, it would have looked really good on her wrist, maybe the humidor as a jewelry box, she always thought the gold nugget was too big and gaudy. So I don't know what she wanted.

Dad was gone and Susanne tried to take Dad's place and become Mother's personal advisor and make decisions for her because that is what Dad did. The only problem was Susanne didn't give Mother any credit for having any smarts at all. She started writing small checks and marked them for various charities, bills, or a loan to herself. Then the checks started getting bigger and for cash and more of them. When Mother got it all figured out, they had a big blow up, and of course Susanne denied all of it and accused different ones of Mother's staff of writing the checks.

Then about five years ago I needed money for some legal stuff and Mother loaned it to me. Susanne got wind of it and went off the deep end and won't talk to me either. So that is the brief long and the short of it all."

"What about Susanne's husband?" I asked.

"Oh, Clinton? Now there's a real charmer for you. He tried to be a politician and got shot out of the saddle real quick, but wouldn't give up and kept trying until he was so financially in debt and reputation ruin that he picked his family up and moved to Florida. Susanne had asked Dad to borrow money and he said no. Clinton decided to go into banking and worked himself right to the very top. I hear he has moved from bank to bank and keeps right on moving. I don't really know his whole story, but knowing Clint as well as I do, and that ain't very well, he is up to his ass in trouble. Excuse me, I want to see if Mother has been moved yet. I'm going to have to get going here pretty soon." He walked to the nurse's station and inquired about his Mother. The nurse went into one of the patient's rooms, when she came out she said it would be just a minute and he could go in.

He came back over and sat down. "Thank you for all the information. If we have any further questions, may I call you? Would home or your office be better."

"I think our conversation is over, I don't think I have any more information that would be of any help to you. I do wish you luck with Susanne. I want to go in and see Mother now and then I have a plane to catch." Daryl got up and started walking away.

"Don't forget about the fax, Daryl. We'll be in touch." I sat there for a few minutes contemplating whether to wait and go in to see Mrs. Compton or come back later. I decided to go see Bob and come back.

CHAPTER 26

When I got to my car I sat there a minute digesting everything Daryl had told me. Trying to analyze it all and come up with a motive he might have had for a confrontation with his mother. I was about to start my car and I caught a glimpse out of the corner of my eye of Daryl running out of the hospital to his rental car. He squealed out of the parking lot and was gone.

I got out of the car and ran towards the hospital, through the lobby and up to the third floor in the elevator. When I got to Mrs. Compton's room three nurses were working on her. She was thrashing and appeared quite agitated. I stepped inside and asked "What happened?"

"I'll be out in a minute, please wait out side," the nurse snapped.

I was waiting outside the room when Doctor Cutter came rushing in. He went in and shut the door. Several minutes went by before the doctor came out. He walked over to me and said, "Apparently, little sonny boy has upset Miss Ellie. The nurse said when he went in the room he was talking to her and then started yelling at her to wake up. All hell broke loose with Miss Ellie, her blood pressure went up, her heart rate accelerated and she started thrashing around. We have her calmed down and she seems to be resting now. Was there anything in your conversation with Daryl that would have indicated this sort of behavior towards his mother?"

"Actually, Daryl hardly spoke about his mother, we mostly talked about his childhood, his dad and Susanne. He was rather anxious to go in to see her because he had a plane to catch. I saw him running from the hospital and he squealed out of the parking lot. I guess I will be the one checking to see who are friends of Mrs. Compton's to visit her, appears 'sonny boy' couldn't be bothered. May I go in and talk to her for a minute?"

"That would be great if you could do that, do you know her friends? Yes, you can go in for a short time."

"The only thing I have is a page I tore out of the front of her phone book when we were gathering medications and information before she was brought in to the hospital. I will see what I can do and I will make the visit quick." We shook hands, Doctor Cutter walked away and I went in Mrs. Compton's room.

One of the nurses was sitting in a chair by Mrs. Compton's bed and looked at me questioningly as I said, "I am Sergeant Weathers with the San Diego County Sheriff's office. Doctor Cutter told me to come in and speak with Mrs. Compton for a couple minutes." She nodded and went out of the room.

I walked over to her bedside, put my hand over hers and leaned down, "Mrs. Compton? I am Sergeant Weathers. I am the one who found you after your accident. Can you open your eyes for me?" I waited a few seconds then said, "If you understand me, squeeze my hand." Nothing. I sat down in a chair, still holding her hand and started talking. "I talked with Daryl today, he seems like a nice son. Do you remember him coming into see you?" I thought I felt a finger move, but when I asked her again there was no movement. "My partner and I are going to Florida to see Susanne and Clinton. It is nice in Florida, I hope we have a good trip. Would you like to go with us? You could see your grandchildren. Daryl told me you have three, is that correct?" Again nothing. "Mrs. Compton, I am going to go now, I am going to contact your minister and some friends to come by and see you, will that be alright with you? You take care now and I will try to stop by tomorrow before we leave for Florida." I leaned down and kissed her on the forehead and said , "Goodbye."

When I got to my car, I called Sam and he answered right away, "Hey there, how's it going?"

"Hi, Just fine and you? How'd it go with Daryl?"

"Very interesting, I'll tell you all about it later. Right now I am going by the station, give Dawson my report and put in for our trip to Florida and Chicago. And set up security for Mrs. Compton at the hospital."

"So do we still need to go to Chicago after your conversation with Daryl?"

"I'm not really sure, I suppose it depends on what we get from Susanne and Clinton, and the fax I get back from Daryl."

"Would you please wait and let me go in with you to talk to Dawson?"

"Okay. Let's see, it is ten thirty now. I'm going over to Bob's for a few minutes, I'll meet you at the station at eleven thirty. After we meet with Dawson we can catch up during lunch. See ya in an hour."

CHAPTER 27

I drove to Bob's and was greeted at the door by Penny. She always has a smile and looks so fresh, even though I know she has got to be exhausted. "It is so good to see you, Brenda, Bob will be disappointed to have missed you. Please come in and sit down. Can I get you something?"

"Bob isn't home? Everything okay?" I asked.

"Oh yes, Bob is doing great. He is over at the clinic being fitted for a new prosthesis. His doctors finally convinced him to at least give this another try. There is a new model that he believes will be just the ticket for Bob. Bob even seems to be a little excited about it." Penny said with tears in her eyes.

"Penny that is wonderful news." And I gave her a big hug. "I really can't stay too long, I just wanted to stop in and say Hi and chat a little while. Tell me how things have been going."

"Well, you know Bob has been going to a psychiatrist off and on for about four years. Brenda, I love Bob with all my heart, and I would do anything for him, and have. But his depression got to be more than I could handle. He started getting angry with everything I did for him, started yelling at the kids for no reason and it got to be too much for us. So I packed up the kids and we left and went to my folks for a couple weeks. I told him if he wouldn't help himself then I was done trying to help him and was not going to let him mistreat the kids anymore. I never called him, he called my parents and talked to the kids, but I refused to talk to him. Then he called and begged me to come home and promised he would make some drastic changes, but he couldn't do it without me. I came home and left the kids at Mom and Dad's and here I am. So far everything is going great. It is like the old Bob is back. He's going to physical therapy everyday, been seeing his psychiatrist twice a week, helping around the house and even trying to get outside and help in the yard. It is amazing, so far. The kids are having a wonderful time with my parents and my parents having just as much fun having them there. So I am going to leave them there for awhile and see if this change lasts. So far so good. How about you, how is everything going with you?"

"It's going good. Sam and I are working on a case right now where an 89 year old woman was shot in her home. The whole thing is rather weird. Anyway, we are leaving tomorrow night for Florida to visit the daughter and son-in-law. For some reason they have been unreachable by phone and we intend to find out why. I met the son at the hospital, but will do a follow up visit in Chicago. We could be gone about a week. Hopefully, less."

"How is the relationship going with you and Sam?"

Trying to act nonchalant I replied, "We are partners, Penny, and we get along very well. Certainly, not the relationship I have with Dawson."

"Brenda? You might be able to fool some people, but you certainly can't fool me. Sam is crazy about you, and even if you won't admit it to yourself, you are crazy about Sam as well. Don't let him go."

"You know the department policy, we can't afford to be anything other than partners. Dawson has already made some accusations and watching us like a hawk. It would please him like nothing else if he could fire me over this. And I won't let it happen. So, like I said, Sam and I are partners and get along very well." I stood up and smiled, "Penny, I really need to get going. Please give my love to Bob and I'll be in touch when we get back off this mission."

Penny gave me a big hug and said, "It was so good to see you and Bob is going to be disappointed. Just remember what I said, don't let him go."

CHAPTER 28

I got in my car and headed for the station and my phone rang. "This is Sergeant Weathers."

"I suggest you watch your back. You are getting way too nosey." My phone went dead. I checked calls received and it came up as Private Caller—number unknown.

How the hell did this person get my cell phone number? I had given Daryl my card this morning. Could it possibly be him? I drove on to the station, parked not checking to see if Sam was in the parking lot or not; and went straight to the dispatcher. "Have there been any calls for me in the last day or two?"

The dispatcher checked the call list and said, "Yes, a call came in this morning at 10:45. I was out on break then. What's up?"

"I need to talk to whoever took that call. Apparently, she gave out my cell phone number rather than take a message. Who was on duty then?"

"It was Officer Stan Johnson, he has been placed on desk duty because of a back injury or something. Let me page him and see if he is still here. He may even be on half time duty." She paged him a couple times and another officer called in that he was gone for the day.

"Would you please call him on his cell, I really need to question him about that caller."

She called Johnson then handed me the phone. When he answered I said, "Stan, this is Sergeant Weathers. Do you remember anything about the call that came in this morning at ten forty five for me?"

"Yes, she said you had given her a card but she didn't have it with her and needed to get a hold of you right away."

"Did you ask her name or did she give you her name?"

"No, I just figured you knew her if you had given her your card."

"Stan, I did not give a woman my card, and it is customary to ask

77

for names and not give out cell numbers just because someone asks. This is totally unacceptable."

"Brenda, I am so sorry, I guess I just didn't think."

"Stan, as an officer of the law, you can not afford to "not think" at the risk of others. I am going to write you up for this, and give it to the Captain. This can't happen again. You know better."

I turned around and started for my desk as Sam was walking in the door.

"Hey there, Brenda, I saw your car in the parking lot so I came on in. Everything okay? You look upset."

The dispatcher was looking first at me then at Sam and waiting for a reaction from one or the other of us. I said, "I'll explain all of this later, right now we need to go in and see Captain Dawson." I looked at the dispatcher, "Would you let the Captain know we are here to see him. I believe he is expecting us or at least me."

We walked into Dawson's office and I think he was surprised to see Sam with me, but he recovered well, and asked us both to have a seat.

"I have a few things to discuss with you Captain, here is my report first. I believe that Mrs. Compton should have around the clock security for awhile. There are some incidents that have happened that makes me feel she is not safe. They have moved her from ICU into a private room and Doctor Cutter agrees it could be necessary for awhile. I would like your approval on this. Then, Sam and I would like to make a trip to Florida to question Mrs. Compton's daughter, Susanne and her husband Clinton Farrell. So far they have either been unavailable to talk to us on the phone or have refused and we don't know which. Our only contact has been with the Nanny. Then we want to go to Chicago and question Daryl Compton, the son, further. Especially after this last incident. I talked with Daryl at length this morning at the hospital. I requested receipt copies of his plane ticket, hotel registration, names of those he socialized with at the cocktail party, banquet and in the bar at his hotel afterward. I gave him my card and asked him to FAX the information ASAP. When I got in my car after visiting Bob's house, my cell rang and a male voice said and I quote, "I suggest you watch your back, you are getting way too nosey." It came up as private caller, unknown number. What is really confusing to me is that I have only given my card to Daryl. Stan was on dispatch and told me it was a woman called in for my cell number that I had given her my card and she needed to give me some information I had requested. I never gave my card to a woman, this all happened within a two hour period. I am filing a report on Stan Johnson, he knows better than to give out phone numbers without asking for a name and if not satisfied then just taking a message. This is not policy or procedure and I want this report in his file." I sat there and waited for Dawson to take this all in. I looked over at Sam to see his reaction and he appeared to be expressionless, as though he was trying to comprehend it all himself.

Dawson cleared his throat and said, "Let's take this one step at a time. First, I'll approve security for Mrs. Compton. We have a couple of security companies we can use. We don't have enough officers in the department to let go, besides the 'rent a cop' so to speak are less money. Check with the front desk for companies and get someone on duty right away. Now let's go to this caller. You said a female called the station to get your number, but your caller was a male?"

"Yes, that is correct. The only person I have given a card to in months is Daryl Compton, and that was just this morning about ten fifteen, he was supposedly on his way to the airport for a one o'clock flight. That can certainly be verified. Then I went over to Bob King's and stayed about a half an hour or so. When I got in my car to come here is when I got the call from a male voice and it was not a distorted voice. Like I said it showed up as a private caller and unknown number."

"There isn't much we can do about the call unless he calls again. I don't think you need to file a report against Johnson, it was an honest mistake."

"With all due respect Sir, I feel it is a reportable incident and I want it in his file." I said firmly.

"Sergeant Weathers, I will not accept the report."

"Sir, please don't force me to go over your head. This is my life he made an 'honest mistake' with. Considering all else that has happened in the last four days to me, I can't afford 'honest mistakes', Sir."

Sam stood up and addressed the Captain, "You know she's right Captain. I think it is in the best interest of the department to appropriately file the disciplinary report on Stan Johnson. You really don't have a choice."

"I have all the choices, Sam, and I don't believe this is your issue. So back off." The Captain retorted.

"Sergeant, I believe we have work to do and some packing if we are going to be leaving tomorrow night. We better get going." Sam took my arm and we started for the door.

"I have not given approval for you two to go gallivanting off to Florida and Chicago Detective Davis." He snapped.

"We have a case to solve. So with or without your approval, Sir, we will be leaving on the red eye Friday night. You will have our agenda as well as the discipline report on Johnson on your desk before we leave. Remember, you have choices as do we." And we walked out the door.

I stopped by my desk and grabbed a few reports and we left the precinct.

"Let's grab some lunch and go back to your house to work. What sounds good to you? Sam asked.

"I don't care, how about a couple tacos or a taco salad? Yah, a taco salad sounds good to me? Will you pick up lunch? I need to stop by the store for a second."

"Sure, see ya in a minute." Sam said and we went to our own cars.

CHAPTER 29

As soon as Sam drove out of the parking lot, I reached in the glove box and got my last cigarette. This is certainly not the time to try quitting, I said to myself. I stopped by the 7-Eleven and purchased a carton of Coastal ultra light 100 cigarettes. I put them under the seat of my car, opened one pack and stuffed it in the bottom of my purse. What the hell am I doing? I am twenty one and I can do as I damned well please. I lit one and started out of the parking lot when my phone rang.

"Sergeant Weathers."

"This is Detective Matt Scott, I have just confirmed the yellow Hummer is a rental from Enterprise Rentals. The rubber off the curb is a match to the tire. They are checking records now on the person that had rented it on May 1st. Brenda, I will get that information to you as soon as it comes in."

"Matt, good job, that is good news. I will be anxious to hear your results. Thank you so much, keep in touch."

Sam was already at my house and had the taco salads set out on the picnic table. I walked over to the table and set my stuff down. Before I had a chance to tell Sam about Matt's call, he noticed the cigarette in my hand. He started to make a comment, I raised my hand and said, "Now is not the time to get into an argument about my smoking. I just got a call from Matt Scott and they have a match of the rubber to the Hummer, it is a rental from Enterprise. They are checking who had rented it right now."

While we ate we discussed the phone call I had received, we didn't come to any conclusions as to how to deal with it since it was non-traceable. We talked about the conversation with Dawson and what an ass he is, but then that is no great surprise. We agreed to go ahead with our planes as we had spelled out to Dawson, and ignore the rest of his conversation until we heard otherwise. I filled out my complaint report on Detective Johnson and made three copies, one for my record keeping, one for Dawson's mail box and the other for DHR, (Department of Human Resources).

Sam continued making calls to Susanne and Clinton Farrell. I pulled out the phone number list I had torn out of Mrs. Compton's phone book on that first day. I had not looked at it since.

The first number I tried was the Reverend Paul Stearns. A woman answered, "Stearns residence."

"Mrs. Stearns, I am Sergeant Brenda Weathers with the San Diego County Sheriff's Department. Is Reverend Stearns in that I may speak with him?"

"Yes he is, one moment and I will get him."

"Paul Stearns speaking, how may I help you?"

"Reverend Stearns, I am Sergeant Brenda Weathers and I need to ask you a few questions. First, is Mrs. Eleanor Compton a member of your church?"

"Yes she is, what is this all about?"

"There has been an accident and I would really like to talk to you in person rather than over the phone. Is there a time I could meet with you this afternoon?"

"Is Miss Ellie alright?"

"She is in the hospital and stable, please, may I come to your office and discuss this with you?"

"Yes of course, let me check my schedule-----------I have an appointment at two, I will be available at two forty five. Will that be soon enough?"

"That is perfect. Where shall I meet you?"

"Do you know where the Trinity Lutheran Church on Henrici Drive is in North East Rancho Bernardo?"

"Yes I do, it is actually not very far from my house. I will see you at two forty five. Thank you so much for seeing me on such short notice."

Sam still had not gotten through to Susanne. However, his contact,

Fred, in Chicago was searching for information on Clinton Farrell and had come up with some very incriminating information regarding bank fraud. According to the Nanny, Clinton was still out of the country. Where, could not be confirmed. However, the search would continue.

I checked the list again and decided to wait on making any other calls until after meeting with the Reverend. Sam was on the phone again, I cleaned off the picnic table and went in the house. After cleaning up the kitchen which didn't take much, I got out my suitcase and started laying out clothes to take on the trip. I started some laundry and one thing lead to another. To kill time until my meeting with the Reverend I decided to clean house. I dusted the furniture of the residue from the finger print powder, ran the vacuum in the living room that rarely gets used, just for show I guess.

When I left for my appointment, Sam was on the phone, we exchanged waves. I arrived early and waited in my car until I saw a couple leaving the Reverends office. I waited a few minutes and then went in.

Reverend Stearns greeted me, "Nice to meet you Sergeant Weathers, please come in and have a seat. Tell me about Miss Ellie."

I repeated the whole story I had told so many times, now, all the way to the event at the hospital this morning. I did leave out the ordeal at my house and the strange call I had received.

"Poor Miss Ellie. Do you have any ideas of who could have done this?"

"I'm sorry, at this point we don't have a clue except for the yellow Hummer and that is in the process of being checked. So far all we know is that it was a rental."

We talked for more than an hour, he gave me names of Miss Ellie's very good friends. He said he could take care of contacting them and choosing only a couple to go visit her. We discussed the relationship with her two children and confirmed the estranged relationship with Susanne. Even though Miss Ellie didn't talk much about Daryl, his opinion was that it wasn't all that rosy either. The Reverend felt the only thing either of her children wanted from her was money, and she had plenty. He promised he would see her immediately after our meeting.

"Would you have any idea who Mrs. Compton would have been expecting for dinner that evening of the accident? The table was set for two when I entered the house."

"I don't know. Miss Ellie was in church on Sunday, we had a lunch social after services. She stayed until almost the end and was in a very cheerful mood. I can ask some of her friends to see if they knew who she would be meeting, if you like."

"It seems rather strange to me that no one has inquired to you about Mrs. Compton, considering the house is taped off as a crime scene. If someone had gone by to see her, wouldn't they call you?"

"Oh, absolutely. But, Miss Ellie, even though she is very social, she is also very private. So it is not out of the ordinary that she would not have anything planned this week. She can be a little on the eccentric side when she wants to." He said with a little chuckle.

"I won't keep you any longer, I appreciate anything you can do. Here is my card, please feel free to call me anytime. I will be leaving town tomorrow night, but my cell phone is always with me and always on. I am going to go see Mrs. Compton before we leave. Thank you so much for seeing me and doing what ever you can. It is a pleasure meeting you, and who knows, maybe I will just show up in church some Sunday."

"That would be nice," he said and smiled, "It has been my pleasure to meet you as well, I will be in touch." We shook hands and I left.

CHAPTER 30

I got in my car, sat for a minute and went over the Reverend's and my conversation. I couldn't quite put my finger on it, but the Reverend appeared too calm and too eager to give out information. Could the church be in financial straits, was he the caller or could he be in financial trouble? Stranger things have happened. Guess I would just have to wait and see who rented the Hummer.

I went to San Diego Security, Inc. and set up twenty four seven security, immediately, for at least two weeks, for Mrs. Compton. I got the copy of the contract and requested a copy also be sent to Captain Neil Dawson.

When I got home, Sam was gone and had left a note on the kitchen counter. "Call me when you get back. I am curious about your conversation with the Reverend. I have information from Fred, regarding Clinton. Would you have dinner with us tonight? Maybe spend the night ☺? Love ya, S."

I checked the clock and it was now five thirty. I wasn't hungry and I know how Sylvia cooks, a lot of delicious food. I decided I was going to pass on dinner. Sam needed to be with his kids tonight since we would be gone for who knows how long. I had a lot to do that evening and it was just better that I stay home. I would get Spook to spend the night and I would be just fine. All of a sudden I heard scratching on the slider and the familiar 'Woof'. "Spook you must have mental telepathy, I was just thinking about you." I opened the door. "Please do come in."

I called Sam, "Hey there. I just got home. I stopped by San Diego Security and arranged for two weeks of security for Mrs. Compton. I haven't heard from Matt yet, so I may just take a run by Enterprise and see if I can speed up their search. Shouldn't be that difficult, were only talking about four days ago."

"How about dinner? We can deal with Enterprise in the morning.

Besides, I want to hear all about your meeting with the Reverend." Sam said in his pleading little boy voice.

"Sam, I have so much to get done before we leave tomorrow night. I am going to pass on dinner and the sleep over. My conversation with the Reverend went fairly well, although I did leave with a strange feeling about him. He was going to the hospital to meet with Mrs. Compton and he is also going to call a couple of her friends to make visits."

"What kind of strange feeling? What do you mean by that?" Sam asked.

"I don't know, he just seemed to be too calm and too helpful and too eager to go to the hospital. I know that is his job, I just had a funny feeling. It could very well be nothing, but you know stranger things have happened."

"Yah, I know. So I guess tonight is a no, is that what I heard from you?"

"Yep, afraid so. Too much to get done. I'll call you if anything new comes up, okay? What did you find out from Fred?"

"Well, it seems Mr. Clinton Farrell is on the run and has been. He seems to have just kept one step ahead of the Federal Reserve for several years. They couldn't positively nail him, came close a couple times, but it appears he is a tiny bit cleverer than the Feds. He has since gotten himself involved with the Mafia and now it is a race to see who catches him first. My personal opinion is Mrs. Compton doesn't even come close to having enough to bail him out if he got it all. I think we still need to make the trip to visit Susanne anyway."

"Some pretty juicy stuff huh? I am going to make a run over to Enterprise before they close at seven and I will call you later, okay?"

"You got it. I made reservations at the Residence Inn for us. Seemed to be fairly close to the address we have for the Farrell's. I made our plane reservations and car rental. So we are all set there, and I used the County's credit card, that ought to stick in Dawson's craw very nicely." Sam said with a laugh.

"You really know how to turn the knife don't you? Good job. Gotta get goin, will call you later."

I called Matt to see if he had heard anything from Enterprise and he said he hadn't. "Matt, I am going to go over there and see if I can speed up the process. You want to meet me there?"

"I can't right now, I am at an accident and can't leave. Go ahead and give me a call later. Gotta go."

I let Spook out of the house and gave him a pat on the head. "I'll be back in a little while. You stand guard now."

CHAPTER 31

When I arrived at the Enterprise office, the staff were just sitting at desks chatting and waiting for seven o'clock. As I stood at the counter, no one seemed to be in much of a hurry to wait on me. "Excuse me, who is in charge here?"

A petite blonde said, "I am." And made no attempt to get out of her chair.

I took my finger and motioned her to come to the counter. As she did, I showed her my badge and said, "I am Sergeant Brenda Weathers, I am here to pick up the results of the person who had rented a yellow Hummer on or about Monday, May 1st. Do you have that ready for me?"

She got her business composure and attitude in order and replied, "I don't believe that is quite complete."

"Well, then let me see if I can help you with that. May I see your rental schedule?"

"I'm afraid I can't do that, Ma'am. Our rentals are confidential."

"Let me explain the importance of this Ma'am. I can have a warrant here before closing or shortly after if you wish to press the issue. I do not give a damn about any of your customers except the person that rented the yellow Hummer on Monday, May 1st. The Hummer has been identified and has been quarantined for future rentals until the Sheriff's office has released it. Do we understand each other?"

"Yes we do." She nervously replied.

"Good. Now may I see your rental schedule for Monday, May 1st?"

She went into the other room and came out with a large book. Then she turned to the computer on the desk and started typing. The two others in the office seemed to have forgotten what they were talking about and sat as though someone had shoved a sock in their mouths.

"Here it is. Todd B. Thompson. All the information you need. Address, ODL #, DOB, and anything else you might need. Let me print this off for you." She pressed print and walla, there it was.

"That was rather easy, don't you think? Now there is just one more simple little task and that is a copy of his signature from this book right here. Can you do that for me?"

She grabbed the book went to the copy machine and had to turn it on. "It will be just a minute for it to warm up."

"Not a problem, I can wait."

She gave me the copy with a smile and said, "Will that be all?"

"You have been more than helpful and I do appreciate it Miss, what was your name, I don't believe I got that."

"Sara, Sara Smyles, with a y."

"Thank you Sara Smyles, and you keep smiling." And I walked out of the office.

I sat in my car reading all the information. This was a fifty three year old from Portland, OR. What ever could the connection be?

Spook met me in the driveway when I got home. Instead of going in I went over to Karyn and Daniel's.

Karyn greeted me at the door and invited me in, "How are you doing, Brenda? You have really been busy, either your partner is there or you are gone. Everything, okay?"

"You can't even imagine. I'm okay, just up to my neck in all this. I wanted to know if Spook could spend the night? I will be leaving tomorrow night for Florida, then Chicago and maybe on to Portland. So not sure how long I will be gone. At least a week I have a feeling."

"Hey no problem, Spook spends most of his time at your house even when you're not home. I think this transition is going to go very well for Spook. Daniel will be leaving in less than two weeks. He is helping me get ready for a big garage sale. Sorting for Good Will, garbage and the sale. The kids are even getting in to the action, they think they are going to get rich by selling some of their toys." She said laughingly.

"The realtor is listing the house by the first of the month. Sure hope it goes fast, I'm not going to like it here without Daniel."

"I bet you don't, but you have the kids so you really aren't alone. Sorry I can't stay, I have a ton of stuff to get done before we leave tomorrow night. Thanks for letting Spook have a sleep over." I said and smiled as I went out the door.

Spook and I went in the house and I locked the door behind me. I called Matt with the information from Enterprise. He didn't answer, so I left a message. Sam was about as confused over this new person as I was. We talked for awhile and then I told him I needed to get some stuff done. "Before you hang up, I made out an agenda for Dawson, guess I better add Portland as a maybe. You get your report done on this Todd guy and I'll come by and get it all and drop it off at the precinct in the morning and you won't have to bother with it. If Dawson has anything to say, he can say it to me. How does that sound? Are you going to be okay there by yourself tonight, Bee?" Sam asked with concern.

"Yes, my new room mate is making another trial run with me tonight. We'll be just fine. You get a good night sleep and I will do the same. Talk to you in the morning."

My cell rang almost immediately. I started to answer as usual, but heard instead, "I just called to say I Love You, I just called to say how much I care, I just called to say I Love You, and I mean it from the bottom of my heart". And the line went dead. Oh, Sam you are way too sweet.

CHAPTER 32

I finished up the laundry and packed my suitcase except for my cosmetic bag. I fixed a bowl of cereal and a piece of toast. Spook and I settled back to watch T.V. and did our usual fall asleep. I woke up at 11:03 and went to bed. Spook found his spot on the bed, head on the pillow next to me. "Okay this may work for tonight, but I think on a permanent basis we are going to have to figure out something different, buddy ole' pal of mine."

I woke up early and Spook had not moved a muscle. I let him out and put on the coffee, got the paper from the front porch and found there were five other papers lying there. Not a good thing to leave. Which reminded me to stop the paper. Mail wasn't an issue as I had a Post Office box that I needed to empty today. Probably ought to pay bills as well. Wow! I sure have let a few things slip by me this week, but then I guess I have been rather busy.

I poured coffee and was reading the paper and there was a knock on the slider. "It's me, Sam."

"Good morning, I hoped you would have the coffee on, I rushed out of the house without any. How was your night?"

"Great, Spook and I slept like babies. He on one pillow and me on the other. Yah, I know, we will have to figure things out differently when it becomes permanent. Here are my reports for his honorable." I said. Got up and poured Sam coffee.

We went over our strategy for the next several days. Talked over some of the happenings of the last four days. "Our flight leaves at ten thirty, why don't I come by and pick you up at seven, go out and have a nice dinner before we have to check in? Will that be alright with you? You can take it easy the rest of the day, you certainly do deserve it."

"I do want to go by the hospital and see Mrs. Compton and be sure security is in position. Dinner sounds great. We'll be in touch." And I leaned over and gave him a kiss.

"Careful, now, you aren't dressed, and I would be willing to bet the bed isn't made yet."

"Get out of here. We have plenty of time to catch up on that. See ya later." I said and gave him a light punch on the shoulder.

I took a showered, got dressed, fixed a soft boiled egg and toast for breakfast and read some more of the paper and another cup of coffee before going to the hospital. There was a novel on the coffee table I had been reading on for about six months and put it with the rest of my carry-ons. I doubted I would get much reading done, but just incase.

I stopped by the nurse's station and asked how Mrs. Compton was doing.

"She is actually about the same. Everything looks good except she just won't wake up," The nurse said. I glanced over and saw a police officer sitting beside her door.

"When did the first officer come on duty?"

"Let me look at her chart. We record everything and all of her visitors, including you Sergeant Weathers." She smiled and flipped a couple of pages, "Here it is. First officer came on at 4:00 p.m. and they changed at midnight and again at 8:00 a.m. Looks like eight hour shifts."

"Have there been any other visitors?"

"Only one, and that was a Reverend Paul Stearns. He was here about five thirty and only stayed for about twenty minutes. Miss Ellie got a little restless while he was in there, but settled down when he left."

"Thank you, I am going to go in and will probably stay about the same amount of time."

I went in her room and slid a chair up close and held her hand. "Good morning Miss Ellie. Remember me, Brenda Weathers? I have been in to see you every day since your accident. Who were you having dinner with the evening of the accident? Was it Reverend Stearns? I went by and visited with him yesterday, he seems like such a nice man. Don't you agree? Miss Ellie, can you squeeze my hand? Can you move a finger? Would you move a finger for me Miss Ellie? You have been sleeping now for four days, don't you think it is time to wake up and talk to me? I want to help you, but if you won't talk to me I can't help you. Who is Todd Thompson?" I felt a slight movement with her hand. "You know Todd Thompson don't you? Can you wake up and tell me who Todd Thompson is. Miss Ellie, who is Todd Thompson?" Her hand moved again ever so slightly, but a definite move for the second time.

The nurse came in the room. "Miss Ellie's blood pressure is raising, did you say something to upset her?"

"Actually, I have been just talking randomly, but there is a name I keep repeating and that seems to be the cause of the blood pressure increase. I will go now and won't be back for about a week. I will be calling in and checking on her daily. Maybe in a week there will be a significant change. I sure hope so." I got up and left.

I decided to leave this information for discussion either over dinner or the plane trip.

PART II

SUSANNE FARRELL
AND
DARYL COMPTON

CHAPTER 33

Sam and I stopped at a very nice restaurant for dinner not far from the airport. The table had a beautiful vase with six red roses and there was a chilled bottle of Dom Perignon. We sat down and I looked across the table at Sam, he had an innocent unconcerned expression look about him as he was reading the menu.

"Sam, what is all this?"

"All what?"

"This." I said and pointed to the roses and the chilled bottle. "Are we sitting at the right table?"

Sam chuckled, "This is just my way to say I Love You. Do you have a problem with it?" And he reached across the table and held my hand with that beautiful smile.

"I'm not sure; this just isn't our normal dinner setting." I smiled suspiciously at Sam.

"Just relax and enjoy dinner, we have a very busy week ahead of us."

"Thank you, the roses are beautiful. How am I going to get these on the plane without ruining them?" I asked.

"The attendants have a place in the front where they can store them, what we don't drink of the Champagne we will carry on and drink on the plane. AND I have already set that up with security; they will take it for us there and give it to the attendants."

"That is quite out of the ordinary isn't it? What happened to the two ounce rule of the airlines?"

"I just happen to know someone that is sneakier than me and is handling it." He said with a mischievous smile. "I doubt there will be any left, so not to worry."

The waiter poured a sample and Sam tasted for approval. Sam

nodded and the waiter filled our glasses. Sam lifted his glass, as did I, and said, "To us and a successful trip." And we clinked our glasses.

I took my first sip and saw something in the bottom of the glass. I sat my glass down and was shocked by the sight of a ring. "Sam, what is this?"

Sam was out of his chair and on one knee, "Brenda Lou Weathers, will you do the honors of being my wife, spend the rest of our lives together? Brenda, will you marry me?"

I sat there in total shock, I didn't know what to say, I know what I wanted to say, but now was not the time. We had so much at stake and we couldn't risk it. I started to cry and before I could come up with a viable argument I had said, "Yes, Sam Davis I will marry you and spend the rest of my life with you." Sam took the ring out of the glass and put it on my finger. And then I heard the whole restaurant applaud with whistling and yelling congratulations. Sam stood up and gave me a kiss and returned to his chair beaming.

"Sam, this is absolutely gorgeous, and it fits perfectly. How did you do this? I am stunned, it is beautiful."

I was afraid of the decision we had just made and repercussion it was going to have with the department. "Sam, how are we going to handle this with Captain Dawson?"

"Well, I am thinking that we need to think about this. I don't remember ever reading anything about marriage in the Policy and Procedure Manual. When we get home let's check it out, in the meantime, let's enjoy." Sam raised his glass again, and we said "Cheers."

We finished our dinner, laughing and joking about most anything. It was apparent the Champagne was taking its toll on me. Unfortunately, when dinner was over, there wasn't any Champagne left. We had drank the whole bottle. This was going to be better than any sleeping pill I had planned to take.

CHAPTER 34

As we boarded the plane the attendant took the vase of roses and put them in a safe place. We were all settled in our seat and as luck would have it, we had three seats to ourselves. While we were waiting for take off I thumbed through one of the propaganda magazines and found an intriguing article about an old Chicago hotel that had recently undergone a complete renovation. The pictures of the lobby, the lounge and restaurant were amazingly decorated as well as the different available suites and rooms. I leaned over to Sam, "Look at this, isn't it gorgeous? Read the article they have all kinds of activities going on, one of which is a daily wine tasting during happy hour. Maybe we ought to check this out when we leave Ft. Lauderdale?"

"Yeah okay. I'll read it." He said it without much enthusiasm and acted more preoccupied than with interest to my suggestion.

When we were airborne Sam leaned over to me and whispered in my ear, "You want to join the Mile High Club?"

"You are kidding?"

"Not at all."

"Well, I'm not interested in the membership. We've had too much Champagne and I think I am going to sleep all the way to Florida."

Sam gave me his childish, lip out, pout. "Okay then, you just wait until we get to the Hotel. You don't know what you are missing."

"You sound as though you are a chartered member of the Mile High Club. Just how experienced are you?" I said, giving him a suspicious, teasing look.

"You have no idea. Sure you don't want to give it a try?"

"Yes, I am sure." I got my book out of my bag and started reading. Sam grabbed his book and started reading as well.

I read about ten pages and started getting sleepy. "That Champagne worked better than a sleeping pill, I'm going to the restroom and then sleep, excuse me please."

As I opened the door coming out of the restroom, Sam rushed in and closed the door very quickly. He was laughing as he grabbed me and started kissing and groping my body. He dropped his pants and sat on the toilet, and pulled my panties down and I stepped out of one leg. Sam pulled me down on his lap; his hands were searching sensuously and found all my hot spots. Sam whispered, "I love you, you are the love of my life." The passion was rising, it wasn't long until Sam was inside me and we were lost in the moment. Kissing and undulating we soon climaxed at the same time and relaxed for a short moment. Then Sam said, "Welcome to the Mile High Club, my Darling."

I stood up, cleaned up and got dressed. This seemed like much tighter quarters than it was a few minutes ago. I gave Sam a passionate kiss and said, "I love you with all my heart, too." I opened the door, stepped out and quickly shut the door. I returned to my seat nonchalantly, picked up my book and continued to read. A few minutes later Sam returned to his seat with an impish smirk. "Welcome, my dear, welcome." And he settled into his book.

It wasn't long until I put my book down and was sound asleep. I was wakened by the Pilot announcing, "Ladies and Gentlemen, we are now making our descent into Ft. Lauderdale, FL. It is 6:30 a.m. and presently sixty eight degrees. We hope you have enjoyed your flight with us and will choose to fly with us for your future travels. Attendants, please prepare the cabin for landing at this time." The attendant then came on over the loud speaker, "In preparation for landing please put your tray table up and return your chair in its upright position." And they started their trip through the cabin.

CHAPTER 35

After landing, Sam grabbed the vase of roses and I made my way to luggage pick up and Sam went to get our rental car. I rented the wheeled cart, now $3.00, what happened to the $2.00 it used to be? Guess times are hard all over, I chuckled. Sam picked me and our luggage up and we headed for the Residence Inn. We checked in and settled into the room, room my ass. This was a two bedroom apartment, completed with a fully supplied kitchen, living room with a big screen T.V. and two large bathrooms. "I could live here very nicely, pretty fancy wouldn't you say?"

Sam walked over to me and put his arms around me and said, "I am the happiest I have been in a very long time. I want to shout to the world how much I love you."

"I love you too; I am still in shock that I said yes so quickly." And I looked down at my left hand and admired the beautiful ring. "I am going to get in the shower and then we need to bring each other up to date before we start the day." Sam agreed.

By the time I got completely dressed, Sam had gone out and brought back a carafe of coffee and blueberry muffins. "This should get us through the morning until lunch. Now let's bring ourselves up to date."

"I told you about going to Enterprise and getting the formation on the driver of the Hummer. He is Todd B. Thompson, fifty three years old, Oregon driver's license and lives in South West Portland. I got the rental signature and phone number, but it appears it is a cell number. I went to the hospital to check on Mrs. Compton and the only visitor she'd had was Reverend Stearns, he only stayed for about twenty minutes according to the nurse. While I was talking to Mrs. Compton I mentioned Todd Thompson's name a couple of times and she responded by moving a finger and then her blood pressure elevated and the nurse came in and I had to leave. So I am guessing there is much more to this Todd we need to pursue. How did your day go? Besides flowers and ring shopping? You had to have been a very busy little boy, my dear." And I laughed.

"Yah, pretty much." Sam smiled and continued. "I never did get through to Susanne, but I have a feeling she is home. The nanny was acting rather strange the last time I called. So I would like to make an unannounced visit to the Farrell's. I think the sooner we do that the more surprised we might catch her and maybe Clinton as well."

"Sounds good to me. You ready to go, I am?"

"Sure am." Setting up both our laptops after Sam ran Map Quest and got the map and directions to the Farrell's house and hit print. We picked up all our stuff and went to the car.

When we got in the car Sam discovered there was a GPS. This was going to be better than Map Quest.

We drove right to the Farrell's without any difficulty or wrong turns. As we made the turn up the driveway, I gasped at the beauty of the home. Actually, this wasn't a home it was a mansion. "Wow, I wonder who financed this place. I don't believe I have ever known a banker who lived quite this well."

"I'm thinkin we sure made a wrong choice in professions." Sam rang the door bell and waited and rang it again. The nanny answered the door, "May I help you?"

"Yes, we would like to talk with Mrs. Farrell, please. I am Detective Sam Davis and this is my partner Sergeant Brenda Weathers."

"I'm sorry, Mrs. Farrell is not at home. You'll have to come back later." And she tried to shut the door.

Sam was very quick and put his foot in the door and pushed it open, "I have reason to believe Mrs. Farrell is home and it is imperative that I speak with her."

The nanny raised her voice and said, "I told you Mrs. Farrell is not home, now you must leave."

"I can't do that. I---------." Sam was cut off by what appeared to be a teenager of about fifteen years old.

"Is there a problem, Maria?" He said.

"I told them Mrs. Farrell is not home and they should come back later, and they won't go." She said in her broken English.

The teenager stepped forward and said, "You heard Maria, Mom is not home."

Then a little voice spoke up, and we looked down to a child of about seven years old. "Yes, she is Tommy, I was just upstairs. She is in her room. I will go get her." And he turned and ran away from the door. Maria and Tommy exchanged looks and stepped aside and Tommy said, "Please come in, I will go upstairs and get Mom."

Maria gave us a "Humph" and briskly walked out of the room.

Sam and I exchanged looks and were astonished at the exquisite furnishings in the foyer and what we could see of the living room.

We watched Mrs. Farrell stroll down the staircase, and walk towards us, "To what do I owe the honor of this visit Detective Davis?"

"It appears you remember my name, but couldn't remember to return a phone call, Mrs. Farrell. Would you care to explain?" Sam asked.

"Your call just said Mother was in the hospital in stable, but serious condition. I saw no need to return the call until she was dead. When did she die? I assume you are here to offer your condolences." She said very sarcastically.

"Mrs. Compton is not dead, Mrs. Farrell. She is improving slowly, all of her vitals are good and she is in a very stable condition. However, she won't wake up. The Doctor believes she is in a sub-conscientious coma, meaning she is not ready to face the trauma of the accident." Sam explained. "We believe she knows who the intruder is and is not ready to face it."

"What intruder, what are you talking about? And please call me Susanne. Mrs. Farrell is my mother-in-law and I don't like the reminder."

"I am going to let Sergeant Weathers explain that to you considering she was first on the scene." He nodded to me to take the lead.

I told her everything from the beginning to the end including the Hummer being rented to a Todd B. Thompson. "Do you have any idea who this man is?"

"No, I have never heard the name. But you need to understand, Mother and I haven't had any contact in several years. In fact I think it is coming up on eleven years now. She hasn't even met her youngest grandson, and the other two were three and sixteen years old the last time she saw them."

"Do you and your brother, Daryl, ever get together?" I asked.

"That whiney little spoiled brat. No. I have no reason or desire to get together with my brother. He may as well be dead as well as Mother."

"Those are pretty strong feelings, Susanne. What happened?" I asked.

"I really don't think it is any of your business what happened with our family. Now unless you have any further questions of me, I believe our business is over and I would like you to leave."

"You are right, it is none of my business, I apologize. Susanne, where were you on Monday, May 1st about 5:30 p.m.?"

"You are kidding of course. You don't actually believe I was in San Diego with the intent to kill my own mother, do you?" She exclaimed.

"It doesn't matter what I think, Mrs. Farrell, please answer my question."

"I was right here at home." She answered.

Sam interjected, "That is really odd, your nanny repeatedly told me you were out of town."

"I always tell Maria to tell callers I am out of town if she doesn't know who they are and then I check caller ID and return calls I want to." She snapped.

"Then I would like to speak with Maria. Please call her back in here." Sam said and Susanne started to leave the room. "Excuse me, you can use the intercom I noticed right here on the wall."

"Alright, I was out of town, I was in Los Angeles at a church retreat. I left on Sunday morning and returned yesterday. You can check with my pastor and the members I attended with." She retorted.

"I will, I need the name and phone number of your Pastor, names and numbers of those you attended with. I want a copy of the receipt from your airline ticket and the receipt where you stayed—check in and check out. And I would like to have that now." Sam requested.

"I can't possibly produce all that right now. It will take me some time." Susanne said with her hands on her hips.

"Not a problem, we have all kinds of time. Don't we Sergeant?"

"Nothing but time." I replied and crossed my arms in front of my chest.

Susanne started up the stairs, "Excuse me, where are you going?" Sam asked.

"I am going to my office to get the information you are requesting." She replied.

"Perfect, we'd like to join you if you don't mind. I would really rather not stand the whole time you are putting this together. Sitting for us would be much more comfortable." Sam said with a smile.

CHAPTER 36

Susanne turned on her heals and started upstairs with both myself and Sam hot on her heels. We each grabbed a chair and sat while she rustled through papers, made copies, went through the phone book, rustled through more papers and got more frustrated as the time passed. Sam and I sat patiently watching her and making small talk. Occasionally Susanne looked up and gave us a cold glare. It took her about an hour and a half to produce all the information we had requested. Susanne put it all neatly in a folder, handed it to Sam and said, "Are we done now?"

"Not quite, we would like to speak with your husband, Clinton. Is he here?"

"No, my husband is out of the country and at the moment I can't tell you where he is."

"Where was he and when did you last speak with him?"

"I don't know what my husband has to do with this." Susanne snapped.

"Maybe nothing, but we will still need to speak with him."

"Actually, my husband and I have been separated for about three months. He is off flitting around Europe with his new little blonde twenty eight year old bimbo girlfriend. So, to answer your question, where is Clinton? I don't know nor do I care. When did I last speak to him? The day he left for Europe with the bimbo and I don't care if I ever do. The children and Maria think he is away on a business trip and I prefer it that way. Are we quite through?" Susanne asked.

"Do you think there would be any reason that Clinton would have gone to see your Mother?" Sam asked.

"Absolutely not. Mother and Daddy never did like him. And Mother doesn't have enough money to bail him out of the trouble he is in if she were dead and he got it all. I can assure you he won't get a penny."

"There is just one more question. Did you hire someone to kill your mother?" Sam asked. That was certainly a question I hadn't expected and with Susanne's reply, she didn't either.

"Detective Davis, I can assure you I did not hire someone to kill my Mother nor did I go to San Diego to kill her myself. If you would please leave, and now, I would appreciate it." Susanne snapped at Sam.

"Thank you, Susanne, you have been most helpful. If we have any more questions we will call. So I suggest you not leave town and answer your phone when we call. By the way, what do you know about Todd Thompson?"

"I've never heard the name. Why are you asking me about this person again?"

"Just a name that has come up that has become a person of interest. Thanks anyway, but if you do remember something, just give me a call." Sam said smiling and we walked down the stairs and out the door to the car.

"Wow, what a pistol. I'm thinking Mrs. Compton should be happy her daughter doesn't have any contact with her. That last one was a surprise; if she hired someone to kill her mother."

Sam smiled at me and said, "It never hurts to ask. Some times the reaction and answer is a dead give away."

"So what do you think?"

"She is certainly in a precarious situation now with Clinton off playing around. Anything is possible. I will be checking out her alibi for sure."

CHAPTER 37

We stopped by the grocery store and picked up a few items for the suite at the Inn. Then the liquor store, an absolute necessity, and went back to the Residence Inn. I fixed sandwiches while Sam arranged both laptops for the afternoon's work.

My first call was to the hospital to check on Mrs. Compton. The nurse reported she had had one visitor, a friend and neighbor that had stayed about an hour. Mrs. Compton's condition hadn't changed much. She did seem to be a bit restless when her neighbor was in the room. But as soon as she left she settled back down. The nurse thought with more company she might start waking up. "Do you know this friends name?" I asked the nurse.

"I will have to look on the chart--------let's see, oh here it is, Nellie Goodman. And I see Paul Stearns was in as well, Sorry I didn't see that one at first."

"How was she after the Reverends visit?"

"Not so good. She seems to get agitated when he visits, nothing to be alarmed about, just a little restless."

"Thank you very much for your help. I will call back either later today or tomorrow. I am out of town for a few days so I will not be in, but if it isn't a problem I will be calling in periodically. Is there a chance someone could call me if Miss Ellie does wake up?" I gave the nurse my cell number.

"That won't be a problem at all. I will make a note of it." And she hung up.

Sam was calling from the list Susanne had given him and I placed a call to Nellie. Her name was on the list I had torn out of Mrs. Compton's phone book.

Nellie answered right away, I identified myself and asked, "Do you have a few minutes that we might chat about Mrs. Compton?"

"Why of course my dear. I am so shocked about Miss Ellie. Why I just never."

"Yes, I know, it is pretty tragic alright. How long have you known Mrs. Compton?"

"Well, let me see. Harold and I moved to this house in 1952. We didn't socialize for the few years, Harold was busy starting a new business and Blake was really busy with his law firm. Seemed like he was out of town a lot for trials in other cities. Miss Ellie hated staying alone and the older Susanne got the more she hated it. Susanne was a handful, that girl, she could get into trouble without even trying. I felt sorry for her most of the time. Her Daddy was pretty mean to her. And then when Daryl came along, he totally ignored Susanne and devoted all his time to that boy. It's no wonder those two turned out like they have."

I could see this was going to require an afternoon visit, so I decided I better shorten up the conversation. "Mrs. Goodman, I would love to visit more with you about the family. It sounds like you and Mrs. Compton are pretty good friends. Did she respond at all to you when you went in to see her?"

"Well, I thought she was just sleeping, so I touched her arm and said 'Miss Ellie, its Nellie. I came to visit for awhile, you can wake up now'. She didn't open her eyes so I leaned down to her ear and said it again louder in her ear. She didn't have her hearing aids in you know so I thought she didn't hear me. She frowned and moved her head away from me. I think she heard me."

"Ah, maybe that is why she isn't waking up, no one has put her hearing aids in and she isn't hearing anyone? Will you be able to visit her again?"

"Oh yes, I can visit any time, well, lets see I play bridge on Tuesday, then the Knitter's Guild meet on Monday and Thursday. But I will sure go see her those other days. The Reverend was there the other day when I was in, so I left right away."

"Oh good, Reverend Stearns seems like such a nice man, don't you think?"

"Well, if you must know, I don't like him. I think he is money hungry. He is a charmer, alright. He is always asking Miss Ellie for money, and she gives it to him. Between you and me, I think he is a scoundrel."

"Mrs. Goodson, is there----------"

"Please call me Nellie."

"Okay, Nellie, are there anymore of Miss Ellie's close friends that can go visit with her?"

"Well, let me a think a minute. Oh yes, Betty Anne still drives, she and Miss Ellie are good friends, and me too I guess. I will call her and tell her what has happened. In fact, I have told a lot of people about poor Miss Ellie, so there could be others that go see her. You see not everyone drives anymore at our age, and some have moved into retirement centers. I will make some calls."

"Nellie, that is really nice of you, however, I don't believe the doctor wants a whole bunch of people coming to see her. So you might want to keep it to just a few, okay?"

"Oh sure, I understand."

"I need to go now, I am looking forward to meeting with you when I get back. I will give you a call and maybe I can drop by for afternoon tea?"

"That would be nice, but I don't drink tea in the afternoons, it keeps me awake at night. I have cocktails at three o'clock, just one, well sometimes two. So please come by for cocktails with me at three."

"Sounds good, I will call you when I get back. Thank you for your help, Nellie. Bye now."

"Wow that was certainly an interesting conversation with Mrs. Goodman." I said to Sam. "I'm sure it will be an all afternoon visit with dear ole Nellie when we get back. How are you doing?"

"Interesting. I have confirmed Susanne did go to Los Angeles. So far I haven't talked with anyone that remembers seeing her at any of the events on the schedule. But they also say she could have been there, just in other parts of the retreat. I am thinking at this point, either she didn't attend any of it and met up with someone else or she made a fast trip to San Diego. I'm not done yet, so I'm not making any final conclusions."

"Maybe you need to check credit cards for other airline flights. You know the ones she forgot to mention. I don't really think I am considering Susanne as the intruder, she doesn't fit the size of the person I saw leaving Mrs. Compton's house. But who knows what else we are going to find out about those two."

"Oh Yah, I'm thinkin the door is opening wide for all kinds of weird links, may not necessarily help us solve our case, but could solve some others." And he laughed.

I looked at my watch, it was three thirty. I stood up, stretched and said, I am going to go in and take a short nap. Don't let me sleep more than an hour and a half, please, or I won't be able to sleep tonight at all."

"Sounds good to me, maybe I will join you."

"Only if a nap is on your mind."

Sam swatted my behind, "Spoil Sport."

I woke at 5:35 and Sam was still sound asleep beside me. I got up and showered and dressed for dinner. Then I woke Sam. While he was showering I made us each a cocktail and fixed a plate of cheeses and crackers.

CHAPTER 38

Periodically I had looked at the sparkling diamond ring on my finger; a two carat marquee cut solitaire. Still in shock over how this had happened so rapidly. I knew as soon as we got home it was going to go back in its little box. I also knew we couldn't share this news with anyone at the risk of losing our jobs. Sam was pretty sure there wasn't anything in the Policy and Procedure Manual about married couples or otherwise. He just thinks it is another ploy of Dawson blowing smoke. However, I was assured he would find out for sure.

We went to a restaurant that was within walking distance of our Inn. Sam ordered another bottle of Dom Perignon. I think he was hoping for success tonight as he had on the plane. What a conniver, I was thinking to myself and smiling.

Sam caught my smile and said, "What are you smiling about?"

"I was just wondering your motive about Dom Perignon two nights in a row?"

"It sure worked last night, why not?" He laughed and started reading the menu.

We had a nice dinner discussing various issues of the case. Then the conversation got more serious when Sam brought up our future and the plans he had hoped we could fulfill. I listened intently as though he were talking about a couple he knew, his best friends. I started laughing and he stopped and said, "What is so funny?"

"You are talking to me as if you are telling a story that happened to two other people. This is us, don't I have any input into what is going to happen to the most important time in my life? You are setting the stage as though it is already signed sealed and delivered. I think you ought to back up and start from the beginning. It is very apparent you have given this a lot more thought than I have. Remember? I am the one you asked to marry just last night."

112

"You're right, I'm sorry Bee. I'm so in love with you I don't want us to ever be apart. Can you understand that?"

"Of course I understand your feelings. But do you understand how much this involves to get there? We have a case to solve, we each have a house to consider, you have children front and foremost, then there's Sylvia and my new room mate. And probably most important is our jobs. Sam, we have a whole lot to think about before 'D' day."

"You are way too practical Bee. Guess I've mostly flown by the seat of my pants and for the most part have come out on top. I know what you are saying, but I don't really see much of a big deal out of any one of them. It will all work out as we go. We can make it work. Okay?"

"Let's get this case done before we try to concentrate on any of the others."

The waiter brought the check to our table and finished pouring the Champagne in our glasses. Sam reaches across the table and held my hand and admired the diamond ring, smiled at me and said, "You are the love of my life, and I want to take care of you forever."

"I know, Sam, we'll get there, it just takes time."

We left the restaurant and decided to take a walk on the beach. The beach was about three blocks from the Inn and restaurant. It was a gorgeous night. The sun had already set and the moon was so bright it lit up the whole sky, the reflection off the water was almost blinding. We strolled holding hands and watched other couples doing the same, however, most of them appeared much younger. Sam over forty one and me almost thirty six we laughed at the fact we were senior citizens to most of them.

When we got back to the Inn, Sam poured us each a glass of wine. I went into the bathroom and changed into my bathrobe. Sam had turned on the news, but was paying no attention to it, instead he had opened the drapes to the deck off the living room and was standing outside on the lanai admiring the view. As I joined him I gasped at the beautiful view we had.

"Sam, this is a wonderful view. I had no idea we had all this."

"I didn't either; we just came in this morning, threw our suitcases in the bedroom, made a few phone calls and left. We lucked out wouldn't you say?"

"Absolutely, look at that moon; he is smiling down on us."

"He sure is and saying 'You two go for it, time is a waistin'." Sam pulled me in closer and we just stood there drinking our wine and drinking in the view.

We finished our wine and retired for the night. Well, not quite. It was the most tender and gentle love making yet for us. Both completely spent we fell asleep in each others arms. I was wakened by Sam a few hours later with another urgency for love making. I glanced at the clock as Sam snuggled up to my back, it was 3:03 a.m. It seemed as though only a few minutes had passed when there was a knock on the door, "House keeping". I looked at the clock and it was 8:30 a.m. I groaned and went to the door. "We're okay, we don't need anything today." When I was sure she was gone I put the Do Not Disturb sign on the door and crawled back in bed. After all, it was only 5:30 a.m. West Coast time.

I had gone back to sleep for a couple hours and was getting up to make coffee and read the paper. Just as my feet hit the floor, I felt an arm around my waist and pulled me back into bed. "Where the Hell you think you are going my sweet lil chick-a-dee? I have a morning surprise for you."

"Ha Ha, I'll bet it is no surprise. Just the same ole thing."

"Same ole thing? Well, well, let's see if we can spice this same ole thing up a bit." Sam was laughing and pulled me back in bed and did he ever spice it up. While we were laying in each others arms afterwards, I started chuckling to myself. If we keep this up I am not going to be able to walk off the plane. A visual that made me laugh out loud.

"What are you laughing about?"

"I was just thinking, if we keep this up at the rate of three times a night until we get home, we are both going to need wheel chair assistance to get off the plane. Now that is a vision to behold." We were both laughing when I got up and went into the kitchen.

CHAPTER 39

The rest of the morning we drank coffee, made phone calls, taking notes and conversing about each call. Not much was accomplished other than not being able to confirm Susanne's story that she had attended the retreat in Los Angeles. She had flown there alright, but it rather dead ended after she had checked into the facility where the retreat was being held. We agreed another visit to Susanne was a necessity.

We were greeted at the door by Maria and her stern familiar being. Without saying a word she left the door open and turned to the intercom to page Susanne.

We waited outside until she invited us in, not knowing for sure if she would. For some reason we had the feeling she didn't like us. Imagine that. Susanne came down the stairs and said, "Now, what? I gave you all the information you asked for yesterday."

"UM, may we come in? We need to chat with you about some issues that are questionable to us."

"What issues? There is nothing that should be questionable. It is all there and nothing more to add."

"That may be. But we think there is. May we go up to your office?"

Susanne sat down at her desk, leaned back in her chair with arms crossed. "Ask away." She said with a smirk on her face.

This was going to be a fun smirk to watch disappear as Sam worked her over. I sat back to enjoy the sparks that were about to fly.

"Well, Susanne, it appears that most of the names you have given us, including the minister, don't recall seeing you at the retreat. Your airline ticket is confirmed and check in at the retreat facility is confirmed. But no one seems to remember you attending any of the sessions. Can you explain this?"

"There were lots of different sessions going on in different rooms. I didn't stay with the same group through out the retreat. It is possible I wasn't even in any of the same sessions as the group that I went with. That is not unusual, you know."

"Why don't you tell me about this retreat? What were some of the topics and what were they about?"

"Oh my God. Are you expecting me to remember all those sessions?"

"As a matter of fact I am. Susanne this was only a few days ago that you supposedly went to this retreat. It can't be that difficult."

She started rustling around on her desk and found a brochure. "Here, read up on it yourself."

That was not a good idea, she had thrown out a game that in no way was she going to win. Sam settled back in his chair and looked at the brochure for a couple of minutes, turning the pages and then said, "This looks like a very good retreat, maybe I will attend one someday. So, on Monday which sessions, did you attend?"

"I don't know, there was more than one."

"I see that. They started rather early, two at 8:00 a.m. till 9:45; two at 10:00 till 11:45 then break for lunch until 1:30. Afternoon sessions, two at 1:30 till 3:30 and two till 5:30, dinner and an evening session from 7:30 until 9:30. That looks like a pretty structured retreat. Seems as though Tuesday, and Thursday were a repeat of Monday and Wednesday so you had the opportunity to attend all of them if you chose to. Why don't you tell me about your favorite one and when it was. Surely you can remember that much, can't you?"

"Detective Davis, just what is it you want from me?

"Susanne, I don't think this should be too hard to understand. All I want is where you were on Monday, May 1st, plain and simple. So far you have not provided me with that information, instead, you have wasted my time and that of others with bogus information that didn't prove shit. So, having said that, can we back up and start at square one. Where were you on Monday May 1st?"

"I flew to Los Angeles; you verified that, I checked into the hotel, you verified that. But I didn't ever go to my room. Instead, I took a cab and went to another hotel and spent the four days with a friend. Yes, it is a male friend and I can't give you his name as he is married. I have been trying to end the relationship. There is just too much other stuff involved."

"You are going to have to do better than that, Susanne, married or not I have to have his name, or I have no choice but to charge you with suspicion of attempted murder of your mother."

Susanne started crying. Sam sat back in his chair, crossed his arms, gave me the raised eyebrow look, and waited for the 'flow of tears' trick to stop. Susanne grabbed a handful of Kleenex, wiped her tears, blew her nose and tried to regain her composure.

"It is so complicated and could get so nasty if this ever got out. Clinton can't ever find out, I made a horrible mistake."

"Maybe you better fill us in. Susanne, you have no choice here."

"Clinton is not having an affair, he is hiding out and on the run. He got us in debt way over our heads and started playing money games in the banking business. This guy came to Clinton and invited him into this investment group with a promise for a quick fast money recovery. Clinton fell for it hook line and sinker, totally out of desperation. When the bank came down on Clinton, he went to this investment group and they of course offered to help and partially did. To keep from being prosecuted Clinton was able to pay back most of the loans he had made with a promissory note to make restitution on the rest, which is a very small amount considering what it was. I can't tell you all of the details of what Clinton is involved in. Not because I won't, but because I don't know."

"So are you telling me your husband is involved with the Mafia?"

"I guess that is who they are. I really don't know. Clinton has been very emphatic about keeping me in the dark in all of this. So I thought Clinton was having an affair and had been seeing other women because of all the secrecy. Then, not intentionally, I got involved with someone. It was innocent at first, someone I could talk to that understood, listened to me and a companion you know? And when I found out Clinton was not having an affair I tried to put the breaks on, it hasn't been that easy."

"Clinton has listed the house for sale with a private realtor of some sort that shows the house by appointment only, only certain days and the children and I have to leave. No real estate signs in the yard and no advertising. I know this all sounds very suspicious, but I have lived like this for the past three years and it is getting worse. I don't know whom I can trust and who I can't, so I don't trust anyone."

"Susanne, I understand your dilemma, I still have to talk to this man. All I am trying to do is clear you from a possible attempt of murder charge. I do not want to get involved with the rest of your life. I want to solve your mother's case. I need his name, number and way to contact him."

She took out a pen from the desk drawer and scribbled down the information and slid it across the desk. "Are we quite through here?" Susanne said.

"One more question for now, anyway, are you sure you don't know Todd Thompson?"

"I have no idea who he is. What does he have to do with all of this anyway?"

"We located the yellow Hummer that was at your mother's house the day she got shot. He was the registered renter of the vehicle from Enterprise."

"So you think he is the one that shot my mother? Then why all the questions of me?"

"We are covering all aspects of this case, Susanne. He is a person of interest as well."

"I can assure you I have no connection to this Todd. I have told you everything I need to. So are we done now?"

"We'll see. Like I said before, don't leave town and do take my calls. We'll be in touch." Susanne stood up and started towards her office door. "That's okay, we'll let ourselves out. I know the way."

When we got in the car I said, "That women is in one hell of a predicament. I can't even imagine being in her shoes." Sam agreed.

CHAPTER 40

As we were driving out the driveway and before we got to the front gate I was looking at the beauty of the place and noticed a couple of horses grazing in the pasture next to the driveway. "Look at those two beautiful horses over there. That reminds me of the days Cindy and I used to have a couple old mares at Grama and Gampa's ranch in Idaho."

"They are beautiful. This is a beautiful place. You never talk much about your grandparents. How old are they.?"

"Grama's eighty one years old and Grampa is eighty two. They still live on the ranch and have hired hands to run it now, a care giver that comes in twice a week to help with their personal needs and they manage the rest of the time. Of course Mom and Dad live fairly close by so they are out there a lot of the time. Grama is involved with sewing projects for the church so Mom goes out and helps her with that. They've planted a garden every summer since I can remember, Grampa keeps it watered, Mom and Dad weed and Candy and I helped weed when we were kids, sort of. Mom always helps Grama put it all up in the fall, either canning or freezing. They are still really active and very young for their age. Grampa is still driving, although Dad refuses to ride with him. They are so cute together. I spent a night with them when I went home for Candy's wedding. Sure brought back some childhood memories."

"I have a great idea. It's Sunday. Let's go back to the room, change clothes, make a picnic lunch and go to the beach for the rest of the afternoon. How does that sound to you? You can tell me about you and Candy and your childhood with your grandparents."

"Perfect, best idea you have come up with all day. Well, maybe not, you might have had one idea better earlier this morning."

We got in the room and started throwing clothes around and into shorts. I was making sandwiches and Sam found a clean box at the dumpster we lined it with the morning newspaper, took a clean plastic garbage basket liner filled it with ice. Grabbed the roll of paper towels, plastic glasses and a couple bottles of wine and threw them in our make shift picnic basket and we were good to go. At the last minute I took a blanket from the closet and two extra bath towels, my book and we were out the door.

It was a beautiful afternoon. Sam found an access road to the beach and drove as far to the end as he could to find a parking place. The parking lots were jam packed. Fortunately, at the end of the road didn't seem to be quite as busy. He let me out with our stuff and parked the car, then we found the perfect spot. We spent the afternoon eating, drinking, napping, reading, playing in the water and of course we both got sunburned. Sun screen was the last thing either of us had thought about. The time went by far too fast and the next thing we knew it was time to pack up and go back to the Inn.

CHAPTER 41

Sam was up early and anxious to call Mike Hunter, the name Susanne had given him. Susanne had given Sam three phone numbers, cell, office and home as a last resort. At 8 a.m. Sam made the first call to Mr. Hunter's cell phone and got his voice mail message. The next call was to the office. The receptionist answered, "Southern Bank of Florida, how may I direct your call?"

"I would like to speak with Mike Hunter. This is Detective Sam Davis of the San Diego County Sheriff's Department in California."

"One moment please."

"Mr. Hunter won't be in until nine o'clock. Would you like his voice mail?" So Sam left another message, the same as on Mr. Hunter's cell phone.

I knew it was too early to make any calls to the West Coast. I wanted to check on Mrs. Compton and find out at the precinct if Daryl had faxed his information to my desk. It was still an hour to early too even call Daryl; we were an hour earlier from him. So here I sat. I decided to put on my swim suit and swim a few laps in the pool. I got a towel, my book and headed downstairs.

The pool was big enough to make doing laps worth while. I have been in pools that made me feel like I was swimming in circles. I got out and toweled off and sat in a lounge, oh my, this was a hard assignment too be on, I thought to myself. I picked up my book and started reading. Wouldn't you know I dozed off and was awakened by Sam.

"I just talked with Mike Hunter and he wants to meet for lunch. Do you want to come along, you sure don't have to?"

"If you don't mind, I think I will stay here and make my calls and you can fill me in when you get back."

Sam leaned down and kissed me, "I would love to fill you in when

I get back. Oh, you're talking about the meeting with Mr. Hunter. I lost my head for a minute."

We both laughed as I got up and walked to the building with him. "See ya later and have fun."

As I was walking into the room my cell phone was ringing. I answered and quickly recognized the voice of my sister, Candy. "Hey there, how was the honeymoon?"

"Absolutely wonderful. We had the best time. Besides all the sex, we really didn't do much. Just hung out at the resort and relaxed. We rented a sail boat for a day and just sailed around in the bay, and of course sun burned our asses off. But Aloe Vera took care of that. Got in on some of the touristy shit a couple afternoons, other than that just hung out. Got a great tan, unfortunately, I have tan lines. We got home last night, Tim had to go to work this morning but I still have this week off to finish getting settled. How about you? What have you been up to? I talked to Mom and Dad this morning for little bit and Dad said you are still having problems with Dawson. That bastard, what is his problem?"

"Oh, you know, he just has an issue with females. It's just that he picked on the wrong one this time. He can't push me around like he can some of the other women. He'll get it figured out one of these days. Actually, Sam and I are in Florida right now working a case."

"You and Sam? My, My Missy. And what is this all about? You of course do have separate rooms? So what's going on with you two?"

I was looking at the diamond ring on my left hand wishing I could tell her the news, but I didn't dare, not yet. "Just business, Candy. The day I got home from your wedding I was witness to a shooting down the road from me a ways."

I filled her in on most of the story, streamlined it considerably and left out the part about the intruder at my house. I told her we would be going on to Chicago and then Portland and home. Candy had met Spook and was thrilled he would be my new room mate. She hated my work and its danger and the fact that I lived alone. So to have a dog as a room mate was perfect.

"When are you going to quit fooling around with Sam and marry him? You aren't getting any younger, and your biological clock is ticking fast away. So tell me, what is wrong with Sam? Why don't you go after him? Is it because he has kids?"

"Hey, how about one question at a time, and how about changing the subject? How's Grama and Grampa doing?"

"You can be such a brat sometimes Brenda. Let's just change the subject if we are getting to close to a touchy subject. So does that mean you two are a thing, or are you just doin the thing?"

"Candy, I am going to hang up on you if you don't stop. If I didn't know better I'd think you have been drinking, but it is far too early in the morning for that. How's Grama and Grampa?"

"They are just fine. Worked all last week getting the ground ready for the biggest garden ever. Mom about croaked when she saw the size Grampa rotatilled. He keeps making it bigger every year."

"That's good for him, keeps him busy and something to do. Only problem is they end up with so much food they can't eat it all. I'll bet they still have frozen and canned food from two years ago."

Laughingly she agreed, "I think I might go out and raid the pantry and freezer. Hey, maybe if I go out to help Grama clean out the pantry and freezer to get ready for this years stuff, she'll give me some."

"Good idea, too bad I am so far away, I'd offer to help, ha ha. Well, kiddo I better get off the phone and get busy. I have a few calls to make before Sam gets back. Thanks for the call and I will be chatting with you soon. I love you and glad you and Tim had a great time. Later."

"Love ya too, later."

CHAPTER 42

Whew, she can sure be a pest. I went in showered and dressed for the day. Checked my emails and answered the ones that were a priority and left the rest. I called the precinct and when the dispatcher answered I asked, "This is Brenda Weathers, is Willy McClain in?"

"Just a moment, let me check. Hey Brenda, how's it goin?

"It's going great. We have been really busy."

"Brenda, Willy isn't here at the station, can someone else help you?"

"Actually, I need someone to check my desk for a fax, there should be a few pages from Daryl Compton."

"Okay, let me put you on hold and see what I can do."

"Brenda, there aren't any faxes on your desk, I checked to see if you had any messages and there was only one from your sister."

"Thank you, I have already talked with her."

My next call was to the hospital to check on Mrs. Compton. I asked for her nurse on the third floor. "This is Sergeant Brenda Weathers, how is Mrs. Compton progressing?"

"Hi Sergeant. This is Katie, I've talked with you before. Miss Ellie is doing better. By that I mean it seems she is trying to wake up. She has opened her eyes a few times; she is very confused as to where she is. She hasn't spoken yet, she gets frustrated and then goes back to sleep."

"Does she react this way with the nurses and with visitors?"

"Not that I know of, the nurses would've charted it. She has only had three different visitors."

"Can you tell me who the visitors were?"

"Let's see, the Reverend was in and Mrs. Goodman, another lady came in and I believe her name was Mary Jane Woods."

"So which visitor does she seem to be more upset with?"

"I guess I would have to say the Reverend. He doesn't stay very long, but she seems agitated after he leaves."

"Is there anyway, one of the nurses could be in the room when he comes to visit? You know, just checking machines or something as an excuse to be in there."

"It will all depend on what is going on at the time, but I will see what we can do."

"Thank you so much. I'll be in touch and you can always call if there are any changes."

My next call was to Daryl Compton. The receptionist told me he was in a meeting, but I could leave a message on his voice mail. I left the message with the urgency for him to return my call.

I went out on the deck and lit a cigarette and admired the view. It didn't seem like I had accomplished a thing so far and it was a definite we would be going to Chicago. I sat there reading my book, waiting for Daryl to call and for Sam to come back. I was really curious how that meeting was going.

It was mid afternoon when Sam came back from his meeting with Mike Hunter and Daryl still hadn't called. I made a couple of small ice cream sundaes with chocolate syrup and whipped cream on top. We sat out on the lanai enjoying the sun while Sam brought me up to date with what he had learned from Mr. Hunter.

"Mike confirmed he was with Susanne for the five days. I have removed Susanne from the list of suspects."

"I didn't think of Susanne as a suspect after we met her. She does not fit the person I saw leaving the house, but there is still Todd Thompson. Anyway, sorry for the interruption. Go ahead."

"Mike is really a nice guy and totally in love with Susanne. He believes Clinton to be a total 'scum bag' and deserves what ever happens. Mike is President of one of the banks Clinton had worked at. In the process of Susanne trying to pay some of the debt down, talking with Mike and pleading not to prosecute Clinton until she suspected he was having an affair. Mike believes Clinton is having an affair and has had others. He says Susanne also believes that even though she told us he wasn't having an affair. He told me stuff he really didn't need to, I guess maybe to justify his relationship with Susanne. But his marriage has been on the rocks for a few years and he and Susanne just fell into the affair for comfort and a need for each other. Apparently, because of Clinton's involvement with this group, if he will turn himself in and turn State's evidence, they have offered him and his family into the Witness Protection Plan. It is really a nasty situation and these guys are very dangerous. He said Susanne is afraid to leave the house, but she is also afraid to stay there. She has had the kid's home schooled for the last two years. Susanne has a tutor come to the house for their schooling. They have a twenty three year old daughter, Jane, they haven't heard from since all of this started. Apparently it was a pretty ugly scene when Jane left home. Tommy, the fifteen year old, is extremely bitter towards his dad even though he doesn't really know what has happened. Susanne is trying to keep all that from the kids. Joey, the little guy, is almost seven years old and finishing the first grade; he is oblivious to the whole situation and misses his daddy terribly. They are all pretty much sequestered in their own home. Maria, the house keeper, is the only one that comes and goes. She runs most of Susanne's errands for her, does all the shopping and occasionally takes the kids out to a movie or a week end away just for some outside activity. When that happens Mike has spent the week end at Susanne's, otherwise they try to sneak away to some secluded place. Mike says he has no plans of letting Susanne go and has already started his divorce and on the tail end of the proceedings. He didn't know why Susanne told us she was trying to break off the relationship or why she said she had made a mistake about Clinton's affair, because none of that was true. So, I'm thinking we are pretty much through here. I think Susanne is in an awful situation, but nothing we need to get involved with."

"Wow, you really had quite the afternoon. Poor Susanne, I guess, or maybe it is more 'poor kids'. So does Mike think he can take Susanne and the kids some place where they won't be found?"

"That is his plan. Even after his divorce he said he will be okay financially. He is sixty seven years old and has retirement from both the bank and the military and with social security they will be just fine. He is adamant he is moving forward with the relationship with Susanne and her kids."

"Does Mike have children?"

"No, ironically he and his wife only had one child that was killed in an automobile accident several years ago when the boy was only sixteen. He said that was the point the marriage started to deteriorate and was on a down hill spiral from there. Sad, that happens so often."

"What a story. I sure never expected all of this. Susanne is apparently a different person than what she has portrayed to us. She came across as tough, snooty and with a 'care less' attitude. Appears as though she is just the opposite."

"I think you are right. So how was your afternoon? Any luck on your phone call to Daryl?"

"No, of course not. He was in a meeting when I called so I left a message for him to return my call on his voice mail. That was about 11:00 his time , so he has had plenty of time to return my call. I called the hospital and checked on Mrs. Compton."

"How is she? Anything knew with her?"

"She has had three visitors, two of her women friends and the Reverend. She has opened her eyes briefly. But the interesting thing is that she seems to get agitated when the Reverend visits. I asked the nurse if one of them could nonchalantly be in the room when he is there, she said they would try. Other than that everything is about the same. I wonder what the deal is with the Reverend Paul Stearns? I guess I will be paying him another visit when we get back in town."

"So I guess we are done here and will be going on to Chicago to visit with dear ol' Daryl Compton. I'll make the plane reservations for in the morning. Better get a place to stay, too. I think it is too cold for a tent."

"I am not looking forward to meeting with Daryl again. He's as big a liar as his sister. Must run in the family. We still have this Todd character to talk to in Portland."

"I'll make the plane reservations, but I have no idea where to stay in Portland, never been there, have you?"

"Let's wait and see how long it takes us in Chicago before we schedule the Portland trip. I have been to Portland. We used to visit Dad's sister every summer. Aunt Julie was younger than Dad and had two kids, Tina, my age and Brad, Candy's age. We used to call Brad, 'Brad the Brat'. They were both really spoiled kids, got everything they wanted, so it appeared to Candy and me. When we would go to visit we always played games by Tina's rules because it was her house, but when they came to visit us we still played by Tina's rules because she was the guest. We laugh about it now, but it wasn't so funny then. After Aunt Julie passed away Tina and Brad moved away and we lost contact for a number of years. It's only been the last five years or so that Tina and I have been in contact again. Anyway, back to your question, I will make hotel reservations. There are several hotels out by the airport, but downtown is so pretty I like to stay there."

"Where was the address we had for Todd?"

"I'll have to check, I got a copy of his Oregon driver's license and that has his address. I'll get it."

"How about a drink, I think we are done for the day?"

"Sounds good, I'll have my usual. Here it is. Wow, Todd lives in Lake Oswego. As I recall that is a pretty ritzy little town. Let's see, the address is The Pointe Apartments on Foothills RD. I have no idea where that is, but I am sure we can find it. I'll make the reservations for two nights. Think we can get him corralled in that length of time?"

"Who knows, it's a start. Here you go my dear, cheers, happy Tuesday."

"Happy Tuesday to you too."

Sam made the plane reservations for Chicago without any problems, but ran into a real log jam trying to a get hotel reservation. Seems there were several conventions going on and one very large convention that booked up most of the hotels. Sam was getting nervous if we were going to find a place that wasn't stuck out in the booney's somewhere.

"I am running out of hotel names for downtown Chicago. You got any ideas? I am stymied."

"Remember that magazine article I gave you to read on the plane, about the old hotel that was recently remodeled and having their grand opening? What was the name? Hotel Allegro or something like that."

"I'll check it out. Oh, I called Dawson and let him know we are going to Chicago, actually, just left a message as he wasn't in."

Since we had an early flight I got my luggage ready to go, closed it up and set it out in the hall by the door. I laid out my clothes for morning and make up bag went in my carry-on. I knew we didn't have a kitchen or even a kitchenette in the Chicago hotel, just a microwave and tiny refrigerator, so I went through the refrigerator in the apartment and put a few of the snack foods in a small carry-on cooler including the can of whipping cream and left a note for house keeping to take the rest.

"Bingo, I got it and pretty reasonable too. I booked it for two nights, I think that will be long enough time to get what we need out of Mr. Compton?"

CHAPTER 43

We landed in Chicago and caught a shuttle to the Hotel Allegro. Sam had changed his mind about renting a car. Who wants to drive in down town Chicago and pay for parking that probably costs more than the car rental.

We had taken a risk for an early check in. Sometimes it worked and sometimes it didn't. When we checked in the hotel clerk told us it would be possibly an hour and half wait before our room was ready. We made reservations to go into the dining room for lunch. We discovered the article, from the airline's magazine of the hotel, to be under rated and less than complimentary as was its beauty. The lobby had a grand piano off to one side all by itself with sofas and conversation chairs placed around the room. That took me back when I had my baby grand piano that I loved to play. I hadn't played in years, actually since Brian and I divorced and I sold it. I hadn't given thoughts to playing a piano in a very long time.

We had a light lunch and by then our room was ready. It was really quite nice with a king bed, a sofa bed, a big screen T.V., two upholstered arm chairs and a table large enough for both our computers. We put our things away and emptied the portable cooler into the little refrigerator. I had decided not to even bother calling Daryl; I was just going to show up at his office. Sam thought it would be best if we both went and I agreed. After all we were in this together.

Sam and I caught a taxi to Daryl's Whacker Boulevard office and took the elevator to the sixth floor. When the elevator door opened it was evident the whole floor was occupied by Compton, Stanton & Associates. Pretty impressive. The huge receptionist desk with a wall of polished mirrors curved around the back of the desk with two good sized trees on each side, was straight ahead of us as we got off the elevator. Before the receptionist had a chance to say anything, I said,

"I am Sergeant Brenda Weathers and this is Detective Sam Davis. We are with the San Diego County Sheriff's Department. We are here to see Daryl Compton."

"I'm sorry Mr. Compton is with a client. May I schedule an appointment for you?"

"No, that won't be necessary, we will wait until his appointment is over and then we will go in to see him. But thanks anyway."

"I am afraid Mr. Compton has a rather full schedule for the rest of the afternoon. We will have to schedule an appointment for you."

"You apparently didn't hear me. We are with the San Diego County Sheriff's Department and we are here to speak with Mr. Compton, and we will speak with him. So if you can relay that message to him, we would be most grateful." I smiled at her and didn't move.

I don't know what she thought I was going to do, but she jumped up as though I might shoot her and said, "Excuse me, I will let him know you are here."

In just a couple minutes Daryl came storming out of his office. I could hear him stomping down the hall and when he rounded the corner he and I made eye contact that was piercing. His greeting was less than pleasant, "What the hell is this all about? I believe my receptionist made it very clear I was with a client and had a full client schedule this afternoon. What the hell are you doing here?"

"Well, unless you would like to discuss the matter right here in the foyer, I suggest we go someplace for a little privacy." I gave him a big smile, "It is your call."

"I need to finish up with this client, then I have only a few minutes before my next appointment." He turned and started back down the hall.

"You might want to cancel your next appointment, we will take more than just a few minutes or your client is going to have a long wait. Again your call." Again I gave him a big smile. He wasn't at all impressed, but continued his stomping down the hall.

Sam and I sat quietly and waited for our signal to go into Daryl's office.

After several minutes had gone by, a woman came sniveling down the hall. She looked as though she had just lost her best friend or even worse. We waited awhile longer, and then it occurred to me there might be another door out. I stood up and walked to the reception desk. She looked up at me as her phone was ringing and then she said, "Mr. Compton will see you now. His office is at the end of the hall."

I smiled and said, "Thank you." Sam and I walked down the hall to his office.

When we entered Daryl's office we got less than a warm reception, which was not at all surprising. He displayed nothing but an angry attitude as he said, "What in the hell are you doing here?"

"Well, Mr. Compton, it seems you may have forgotten to fax the information I had requested from you, therefore, I am here to pick it up." I smiled and crossed my arms, considering he had not offered us a chair and we were both still standing.

"Oh, for Christ sake, you came all the way here for just that? I haven't had time to get that stuff together."

"May we sit down while you put it all together?" Still smiling at him.

"Excuse me; you really think I am going to stop everything I am doing to get such frivolous crap together now?"

Sam and I pulled a couple of chairs together and sat down, "As a matter of fact that is exactly what we are going to do"

"This is total bull shit. I am going to ask you to leave right now and I will get the stuff faxed to you. Now if you don't leave I will call security and have you escorted out."

"We are not leaving until I have it Daryl. And I mean all of it. So you might just as well get busy."

He hit the intercom button, "Miss Hall, call security to my office, please?"

"I wouldn't do that if I were you. Or we will have no choice but to

take you in and charge you with attempted of murder on your mother."
We stood up, pulled our jackets back and Sam showed his hand cuffs
and we each showed our weapons.

"Cancel security, Miss Hill. Would you please reschedule my
afternoon appointments?"

"Thank you Daryl, now let's regroup here and make this a more
congenial meeting and get some business done. I had asked you for
a copy of your receipts for airline tickets, receipts from the hotel and
confirmation of attendance at your convention, names of those you
dined with at the banquet and those you had dinner with and cocktails
at your hotel. I assume you still have that list?"

"Yes, I have it some where."

"Good, then let's start with copies of plane tickets, convention and
hotel receipts. I am sure Miss Hill can come up those quickly while you
provide the list of those you were with at the convention as well as those
you had cocktails with at your hotel."

Daryl called Miss Hill at the reception desk, "Make copies of my
plane ticket, convention and hotel receipts from the conference in L.A.
last week and bring them into my office."

The longer Daryl worked on the name list the more agitated he
got. He would write down some names, cross out one and write down
a few more, cross out two. He got his personal phone directory out
of the drawer and added some phone numbers. He didn't have phone
numbers for everyone and said we were on our own for those.

Miss Hill brought in the copies Daryl had requested and he set
them aside hardly acknowledging she was in the room. Daryl continued
completing his list, which he gave to me about an hour and a half
later.

"Thank you, I appreciate this. When you went in to see your mother
last week, do you think she recognized you?"

"No, not at all. She didn't open her eyes or move as I spoke to her.
Why do you ask?"

"I saw you run out of the hospital and squeal out of the parking lot. When I went in to see your mother the nurses and the doctor were trying to calm her down. The doctor had to give her a shot. What did you say to her that got her so upset?"

"I didn't say anything to her that should have upset her. What is your point?"

"The nurse said she heard you yelling at her and then you ran out."

"I was not yelling, I was merely trying to get her to wake up. She did not have her hearing aids in and I thought she was not hearing me. The reason I was running out of the hospital is because I had a plane to catch. You and I had already discussed that, Sergeant. What is your issue?"

"Mr. Compton, we are trying to get to the bottom of who and why someone went into your mother's house and shot her. Nothing was taken and the weapon used was a small handgun and not powerful enough to kill her. We do not believe murder or robbery was the intent of the intruder. So what was it? We are questioning every possible angle we can and so far the cooperation with you and Susanne has been less than cooperative."

"So what is Susanne's story? I'm sure she had a dandy."

"We have confirmed Susanne's alibi. Clinton is still out of the country, so they say. We may not be able to question him for quite sometime. Mr. Compton, I don't believe you have mentioned your wife, what was her name?"

"My wife's name is Melinda and you leave my wife the hell out of this. She is an event planner and quite frankly a very good one. She has been working for a year on a convention that is going on right now at the Convention Center for Medical Administrators. I can assure you she would have had neither the interest or the time to make a trip to San Diego to visit my Mother. Just leave her out of this!"

"For right now we can do that, in the meantime we are checking out all avenues, and until your story is cleared, you are still a person of interest."

"OH, how special."

"By the way, do you know anything about a Todd B. Thompson?"

"You have already asked me that, and I have never heard the name before you brought it up?"

"Have you called and checked on your mother?"

"Actually, I have not. I asked the hospital to call me if there were any changes. I have been hammered with work since I got back from the conference."

"You know, your mother is eighty nine years old and this has been a traumatic experience for her. I am quite surprised that you and Susanne have not given her anymore attention than you have. I find it rather appalling. But that is my personal opinion for whatever it is worth. Thank you for your help. We will be in touch so keep yourself available."

"Quite frankly, Sergeant, I don't give a damn about your opinion."

"I'm sure you don't, Mr. Compton. You have a great day."

CHAPTER 44

Outside the office building I turned to Sam, "That certainly went well. I wonder how many of these names are going to be valid. Ya, wanna wager on it?"

Sam shook his head, "I have a feeling we are going to be chasing our tails with this guy. I think he thinks he has the upper hand with us. Little does he know. Let's go back to the hotel and start making calls."

By the time we got to the hotel, through all the downtown traffic it was after five. The lobby was buzzing with guests participating in the wine tasting and various kinds of sample cheeses and crackers. We tasted several merlots, pinot noirs and a few brands we had never heard of. Sam and I weren't real big on wines and the expertise of a true wine conisior, but this was certainly more fun than going back to the room and making phone calls. We chatted with a few people making small conversation, then Sam got caught up with some guy he seemed to be very interested in.

I wandered over to the grand piano and was admiring its beauty and shine; I could see my reflection in the polished dust free top. I sat down and gave consideration to playing a couple tunes, then thought better of it. I walked over to the window and watched people scurrying up and down the street, catching buses, hailing cabs, waiting at corners to cross streets and shoppers struggling with multiple packages. I was chuckling to myself how much different a life style this one was compared to my quiet little suburbia town and neighborhood.

"Amazing how fast the pace is here in the middle of Chicago compared to home isn't it?"

I turned around to face a strikingly beautiful woman. "I'm sorry, have we met?"

She smiled and said, "No, actually we haven't. My name is Alexis

Taylor. I believe our husbands are caught up in a deep conversation and I observed you sitting at the piano and was hoping you were going to play. Seems a shame not to have background music. Do you play?"

"I used to, haven't played in many years. My name is Brenda Weathers." I smiled and laughingly I said, "I must correct you, he is not my husband, Sam and I are partners."

"I apologize, that was quite rude of me to make such an assumption."

"No problem, it was an honest and very harmless mistake. Are you here with the convention?"

"Yes we are. I understand we all live in the San Diego area. As a matter of fact our hu---ah---Jim and Sam discovered we live close to the same area, with in fifteen miles or so. Small world isn't it?"

"It sure is a small world. So where do you and Jim live?"

"We live in Del Mar, not too far from The Del Mar Race Track."

"Is Jim a hospital administrator?"

"Yes he is. He is so dedicated and puts in such long hours, I hardly ever see him. He is not a good one to delegate. He would rather do it himself and be sure it is done right than to explain it to someone. I would not like to work for him. I keep hoping these conventions will teach him to be a better administrator, but when he learns something new he never seems to pass it on to his staff. Guess he needs a different kind of management course. What do you and Sam do?"

"We are detectives for San Diego County." I saw the two men walking our direction and when I smiled at them, Alexis turned around and reached out for Jim's hand.

"I see you two ladies have met." Jim extended his hand to me, "I'm Jim Taylor and you must be Sergeant Brenda Weathers? Nice to meet you. Sam and I have had quite the conversation sitting over there."

"Sergeant? Brenda you didn't tell me you had a title," Alexis chuckled.

"Some things are better left unsaid." I looked at Sam, "I would really like to go up to the room and freshen up before we go to dinner.

This has been fun meeting both of you. Hopefully, we can get together sometime soon."

Jim jumped in, "How about joining us for dinner this evening?"

Sam came to my rescue, "I don't think that is going to work for us this evening, we have some calls to make. We should have been doing that instead of lingering, but then we wouldn't have met you two. You have my card, Jim, let's see what tomorrow evening brings, if we are all still here."

CHAPTER 45

We exchanged the appropriate good byes and went up to our room. I kicked off my shoes and plopped down in one of the comfy arm chairs, put my feet up on the ottoman and sighed, "They seemed like a very interesting couple. How ironic they live so close. Which hospital is Jim administrator too?"

"I don't know, guess I didn't think to ask. We got to talking about horse racing, I think they are really into that. Might be kind of fun to go there with them sometime."

We turned on the news and started discussing the Compton's. "You know for all the money this family appears to have, they are about as dysfunctional as some under privileged less educated people. I don't get it."

"As the old saying goes, money doesn't make people happy. Guess this is a true case of that. I don't think either Susanne or Daryl seem very happy. Its like they are blaming everyone else for the troubled situations they get in. We certainly haven't heard much about Daryl's wife, until you asked about her today. Only thing he has shared is that he doesn't have children. At least none that he is claiming or knows about."

I was laughing at the last statement Sam had made when I saw a news bulletin regarding a Chicago banker found after several months search. "Oh my god, Sam, did you see that? I didn't catch the name, did you?"

Sam was at the little bar mixing a drink and hadn't been paying any attention. He immediately came over and sat down to see what it was all about. "I didn't catch any of that. Who were they talking about?"

"I don't know, it went to a commercial break, let's see what comes up next." Of course when you are waiting for something special there are about twenty commercials to sit through.

There it was. A picture of a distinguished looking man with white hair dressed in a dark blue pinstriped suit, white shirt and red tie. The newsman continued, "In the mid seventies he had made an attempt to run for local government without success. Having moved his family to Florida he began his career as a banker with small cap banks. It is believed he had confiscated funds, made inappropriate loans from almost every bank he was employed." Still there was no name, just the picture. He continued as Sam and I stayed glued to the screen. "This man has been clever to have stayed ahead of the Federal government and not get caught. It is also suspected he had further jeopardized his career when he got involved with a financial investment group. However, it has also been suggested he was undercover with the CIA to uncover this financial agency. More details at 11:00. This is Joe Smith with KRX News."

"Well, crap. We still don't know who that was. I don't remember seeing any family portraits at Susanne's other than one that was of her and the three children when the little guy was an infant. Do you?"

"No, I didn't pay attention to pictures. That's not a guy thing." Sam grabbed the remote control and started surfing the channels to see if he could pick the story up on another channel. All he got into was weather and sports.

"So, I'm guessin we will be stayin up for the eleven o'clock news? What a ya think?"

"Oh ya."

"I want to get out of these clothes and get into something more comfortable and casual. Actually, I think I will jump in the shower."

I got up and hung up my clothes, picked out another outfit and got in the shower. I was all soaped up and hair wet when I felt Sam's arms slip around me from behind. "Uh oh, call the cops, I feel there is an intruder in here."

"Oh really, you think the cops are going to help you? I could be of assistance if you really need help."

"And just what kind of assistance do you think you have to offer?"

"Stick around Baby and I'll show you."

I turned around and we fell into wild passionate kissing and groping. The water was still pounding on my back and Sam turned me around and slid me to the bottom of the tub. It was short and sweet and not the most comfortable position I had ever encountered. I finished my shower as did Sam and as I was drying and Sam came out of the bathroom, picked me up and placed me on the bed. "I'm not done with you yet."

Our passion for each other seemed to get more intense every time we made love. Sam was so tender and gentle and eager for both of us to have total satisfaction, and did just that with great success. We laid on the bed for a few minutes wrapped in each others arms and damp bath towels. It was Sam that made the first move, he slapped me on the butt and told me, "Get up and get in the shower, nap time is over."

"You go first, then I'll get in."

I loved his sense of humor. He could be so funny and playful, but still had that serious and business side of him. I think what was most intriguing to me was his dedication to his children, parents and Monica. I know he had called his children everyday that we had been gone and talked to all three including Sylvia. I never, ever heard him hang up without saying 'I Love You' to his kids. Sylvia assured him everything was alright and going well, although they all missed him terribly.

CHAPTER 46

I had yet to meet his parents. I knew Paul and Rita lived north of Seattle around Lake Washington and had a beautiful home on the lake. Sam never really talked too much about their home, but was in constant admiration for his Dad. He thought his Mother to be a little on the neurotic side. Sam had grown up in the Seattle area and graduated from The University of Washington, as did Monica. They had lived in a rural area with acreage and the kids had been involved in 4-H. Sam raised steers and pigs and Monica was in the equestrian program. After Sam and Monica left home for college their parents started talking about down sizing. They certainly didn't need all that acreage and the house was huge with three levels. Of course Sam didn't have any of his steers or pigs as they had been sold at the county fair each year, but when their parents sold Monica's horses, she went ballistic. Sam told the story that it took her a couple years before she would talk to her parents again. Monica didn't have a plan or a place for the horses but she thought she should have been consulted. Of course they laugh about it now, but it was a pretty hot subject then. At Rita's insistence and Paul's lack of a strong objection, they ended up with an elaborate house and huge terraced yard on Lake Washington. In the last few years the house had gotten to be too much for Rita to keep up, so they got a housekeeper. Paul finally relented to a part time gardener. Sam wouldn't say anything to his parents, but he felt his mother had made an extravagant decision on their place that was now taking a toll on them both.

I heard the shower turn off and I got up to lay out some clothes when my cell phone rang. "This is Sergeant Weathers."

"I told you to back off. You are treading where it is none of you business. Now you have pissed me off. Consider this a warning." And the line went dead.

Sam came out of the bathroom, "Next." I was sitting on the edge of the bed and he could tell by the expression on my face something was wrong. "Bee, what's the matter?"

"I just got another call from Mr. No Name, No Number. He told me to back off, I was treading where it was none of my business and now I have been warned."

"What the hell does he want and who is this guy? At least he has no idea where you are. Maybe we ought to call the Sheriff and have a surveillance put on your house till we get back?"

"I suppose, at least have someone drive by and check it out." I just sat there in a state of shock. "Sam, I can't figure this whole thing out. What is it that we are not supposed to find out? There wasn't a murder, there wasn't a robbery, and there have been two un-cooperative adult children of the victim that still has not regained consciousness. And then there is this Todd character that no one seems to know anything about."

Sam sat down on the edge of the bed and put his arms around me, "I don't know either, Baby. This has me baffled too. Let me call the Sheriff and get your house taken care of. You jump in the shower and then let's get out of here and go have some dinner."

"I don't think I feel much like eating, now"

I got in the shower and just stood there for a few minutes letting the water hit my back and trying to think the whole through. When I was done and toweling off Sam brought me a drink and said, "The Sheriff will take care of everything and will call later. Okay? Now will you please relax, there is absolutely nothing we can do about anything from here."

We went down stairs and a cab was waiting for us. Sam gave the driver the address of the restaurant then leaned over and gave me a gentle kiss. He put his arm around me and tried to coax me to relax. When we got to the restaurant several minutes later, we took the elevator to the fourteenth floor, Sam asked the host if he could seat us in a quiet corner. He of course slipped him a bill and we got the best seat in the house. At least I thought so. There were windows on each side of us in the corner and the view of the city was beautiful. Sam ordered a bottle of Dom Perignon, I knew he was trying to get me to relax and get my mind off that call.

"I just can't figure this whole thing out. I have gone over and over in my head and retraced all of my steps from the start. I can't think of anything we could have missed. There is only one thing that I didn't follow up on with Dawson and that is the room that was over the garage when he and I did the initial search of the house. That room was locked and he said he was going to get a lock smith to unlock it or try and pick the lock. I don't know if he ever did and I forgot to follow through."

"Bee, the Captain is the over seer of all jobs, and if he said he was taking care of it, he did. If there had been anything mysterious he would have told you. You can't carry the whole burden yourself."

"I know, there has just got to be more to it or this guy wouldn't keep calling me."

The waiter brought the Dom Perignon, a sample for Sam to taste then he filled our glasses. "Okay, let's have a nice dinner and pick this up in the morning, okay?"

"Okay, but don't forget we have the news to watch at eleven o'clock. I am really curious about that Chicago Banker. I don't recall that Clinton was in the banking business in Chicago. I thought that was where he tried his political career and he didn't start with the banks until he moved to Florida? But then what do I know? Seems like no one tells the same story the same way two times in a row."

"You're right there. Say, have you talked with your parents lately?"

"Not since we left home. I told Dad I would call when we got back. Not much going on with them other than taking care of Grama and Grampa. I don't think I told you Candy called yesterday. They had just gotten home from their honeymoon the night before."

"How was their trip?"

"She said they had a great time, besides all the sex, they rented a sail boat and did the touristy stuff. Tim had to go back to work on Monday, but Candy has this week off to get settled in. She says everyone at home is just fine. I guess Grama and Grampa put in a huge garden, bigger than ever. Mom and Dad about had a stroke when they saw how big it was."

"Why is that?"

"Because they practically do all the work, a good share of it anyway. And in the fall and off and on all summer they are canning and freezing. Grama has canned food in the pantry from two or more years ago, some of it needs to go to the compost pile as well as probably more than half of the freezer. Candy is going to go out and help clean some of it out and maybe take some home."

"Maybe we could go over there and spend a few days and help out. I would love it and so would the kids. I think that would be a great get away for all of us and give Sylvia a little vacation. What do you think? Did you tell Candy about our engagement?"

"No, I think it would be best to wait a while. Besides I would like to tell them in person. So to answer your other question, I think that would be a great idea to spend some time with Grama and Grampa and I know they would love it and love having the kids around. That would be right up their alley. Only problem is, I just had a week's vacation when I went home for the wedding."

"I think once we get this case closed we will both be entitled to a few days off. How many weeks vacation do you have? I have four weeks annually and still have one week from last year, plus come July 1st I have another four weeks, so if I don't use last years week I loose it."

"Hmmm, I have four weeks a year. I am even now with four weeks coming up in July. Do you realize what we are saying here? It sounds to me as though we are work alcoholics."

"Oh ya think? I hear that at home from my kids and Sylvia all the time. No knew news to me. So I think we need to do something about it, don't you?"

"Probably, I know this case has been more stressful to me than any other case I have had in many years. But then I have never been on a case that involved me personally, and I do take this one very personally"

"Let's just put this into a plan and take a week and go visit your family in Idaho. The kids will be out of school in another month and that will give us a chance to wrap this case up. I think timing couldn't be more perfect."

"I think the kids would have a blast. Sean probably not as much as the girls, but he could hang out with Grampa and that would delight Grampa immensely. Sandy and Sara are good at entertaining themselves, but Grama is great to allow them to help in the kitchen baking cookies or creating projects for them. Candy and I used to spend most of our summers with them, even before we moved from San Diego. And after we moved to Idaho we practically lived out on the ranch. Of course we had our horses out there and we rode every chance we got. Unfortunately, there aren't horses there now."

"That reminds me. When we were leaving Susanne's place and you asked me to pull over to watch the horses in the meadow, you said that took you back in years when you and Candy used to ride, you said you would share that story with me sometime. What was it?"

CHAPTER 47

The waiter refilled our glasses and took our dinner orders. I took a sip of the Champagne and was reflecting on those young years and stared out the window at the beautiful view.

"Hello, earth to Brenda, get on your horse and ride back here." Sam said laughingly.

"Ya, right," I smiled in a dreamy sort of way, "I was remembering the summers Candy and I spent on the ranch. We rode those horses every chance we got. We had such great imaginations and made up stories for our rides. We each had a horse, mine was a sorrel mare I named Faith. Candy had a big buckskin gilding she called Buck. Sometimes we would ride bareback and take off across the pasture and head for a camp ground not far away. We would ride as fast as we could yelling, whooping and hollering like a couple warrior Indians, circling in and out around the camp sites, kicking up dirt and dust and beat it out of there just as fast as we entered. Other times we would dress up with chaps, boots and spurs, cowgirl hats and saddled horses and take the same ride through the camp ground. We would slowly ride in and stop at each camp site and ask, in a slow southern drawl, "Have ya seen any calves, we seem to be missin a few?" Of course the campers hadn't seen any, there were no missing calves. That's only two of the many stories we had dreamed up for our entertainment. I remember one weekend my parents let me take my best friend Rachel to Grama and Grampa's. Rachel and I wanted to go for a ride which meant we would take Candy's horse and did she ever get pissed. Grama told us we could go and she packed us a little lunch. We took off and left Candy standing beside Grama crying that it wasn't fair, it was her horse and she didn't give us permission. We were gone for most of the afternoon, ate our lunch and of course spent most of the afternoon talking about boys. We started back to the ranch and as we rounded the bend in the road there is a tree that Candy and I climbed with quite frequency, much to our grandparent's disapproval. Well, sweet little Miss Candy had climbed up in that tree and waited for Rachel and me to return. Just as we got under that tree, she started yelling and hollering. The horses shied and went one direction and we went the other and the horses headed for home. Candy climbed out of that tree and ran as fast as her little legs could carry her back to the house and right to Grama's side. Good news is we were neither one hurt, except our pride. If we could have gotten our hands on Candy we would have beaten her to a bloody pulp. But she was one smart little girl. She stuck to Grama like glue for the rest of the weekend. It's funny now, but sure wasn't at the time."

Sam was laughing so hard at my story he almost choked on his Champagne. We had finished the bottle, eaten the salads and our dinner had arrived. Sam ordered a dinner wine, "I am sure Candy did stay clear of you, I don't think I would want to cross you and expect to live through it."

"Ha! Ha! You just remember that! What time is it? I want to get back to the Hotel in time to see the eleven o'clock news."

Sam looked at his watch, "It's 9:45. Why don't we go back to the hotel and have a night cap in the bar and watch the news there?"

"Sounds good. That is if I can even walk out of here. Good thing we are cabbing it after the bottle of Dom Perignon and bottle of Merlot. I think you are trying to get me drunk and take advantage of me, you bad boy!"

When we got back to the hotel and went into the lounge, we found a table among the few that were empty and each ordered a heated Drambuie with a coffee back. I scanned the room for Jim and Alexis, but they weren't there. The lounge was quite busy and had a jazz band playing soft music in one corner. Several couples were dancing slowly and appeared romantically involved. Sam and I hadn't been out dancing together for a very long time and I was thinking this could be fun that is if I could stay on my feet long enough. The alcohol consumption was taking a tole on me and I wasn't sure just how steady I was going to be.

"How bout it Baby, shall we give it a couple twirls around the dance floor?"

"If you are sure you can hold me up and promise not to step on my toes."

We danced a couple times and sat down and I was looking around for a television set to watch the news. I spotted one in the corner at the end of the bar, but it was turned off. "Excuse me sir," I said to the bartender, "can you turn on the T.V. so we can watch the news?"

The bartender replied, "Sorry Ma'am, as long as the band is playing we have to leave it off."

"Let's take our drinks to the room; he won't turn the T.V. on with the band playing. We can come back down if you want to, but I really want to watch this news report."

"Okay, you go ahead up to the room and I will settle our tab."

CHAPTER 48

When I got to the room and turned on the T.V. the news had just begun.

"Good Evening. This is Joe Smith with KRX News. This morning it was reported that a Chicago Banker was found after a several months search. Clinton Farrell was found shot in a hotel room in Puerto Rico. He has had surgery to remove several bullets from his chest and one in the head. Mr. Farrell was last listed in grave critical condition." There it was again. A picture of a distinguished looking man with white hair dressed in a dark blue pinstriped suit, white shirt and red tie. "So that's Clinton Farrell," I said to myself. The newsman continued, "In the mid seventies Farrell had made an attempt to run for local government without success. Mr. Farrell went to work for the Chicago Bank, however after only one year he moved his family to Florida and continued his career as a banker with various small stockholder owned banks. It is believed he has confiscated funds, made inappropriate loans from almost every bank he was employed. Mr. Farrell has been clever to have stayed ahead of the Federal government and not get caught. It is also suspected he had further jeopardized his career when he got involved with a financial investment group. However, it has been suggested he was undercover with the CIA to uncover this financial agency. Many rumors are attached to Clinton Farrell. We called the CIA and they have refused to take our calls. We have been unsuccessful in reaching Mrs. Farrell, which was reported she and two of their three children are in seclusion at their home in Ft. Lauderdale, Florida. Next we have your local weather and ten day forecast. Stay tuned to KRX News, we'll be right back."

"Oh my God! It was Clinton! Poor Susanne." I was saying out loud as Sam walked into our room.

"Is he dead? What happened?"

"No he's not dead, but chances of recovery sounds pretty slim to none. He was shot several times in the chest and once in the head. The newsmen tried to get hold of Susanne, but reported she is in seclusion. My bet is that Mike has her and the children in hiding somewhere."

We discussed the news report at length and concluded it was not our issue and nothing that affected our case. Our plan was to pursue Daryl Compton's list of alibis in the morning, call on Mrs. Compton's condition and check with department about my house. The rest of the day's plan would be pending on the morning's progress. With all that concluded we decided to call it a night.

Sam went in to take a shower and I went out on the veranda to have a cigarette and admire the view. It was quite chilly but the view was spectacular. I was deep in my own thoughts when Sam came out in the hotel thick white terry clothe robe and wrapped his arms around my waist, "What is going on in that pretty little head of yours?"

"Actually nothing in particular and a whole lot of everything. Just admiring the view and trying not to get bogged down with all this stuff. For such a simple case, or should be, this has turned into one hell of a mess. I wonder how it is all going to turn out. Sure has me baffled and I know you are too."

"It will all come together, Bee, the right answers will come. We are doing all we can and we will get it figured out, we always do. Now let's go to bed and put some other ideas in your pretty little head for a while."

Sam pulled me around to him and we started kissing, he was unbuttoning my blouse and the thought of undressing on the veranda wasn't very appealing besides it being very cold. We moved into the room as Sam was removing my clothing. I was completely undressed and when Sam removed his bathrobe and turned to get into bed I reached in the little refrigerator and grabbed the can of whipping cream. I turned around to see Sam lying there on the bed and his manhood was ready for action. I quickly removed the lid and started squirting whip cream all over Sam's body.

153

"Holy shit! You are in so much trouble little girl, you have no idea what you just started." He grabbed me and at the same time took the whipped cream can away from me and started spraying my body. Licking the whip cream and kissing each other's body became so sensual in parts of each other where nerve endings caused shivering orgasmic experiences. We played with each other until playing was no longer an option. I raised my body to Sam to accept him inside. He was so gentle and slow and firm and we came together as one. I clung to Sam saying, "I love you so much, you are the love of my life, you are the best thing that has ever happened to me. And I want to make your life miserable for the rest of your life." And then I laughed.

"I love you too, and misery loves company. So your challenge is on my dear, I don't think you have it in you to make anyone miserable. But good luck." Then we both started laughing at the looks of us and the mess we had made out of the bed. "Now what are we going to do, you and your brilliant ideas of fun? We can't sleep in this sticky mess."

"Well, let me check and see if there is a set of sheets in the closet for that sofa bed?" I got up and checked the closet, no sheets, so I concluded the sheets were already on the bed. "Okay, lazy butt, get up and help me tear this sofa bed apart and remake our bed." By the time we got the bed remade and each took a shower it was two o'clock. "This is going to be a very short night."

I put the 'Do Not Disturb' tag on the door and climbed into bed. We snuggled close and within seconds were sound asleep.

CHAPTER 49

Sleeping in was becoming a habit on this mission, but then staying up late was rather out of the ordinary as well. When I woke at 8:15 I hit the floor running, in the shower and dressed, coffee made and brewing and at the table with the phone list from Daryl Compton. Sam wondered out of the bedroom in a sleepy haze, "Wow, is there a fire somewhere? Do we have a plane to catch that I forgot about?"

"I just woke up and wanted to get these calls made and get the day going. I want some answers to all this and now. I think we are barking up the wrong tree and going in circles and I intend to find out why."

"I'll get in the shower and join you?" Sam leaned down and gave me a kiss, "Top of the mornin to ya my amazing little girl. Looks like there was wild animal fight in this room last night, and I think you were the wild animal." Handing me a cup of coffee, Sam was laughing and went into the bathroom.

My first call was to the hospital. "This is Sergeant Brenda Weathers; I would like the nurse's station for Mrs. Compton, please." My call was transferred.

"This is Nurse Kelly, how may I help you?"

"Hi, Sergeant Weathers here, how is Mrs. Compton doing today? Any changes in her condition?"

"Sergeant Weathers, there certainly is. She is awake, but is terribly confused as to where she is and what happened. Dr. Cutter was with her last evening and gave her a thorough exam and evaluation. Her wound has healed nicely, all her vitals are back to normal but her memory is not coming back quite yet."

"That is good news. Does she still get agitated with certain visitors?"

"There aren't any notes regarding that, but I also don't see that she

155

has had any visitors in the last two days. Is there anyone in particular you are referencing?"

"Not really, just curious. When Dr. Cutter comes in today, is it possible to get a message for him to give me a call?"

"Of course, I'll make a note of that right now. Is there anything else I can help you with Sergeant?"

"No, thank you, you have been very helpful. I'll be checking in again."

I sat there and went over that conversation in my mind again. I wished I knew more about Mrs. Compton. The friends I had talked with seemed to know her casually and socially, but there wasn't anyone that appeared to be a real close friend. Reverend Stearns is the only one that came across as being her best buddy, but then he is also the only one that irritated her. I wanted to talk with Doctor Cutter, I had been thinking Mrs. Compton could be faking this mental confusion. Surely Doctor Cutter would pick up on this. I was anxious to talk with him and get his take on her condition.

Looking at the list of names Daryl had given me, I contemplated if it was even worth the effort to confirm. I called the hotel where the reservation had been made. It was confirmed he had checked in on Sunday, April 30th and checked out on the morning of Thursday, May 4th. I made one call to one of the six gentlemen Daryl had met in the bar at his hotel on Wednesday evening May 3rd. I saw no need to call the other five men from that group. I made a couple other calls. One gentleman I had left a message and the other said he remembered seeing Daryl at the conference but couldn't specifically remember which day or time he saw him. I called another one and he could only confirm he had seen Daryl at the banquet, which was earlier on Wednesday evening around five thirty. Making one more call only confirmed the same, he was at the banquet, but couldn't remember seeing Daryl any other time, but followed up that it was a largely attended conference and it was possible he wouldn't have seen him at all.

So this was suspiciously leaving Monday, Tuesday and part of

Wednesday with a void and no one to absolutely confirm Daryl's attendance. So where was he and what was he doing? I decided to put this aside for awhile and made a call to Captain Dawson.

"Captain, this is Sergeant Weathers, remember when you and I made the search of Mrs. Compton's house and the room over the garage was locked? Did you get that room unlocked and go in?"

"Actually, Sergeant, I assigned that task to Officer McClain. Didn't you follow up on that?"

"No, I didn't, I didn't know who you had assigned that job too and I thought you were following up on it. With everything else that was going on with the threatening calls and intrusion into my home, I quite frankly forgot about it. I'll call Willy right now."

"You always seem to have excuses don't you Sergeant?"

"No excuses, Sir, just facts. Thank you for your help. You have a great day." He started to say something else but I hung up. There was no need to listen to his crap, I was in no mood.

I was getting ready to call Willy when Sam came out of the bathroom, "How's it going?"

"You are not going to believe this one. Well, on second thought you probably will. Dawson is up to his usual tricks. I called him to see what he found in the upstairs of the garage. He said he had assigned it to Willy and I should have followed up. When I said I didn't know who he had assigned that too and I had believed he had followed up on it. He just came back that I always have excuses. I just hung up on him. I will call Willy and see what he found up there in the apartment. I am getting more frustrated the further we get into this case. I called the hospital and Mrs. Compton is awake, but is very confused as to what happened and where she is. I am wondering if she is clever enough to be faking her mental state? Surely Doctor Cutter knows her well enough to recognize this if she is, wouldn't you think?"

"I think that is great news she is awake and I think it is perfectly understandable for her to be confused considering the length of time she has been in a semi-coma. I would think Doctor Cutter would pick up on that right away."

"I am sure he can, I just have to question this in my own mind. There are too many questioning options out there that have me baffled and I want to survey all of them."

"I know you do. Bee, but I think you are over taxing your brain and over working this whole case. Let's sit back and regroup, reanalyze this situation before we move forward. You have pretty much covered that most of Daryl's alibi is confirmed. Even though there are some gaps I'm not sure they're worth spending a lot of time on. Let's just put this to rest and move on to Todd Thompson in Portland. We can always follow up on Daryl later."

"Shall we get out of here and head to Portland?"

"Let me do some checking on airline reservations, and we'll go from there. Now why don't you quit worrying that pretty little head of yours?" He kissed me and said, "Good morning, I love you." And he just stood there smiling at me.

Sam had that way about him to put things into perspective in a calming way. While I go at things like I am killing snakes and want it done now even though I am totally thorough. Sometimes my patience level is nonexistent which causes me more frustration than necessary. One would think after ten years in this business I would've learned to control my emotions better, but then I had never been an involved character in a crime I was trying to solve. I felt that was the part that had me in a different frame of mind than any other case.

CHAPTER 50

I picked up my phone and dialed Willy. "Hey Brenda, what's up? How are things going where ever you are? Where are you anyway?" Obviously Willy recognized my number.

Laughing at Willy I responded, "Good morning to you, hmmm, I guess it is afternoon there. We are in Chicago right now, but getting ready to go to Portland and follow up on Todd Thompson. So far we are dead ending on all of our leads to this point. However, it certainly has been eventful. I'll fill you in later. My question to you is---did you ever get into that room above the garage at Mrs. Compton's?"

"What room? I don't know anything about it? Why are you asking me?"

"Well, that is interesting. After Captain Dawson and I had made our search of the Compton house to be sure it was clear, we went in the garage and there were some stairs on the far left side that goes to a room or something over the garage. The door was locked and Dawson said he was going to have you pick the lock or get a lock smith to get in."

"Dawson never said anything to me about that. The only thing he told me to do was go with you to gather the items for the hospital and we did."

"So I wonder who he asked. He was trying to put the blame on me that I had not followed up with you as to what was in there. I just talked to him a few minutes ago, Willy."

"I don't know what to tell you, Brenda. I will go out there today it you want me too."

"That would be great. Do you have a lock-pick kit? I really don't want the door kicked in. Take someone with you, I don't want you going out there alone. Give me a call after you get in, please."

"Yes, I do have a kit; if I can't make it work I will get a lock smith. I'll call you later."

"Thank you, I knew I could count on you. Later."

Sam was getting off the phone as I hung up. "What did you find out about a Portland flight schedule?"

"It is looking like our best connection is going to be in the morning. There is a flight in an hour, but we can't make that and all other flights are full. So I booked in the morning."

"That's fine. I called Willy and he said he didn't know anything about checking out that room over the garage. He said Dawson had never said a word to him. He is going to check it out and call me later. That son of a bitch is bound and determined to find cause to fire me."

"You're right Brenda; he is crossing all the angles. It is ten thirty, let's go down stairs and strategize a counter attack over breakfast. May be you'll get some calls back and have better answers."

"Sounds good to me."

We walked in the restaurant and were seated when Jim walked over and asked us to join them. They had gotten there a few minutes ahead of us and were sitting at a larger corner table. Alexis was looking her ravishing best.

"Good morning you two. I hope you had a nice evening. We had a lovely dinner in the lounge, however, with all the wine I had consumed during the wine tasting party, wine with dinner and the after dinner cocktails I was toast and went to bed rather early. Jim continued the evening with colleagues in the lobby bar. I don't know when he came in." Alexis was laughing. Jim only smiled, either because he saw no humor in her rattling on or he was suffering a bit of a hangover.

"We had a quiet night, had some business to tend too and went out for dinner at a real nice Italian restaurant. Stopped off in the lounge for an after dinner cocktail, danced a couple and went up to our room to watch the news." Sam didn't elaborate on the news or the calls.

I laughed and made comment to Alexis, "I think I had over indulged at the wine tasting, too. I'm not really too keen on a lot of wine and it usually gets to me quicker than my usual vodka and water."

The waitress came by and we ordered breakfast, coffee and juices. Jim ordered a Bloody Mary and seemed a little sheepish but made no comment.

"So what are you two up to today?" Jim finally spoke for the first time.

"Actually, Bee has been going at it since eight this morning and we will probably go up to the room and continue to make calls. We could possibly have a repeat appointment this afternoon. Other than that not a hell of a lot. How bout you? Do you still have conferences scheduled?"

"Yes, I have one from two until four and then we are done. They have always in the past had a banquet on the last evening, but this convention has been so largely attended they didn't have a facility for it. First time in Chicago for this event. So the committee decided to hold social hour with hors d'erves at several individual hotels. Never been to a conference that did it this way. Some will be checking out this afternoon right after the last meeting and wouldn't stay for the banquet anyway. It could turn out to be a new concept. We'll see."

"That is different. Never been to a convention that held happy hours at different hotels. But then I have never attended one of this magnitude. I wasn't sure we were even going to get a room in Chicago. We probably wouldn't have except for the grand opening here. Pretty elegant hotel and appears to have reasonable rates even without their special for the opening."

"I agree. I was late making my decision on even attending this conference, so I know what you mean. This hotel is rather impressive."

Our breakfast came and we all started eating. I was amazed the two men had been able to carry on a conversation without the interruption from Alexis. I thought her to be very high maintenance and loved to be the center of attention and trying to control the conversation. So far she had only been an observer. I decided I was wrong, maybe Alexis was the one suffering the hang over.

Alexis finally broke her silence, "Well, I'm going shopping this afternoon. Would you like to go with me, Brenda? I can show you some really neat shops. I've been into most of them a couple of times." She gave me a wink and shrugged her shoulders with a mischievous smile.

"That sounds like fun and I would really love to go shopping with you, but I have work to do this afternoon. Several calls to make, a report to get out and like Sam said, we may have a repeat appointment to make. Trust me, I would much rather go shopping."

"That's too bad, remember, all work and no play makes Brenda a boring girl."

"I can assure you, Brenda is not a boring girl." Sam chimed in and we all laughed.

The waitress brought more coffee and cleared our plates and Jim ordered another Bloody Mary. Alexis raised an eyebrow but didn't comment to Jim's second drink. The thought occurred to me this could be an issue with them, on the other hand this could be a result of the evening before. I know I have at times been guilty of suffering the morning after the night before, but more alcohol was not my cure, just food.

Jim directed his question to both of us, "So, do you attend many conventions in your line of business?"

I was first to answer, "No, we don't really have conventions, per-say. However, we do attend special seminars that are held regularly around the states. For instance, one for Gang Enforcement, Child Abuse or Domestic Violence, SWAT teams and many more, then there are special trainings on the use of various firearms. It just depends on which special field one would be in that could either be a required or elective training. But there is something going on all the time somewhere. Sam and I happen to be in criminal investigation which covers homicides, attempted murders and sometimes theft cases."

"Wow! How exciting is that. I can't imagine sleuthing through alleys looking for the bad guys, breaking into their home for a search or high speed chases. How dangerous. You must get scared all the time and have a real adrenaline rush?" Alexis dramatized.

"It's not quite that traumatic, Alexis. But it can get a bit exciting at times, but most of the time it is routine and can be very boring. Like this case, travel from one side of the United States to the other and get no results or answers we were looking for. That is frustration." I explained.

Just then my cell phone rang and I looked at the number, it was Willy. "You'll have to excuse me, I need to take this call. Sergeant Weathers, here." I got up and quickly walked out of the restaurant.

"Hey, Brenda. This is what I got. I went out to the house and was able to pick the lock and get inside. There is definitely evidence of someone living up there. I snooped around but couldn't find anything that had a name on it for identification. There is a little bit of food in the refer, only a few dishes in the cupboard and it is neat as a pin. Very few clothes that definitely belong to a man, a tall man. We were in and out of there pretty fast. So what do you want me to do? Do you want me to take someone from forensic out there to get finger prints? Your call."

"Thanks Willy. Let me think on this and check with Sam. I don't want this guy to run if he gets suspicious. I'll get back to you."

CHAPTER 51

When I got back to the table Sam was engaged in a conversation that had both Jim and Alexis intently mesmerized. As I sat down Sam said to me, "I was telling them a story about a convention I had attended when I was with the FBI early in my career. We had gone to Phoenix, AZ and stayed at the North Pointe Resort. It was a beautiful resort with at least three swimming pools, but the main pool had the swim up bar and everyday from four to six was half price happy hour. There was another convention there of hair dressers and what a group that was. What a bunch of party animals they were, from ages eighteen to probably some in their sixties. But, my eye caught this threesome that was sitting not too far from my group that had me intrigued. What I thought to be a couple in their early forties and maybe their daughter in her twenties, turned out to be the married couple, the guy and the younger women, and the other lady was single. The older women kept going to the swim up bar and taking cocktails for the three of them. She was really quite attractive and seemed to have quite a sense of humor as they were always laughing. So, when she went up to the bar I decided to do the same and strike up a conversation with her. As it turned out she was a salon owner in a small Central Oregon town, the couple she was with was her salon salesman and his wife. She invited me to join them and I did for a while and we had a great time. After happy hour we went our separate ways for dinner and met back at the pool later that evening. I remember it was June and they had had record high temperature for that time of year. It varied from 117 to 120 degrees during the four days we were there, so the evening swimming was participated by a lot of the conventioneers. The pool ordinarily closed at ten, but because there was such a big crowd management left it open until eleven and then kicked everyone out. I offered to walk the lady back to her room, don't remember her name, but she declined.

But when we all started leaving I noticed she was walking in the same direction as my room, so I walked with her. Ironically she was down the hall several rooms from mine so I did end up walking her to her room." Sam raised both hands as in surrendering, "Honest, I did not go in her room."

"Oh sure you didn't." Jim interrupted and we all laughed.

"No, I really didn't. Anyway," and Sam pointed his finger at Jim, "the next day after our classes, I was in my room getting ready to go to the pool and she walked by my room in her swim suit and towel over her shoulder, my door was open, so when I saw her I invited her in for a drink. She came in, I left the door open," and Sam pointed his finger at Jim again and continued, "We talked about her business some, she was single, had two sons---one lived in Phoenix and the other was in Tucson in the Air Force---but she was really more curious about my profession. We didn't stay in my room very long and joined the pool group. It was our last night for the convention and my Lieutenant had set up a barbeque at the upper level pool by his room for our group. I invited her to go with me and she accepted. We had one hell of a party, pool games and dancing until management came up around midnight and told us we were going to have to shut it down. We quieted all the activity but a lot of us stayed around the pool and told stories. She and I continued talking about our lives and where were going with it. We just clicked and enjoyed each other's company. It was well after one when we finally broke it up. I walked her back to her room, and no I did not go in her room; but we did kiss good night and said goodbye as we were leaving the next day. When I got back to my room I discovered my briefcase and computer were missing. I had left them on the table when we left for the pool earlier. The real problem was that I had case files on my computer, case notes in my briefcase along with my badge and weapon and all of my money. I immediately called my Lieutenant and told him what had happened and he called security and they were all in my room within minutes. We were up most of the night going over my room for fingerprints and questions about the lady that had been in my room, they took both glasses and finger printed them, took the ashtray, she smoked. I was ordered not to tell her about this or talk to her at all. I didn't figure this to be a problem since she and I had already said goodbye and we were checking out later that morning. While I was at the checkout desk, her seminar had broken up for lunch and she was coming through the lobby and spotted me. She was walking towards me with a big smile and I turned and went into the men's room. I waited for a few minutes and when I came out she was still waiting in the lobby, I tried to walk away but she followed me and said, 'Sam? What's wrong?' I told her I was sorry I couldn't talk to her I was busy. I felt bad because I was really rude, and she walked away towards her room. It wasn't long until the desk phone was ringing and when I heard the receptionist said 'Calm down, I will have security down there right away.' I knew immediately that her room had been gone through and I looked at my Lieutenant and he told to me to leave it alone. We walked out of the resort and got in the shuttle for the airport."

"Oh my God! Did you ever hear what happened? Did they ever catch who stole your stuff? What happened to the woman?" Alexis questioned.

"Yes, they found my computer and briefcase and all it's contents except for the money. It turned out it was one of the guys from the resort that came in to turn my bed down and freshen up the room for the night. He just got a little sidetracked with all my stuff. I was in deep shit trouble, that is one thing an FBI agent does not do, is loose his firearm. A hard lesson I learned real early in my career."

"Did you ever hear what happened to that woman?" Alexis asked.

"Actually, I did hear from her, she had called about a week after she got home from their convention, I did not return the call. Then I got a letter from her about a week after that and she explained what had happened when she got home. She wrote that one of her clients happened to be a county deputy that the FBI had talked to when they ran a criminal back ground on her. We found out she was an upstanding citizen, on the city council and involved with the local Chamber of

Commerce and some kind of women's philanthropic organization, so she was not an issue. But we had made that check on her before the resort employee had been picked up."

"OUCH, I bet that was a barn burner letter." Alexis commented.

"No it really wasn't, she took it rather comically, she knew where she was in life, and her client really teased her about it. I didn't answer her letter or phone call and I never heard from her again. She was a cool gal."

"My, My, that is a story I've never heard before." I said to Sam. "You must have been quite the rounder in your younger days?"

"I wouldn't say that, it was just one of those incidents that turned out okay and I learned a great lesson. I was single and having the time of my life during those years, being an FBI Agent didn't allow much time for play and when the opportunity came about I played. Besides, I got married not long after that and then playing was really over."

"That was a fun story, Sam. I would love to stay and hear more, but I am afraid I need to get ready for my last seminar. Hey, what are you two doing for dinner this evening? If you don't have plans why don't we get together later? What a ya think?" Jim asked.

Sam looked at me and said, "I don't think we have any plans. Let's see how our afternoon goes. How about we meet you in the lobby bar around six and we can go from there?"

"Sounds good." Jim replied and we all got up left the restaurant.

"Sure wish you were going shopping with me." Alexis said over her shoulder as we went our separate ways.

"Ya, me too. Maybe next time." I said and we got on the elevator to our room.

CHAPTER 52

"So what did Willy have to say?"

"He got into the room and it is evident someone is living there, a tall man determined from a few clothes in the closet. A little food in the refrigerator, a few dishes, but very sparsely equipped. He asked if I wanted him to have it fingerprinted. I told him I needed to think about it and check with you." The elevator opened and we headed for our room.

Inside our room, Sam asked me, "What do you think?"

"I'm not sure. I don't want this guy to get suspicious and run. I would like to be there when they do all this and I really want to go through that room myself. Damn, I wish we were going home today."

I sat there with my head in my hands rubbing my temples. Frustration was really setting in with a vengeance. I felt like we were getting so close to catching this guy and here we were on the other side of the United States. I needed a cigarette. "Sam, I am going downstairs and go for a short walk. I'll be back in a few, I need to clear my head before I explode."

"Would you like me to go with you?"

"No, I'll be fine, I just need some fresh air."

When I got down to the street, I didn't know which way to go. I went to the corner, turned right and just started walking. I hadn't gone too far and there was a tiny little park, actually not even a park. A small grassy area with a couple of small trees and three benches. It was a little breezy and cooler than I thought it was considering the sun was out. It really was a beautiful day for Chicago and this time of year. I sat down and lit up. People watching has always been an intriguing past time for me. Watching them hustle down the street, taxis darting in and out of traffic honking their horns, hair every color of the rainbow, young boys with pants hanging so low I couldn't even imagine what was keeping them up and I noticed most everyone was either talking on a cell phone or had ear buds in listening to music. It was certainly fascinating and did take my mind off the issues at hand. I was interrupted by my cell phone ringing, I recognized the number being from the hospital. "Sergeant Weathers."

"This is Doctor Cutter, I had a message you wanted me to call."

"Yes I did, thank you so much for returning my call. Have you been in to see Mrs. Compton today?"

"As a matter of fact I just left her room. I'm afraid I don't have much new news for you, Sergeant. She has regained consciousness, but that is about all. She is still in a state of confusion, doesn't remember what happened, she doesn't know visitors or me. I'm going to have to release her from the hospital and send her over to the re-hab center."

"Doctor, I have to ask you, is there a chance she is faking this amnesia? The reason I ask is because someone has been living in an upstairs portion of the garage. I am curious if this person could be why she won't remember what happened, if this person is some kind of a threat to her?"

"I had a psychiatrist in this morning to evaluate her. We haven't connected yet to see the results. That is a very valid question, Sergeant; I have given that consideration a possibility as well. We will be moving Miss Ellie in the morning."

"Can this be kept under wraps? We will not be able to transfer security to another facility and we only have one more day as it is. I would appreciate it if no one knows which center she goes to until we can find out who this guest is that lives in Mrs. Compton's garage. Is this a possible request?"

"I'll do what I can."

"Thank you, Doctor. We are in Chicago right now and should be home on Sunday. We did make connections with both Susanne and Daryl. I will be in touch when we get back. I will let you go and thanks again."

"No problem, have a safe trip home."

I continued to sit on the bench and gaze into the horizon. I lit another cigarette, the sun caught my diamond ring and it gave off a brilliant flash, I had almost forgotten I was wearing the ring. Admiring its beauty and how this all came about, I started to question myself. Was I ready to take on three children and become an instant Mom? Was I ready to take on the responsibility of being a fulltime housewife with a fulltime career? Was I ready to give up my home and my freedom and independence? And what was going to happen about my job? My job was probably already on the line the way Captain Neil Dawson's mind worked and his dislike towards me. I was deep in my thoughts and not coming up with a single answer to any of my own questions.

"There you are. I didn't think you would get very far, nice park you found, Baby. So, I checked the airlines for reservations to see what other options were available. We can take the milk run from here to Portland. Chicago to Denver, no plane change but a thirty minute delay; on to Seattle with a plane change and hour wait. We can leave at four and even with the two stops plus the two hour time change we should be in Portland about eight this evening. Oh, I forgot to mention the flight from here is standby, but we have a chance if we get there early, you want to give it a shot?"

"Before we do all that, let me see if I can track down Todd Thompson in Portland. There is no need to make that trip if he isn't around. I have a feeling he is right there in Mrs. Compton's garage."

"You are probably right, you make the calls and I'll go back and start packing my bag."

I tried the only phone number I had and of course it was not a working number. I called information for the Pointe manager's office. When they answered, I identified myself and asked to speak to the manager.

"Sergeant Weathers, this is the property manager, how can I help you?"

"I am inquiring about one of your tenants, Todd Thompson. Can you tell me anything about him and if he still resides there?"

"I can't tell you anything about him, because there isn't much to tell. He signed a six months lease and moved out the first of April. He didn't leave a forwarding address, he was a very quiet tenant, stayed to himself, never attended any of our complex activities. I don't know what else I can tell you."

"Thank you, may I leave my name and number and if anything turns up will you please give me a call?"

"I can do that." I left my information and hung up.

I went back to the hotel room and told Sam, "We are done here. Change the reservations for San Diego; there is no need to go to Portland, Todd's not there. Let's just go home."

"All righty then, I'll see what I can come up with." Sam started making calls and I decided to go downstairs to the gift shop and see if I could find some kind of trinket for Sam's kids. Not sure where that idea had come from, but it was something I wanted to do. I looked around and found a cute inexpensive watch set for each of the girls. They were both Timex with different colors of rhinestone inserts that circled the watch face. Finding something for Sean was more difficult and then I spotted a bigger watch that was one of those that is water proof for several feet down, had a compass and something else. Sure looked like a boy to me. I made my purchases and three gift bags and went back upstairs.

"Okay, I got another stand bye, canceled the Portland trip. Let's get checked out of the hotel, go to the airport, check in and then we'll have time for lunch."

We started throwing our stuff together. Sam called the front desk and asked for our bill to be ready we were checking out. Then we both remembered at the same time we had committed to have dinner with Jim and Alexis. Sam left a message for them that something had come up and we were leaving, we would be in touch after we all got home.

On our way to the airport I told Sam about my phone call with Dr. Cutter. "So he agreed with you that Mrs. Compton might be faking her amnesia?"

"He didn't really say he thought she was, it was a consideration. He said he had a psychiatrist in to evaluate her. But they are moving her to a re-hab center in the morning. I hope they can keep the move quiet. Security is no longer available to her."

CHAPTER 53

When we arrived at the airport we checked in at the desk to confirm our status. Sometimes showing our badges gave us priority and this time it appeared to have some clout with the ticket agent. We could only hope so. We were counting on being able to get on the 3:35 non-stop flight to San Diego arriving at six o'clock; this would be the perfect scenario. Our second option was two hours later at 5:35 with a plane change in Phoenix and arriving at nine.

The early flight would be a dream come true for a number of reasons, one being Sam would be home early enough to spend time with his kids. I knew he missed them terribly when he was on long trips. Week long trips were unusual, most cases were local, maybe an over night or two but not this long. I was looking forward to being home as well. There wouldn't be anyone to greet me like at Sam's house. Oh, yes there was, Spook would be there.

While we were eating lunch, Sam was reading the newspaper and I was people watching with no particular thoughts going on in my head for a change. My cell phone rang and when I answered it and before I could address myself the voice came through loud and clear, "You just don't get it Bitch. I told you to back off and I mean it. You are treading on grounds where you do not belong. Mind your own business or you are a dead Bitch." My cell phone went silent. I dropped the phone on the table and when Sam looked up from his news paper he knew immediately who the call was from.

"It was him wasn't it? What did he say to you?"

I repeated the call best I could, "This is the first time he has actually said if I don't back off, I'm dead. He knows we have been to the garage apartment. He knows we know who he is now and that he is living over the garage."

"I agree on all counts."

"I'm afraid he's going to run and go underground. Damn it! I'm going outside for a few minutes and give Willy a call and let him know we are on our way home. We still have an hour and a half before flight time."

I looked at my watch and started to walk away and Sam grabbed my hand, "Bee, we are going to get him you know."

"I know." And I walked away.

Outside I found a bench and sat down, lit a cigarette and called Willy. I let the phone ring until I got his voicemail and I left a message to call me. I opened my brief case and pulled up my report page and continued bringing it up to date. The last thing wanted to do was not have the report done and on Dawson's desk Monday morning, first thing. Man, I was dreading this meeting all ready. I needed to have my ducks all lined up and ready for battle. I typed a few lines and my cell rang. It was Willy.

"Hey, Willy. Just wanted to let you know we will be home tonight. Depends on whether we can get on this next flight or wait until the 5:35 flight. Anything new there?"

"No, I've been waiting for you to tell me what to do next. Dawson called me and was really angry when I denied knowing anything about his request to go into that room. He told me I was turning out to be as incompetent as you."

"You are kidding. What an ass. What is his problem?"

"I don't know. But I am hearing all kinds of rumors from the guys that he is really starting to lose it. I wouldn't worry about him Sergeant; I think he is paving his own street."

"I sure hope so; I would like nothing more than if he were removed as Captain. That would make my day, big time."

"I hear ya, and you are not alone with that thought. Don't count on it, he is one shrewd man."

"How well I know that. Well, I need to go; I just wanted to check in with you for any updates. I'll be home all week end if you want to stop by or call me. Thanks for everything, Willy, you are a jewel. Catch ya later."

"Thanks, later."

I closed my computer, glanced at my watch and decided I had time for one more cigarette before going in. Damn, I was getting right back into this smoking, I was doing so well until this case came along. When this is all over I will go back on the patch or maybe try that pill or maybe hypnosis. Besides, if Sam and I were going to continue this relationship smoking was out of the question. He really hated it. But then most reformed smokers were the worst critics.

Out of the corner of my eye I noticed a man standing a little ways away, and I thought he was staring at me making me terribly uncomfortable. He was dressed in a black suit, black hat and sunglasses. He walked over to the bench I was sitting on and sat down, "You have a light?" I looked up at him and he gave me a forced grin. I reached down and got in my purse and handed him my lighter at the same time moving my purse to the other side of me. I was putting my computer back in my case, he gave me my lighter, "Thank you, you traveling far today?"

"Just going home."

"Oh Ya? Me too."

"Have a nice trip." I put my cigarette out and went in to join Sam. For some reason this guy made me really nervous. Was I getting paranoid? I had the eerie feeling this guy was Todd Thompson. Why? There was no way he could know where I was, or could he?

Sam was still reading the paper with a cocktail in front of him. I sat down, "Where did you get that? I think I will join you and have one. I just had a weird experience while I was outside." I raised my hand, the waitress came over to our table and I ordered a double vodka water. Sam raised his eyebrow at me and ordered a double scotch water.

"What happened, you look as though you saw a ghost?"

I told him what happened. Sam's expression didn't change, "Bee, you are imagining that it was Todd. There is no way he knows where you are, what you look like and furthermore, you have no idea what he looks like. Baby, you have to relax, don't go ballistic on me now." And he smiled.

Startled by Sam's statement to me, I leaned over and quietly said, "Sam, I do know what he looks like. I have his Oregon Driver's license that has his picture." I started going through my file in my briefcase and continued, "I have concentrated so much on the address I haven't really looked at his picture. Here's the file." I studied the picture for a minute, "I can't tell, the guy outside had on a black hat and dark sunglasses, it covered most of his face. I don't know if it was him, it was just an eerie feeling I got. Maybe I am getting paranoid."

"Bee, you have every right to be suspicious, this guy has taunted you from the get-go. I would not call it paranoia. Let's go to the gate."

We finished our drinks and went to our gate for departure. Our luggage had been checked and we could only hope we made this flight. We checked in at the desk for cancellations, of course there were none. Sam reminded the airline agent we were on stand by and we laid our badges out on the counter, just for her observation. We'd see if it worked.

"While I was outside I called Willy. Dawson is on the warpath and making everyone's life miserable again."

"So what is Dawson up to now?"

"Dawson called Willy into his office for an update on the upstairs room and what he found. Willy told Dawson he had never requested him to check that room out and he told Willy he was as incompetent as I was. Willy thinks Dawson is losing it; his phrase about Dawson is he is paving his own street. But we both conferred he is too shrewd to get caught. At least he thinks so."

CHAPTER 54

I pulled my computer out again and started working on my report. I was almost done when the airline agent announced they would start the boarding process in fifteen minutes. I put my computer in Sam's lap and asked him to go through and proof it, make changes, add ons, deletes or anything else he thought necessary. Then I hoped we were done with it. Sam had all the receipts organized and clipped together, so all we needed to do was print the report and turn it in to the Captain on Monday morning.

Sam had just finished proofing when the agent announced boarding would begin. First was anyone needing assistance or those with children, next was the A boarding passes, then B boarding passes, followed by C boarding passes and the rest fell in the D category. That would be us, on stand by.

We waited until the waiting area was empty and for the agent to let us know if we were on or not. She finally came up the ramp from the plane and told us there were two open seats; even though they were not together we didn't care. We took them. It wasn't until the door was shut to the plane that I breathed a sigh of relief. I let Sam take the first seat because it was an aisle seat and more leg room for him, I took the seat farther back that turned out to be a window seat and only two seats, so I was clear in the back of the plane. Perfect, now all I needed was a pillow and I would be sleeping all the way home.

The lady sitting next to me sat as though she were frozen. She sat with her head plastered against the back of the seat, her hands tightly folded in her lap and tears streaming down her cheeks. I leaned over to her, "Are you alright?"

"I'm fine. Thank you."

"Are you afraid of flying?"

"I hate it and I really hate sitting in the back of the plane, but I will be just fine."

"Would you feel better if you were sitting farther forward in the plane? My partner is sitting mid-way forward and I am sure he would switch with you if that would help."

"I don't want to be a nuisance; I go through this every time I fly, I will be just fine, but thank you for your concern."

"Okay, but if you want to change seats, just let me know."

We taxied out and the captain came over the loud speaker to inform us we were in line for take off, there was the usual heavy amount of air traffic considering the time of day, so sit back and relax we will be taking off shortly.

I took out my book and started reading and the woman next to me started shaking uncontrollably. I put my hand on her arm, "Take some deep breathes, slow deep breaths, you need to relax."

"I can't." And she started sobbing.

"Talk to me. What is your name?"

"Marlys."

"That is a very pretty name. What do you do? Tell me about yourself."

"Thank you; I am a model, twenty nine years old, not married and terrified of flying."

"Let's not talk about flying. Do you live in San Diego?"

"No, I was raised in San Diego and went to modeling school, but I live in Chicago now and work for a couple of the large clothing stores. I am going home for my Grandfather's funeral. He was only sixty nine, he had walked to the store only two blocks from their home and he was hit by a car while in the crosswalk and the driver never stopped. This has really been hard on Grandmother and my parents. I'm sure my emotions have a lot to do with this trip."

"How horrible, I am so sorry. Have they caught the driver?"

"Not that I know of. There were several witnesses, but so far they have not found the car or the driver. Grandmother is taking this really hard; Mom has taken her to their house and she wants to go back home. It is not a good situation all the way around."

We continued to talk through take off and most of the trip to San Diego. She had finally settled down and relaxed, we had a couple cocktails which I know helped her a lot. Sam came back and visited with us a couple times. The flight was quite smooth and landing was without a glitch.

Marlys walked to baggage claim with us and I gave her my business card as we each went our separate ways, "Please give me a call if I can do anything for you. I mean it Marlys, if you need anything, please call."

"Thank you so much, you made my flight so much easier. It was a pleasure meeting both of you and I will call if I need too."

Marlys rushed off to the open arms of a man we assumed to be her father. We waited for the shuttle to take us to the car.

Sam took me home. "Let me go in with you and check it all out. I really hate leaving you here alone tonight."

"I know, I have gotten accustomed to having a real partner this past week and I have to admit it was really nice. But we will work through all this with time." Just then Spook came rushing through the door and was so excited to see us, he couldn't decide who to go to first. "I guess I won't be alone tonight after all." And we both laughed. "You need to go home to your kids; they need you since you have been gone for a week. I will be just fine; Spook is here, my new body guard. I love you and we'll talk in the morning."

Sam put his arms around me, "I miss you already. I know we have to take this slow, but I can't help myself that I want everything to happen now. I love you too, and we will talk in the morning." I stood at the end of the patio and waved until he turned to go down the street.

CHAPTER 55

I took my suitcase to the bedroom and had just set it on the bed when my cell phone rang. I looked at the face of my phone and saw that it read, 'Private – Unknown Number'. I didn't answer it and turned my phone off. I hate turning my cell off, but if anyone needed to get a hold of me they could call on the land line. I did not want that call, not tonight.

There was a knock on my sliding door, and Spook went to the door waging his tail. I peeked out and saw it was Karyn and Daniel. "Hey you two, what's up? Come to take my playmate home?"

"Nah. We saw the lights on so thought we would come over and check it out. But I can see Spook already has." Karyn said patting Spook on the head.

"Actually, we are glad to see you home. We had an offer on the house on Wednesday, I flew home yesterday, we counter offered today and they accepted late this afternoon. Unless something goes wrong with their financing, which has been pre-approved, we just sold our house." Daniel gave his wife a loving squeeze. "So, we came over to ask if Spook could stay with you till we get back. We fly out tomorrow and Karyn will be back later in the week. The kids are staying with friends, so they can finish the school year."

"That is great news. I am so excited for you." And I gave them both a big hug. "Of course Spook can stay here with me. I am thrilled to have him and thrilled for you, too"

All of a sudden Karyn grabbed my hand, "Oh My God! What the hell is this, Brenda? Who is the lucky guy?"

"Karyn, I have to trust you to keep this quiet. This can not get out or I could lose my job. Department Policy. You have to promise."

"Of course we will keep this to ourselves, besides we are leaving town, so no problem. It's Sam isn't it?"

"Yes it's Sam. He proposed the night we left for Florida. I still can't believe I accepted. He sure caught me off guard. We have a long ways to go before any wedding date is set. This could be a very long engagement."

"Congratulations and we better get an invitation to the wedding."

"Of course you will, but don't start planning your trip yet." Karyn and Daniel both gave me a big hug; we were laughing as they examined my ring more closely.

"Honey, we need to get back to the house. We left the kids watching television and no telling what they could be doing now." We said all the appropriate congratulations and see ya later, "You take good care of Brenda there buddy." They each patted Spook on the head and went home.

"Well Spook, guess it is just you and me baby."

The rest of the evening I spent putting my stuff away, doing laundry, checking the mail, finally sat down with a drink, flicked on the television and breathed a sigh of relief to be home again.

Sam called, "Hey Baby, what's up? I called your cell three times and your voice mail keeps coming on. Everything okay?"

"Oh, ya, I decided I didn't want any calls tonight and those that are important know my home phone and would call on the land line, and you did." I didn't bother to tell him about Mr. No Name's call that I didn't take and I didn't check the voice mail. "So how were the kids and Sylvia?"

"Everyone is just fine. They are all trying to tell me about their week at the same time. We finally got through it one at a time. No catastrophes, even Sylvia said the week went well. So what are you doing? I miss you terribly."

"I miss you too. I just finished putting all my stuff away and doing laundry, you know the stuff one does when they don't have a house keeper." I laughed, but I knew I shouldn't have made that last statement and I was right.

"Well, you know we can fix that real easy and real soon." We talked for a few minutes and then said our good nights and hung up.

PART III

TODD THOMPSON

CHAPTER 56

Startled, I was awakened by a something cold and wet touching my cheek; I opened my eyes and was staring in the eyes of Spook. He was stretched out, head on the pillow and wagging his tail.

I glanced at the clock, "Oh My God, I can't believe I slept in this late. Okay, Okay I'll get up. What are you doing lying up here on my bed? Your bed is right here on the floor." I scratched the top of his head and got out of bed and Spook jumped down and headed straight for the door. I guess I better start addressing the sleeping arrangement here real fast. Although I thought I had it figured out with his bed beside mine, he apparently had a different idea sometime in the night. I'll get it taken care of.

I put the coffee on and decided I better check my cell phone messages. Sure enough I had seven, three from Mr. No Name, three from Sam and one from Willy. I deleted all the messages except the one from Willy, "Hey Serge, better give me a call as soon as you can, things are getting pretty nasty at the office. Later."

I hit the return call number to Willy, "Hey Serge, did you get my message?"

"Sure did. We just got home last night, I turned my cell off so didn't get your message till just now. What's up?"

"Rumor has it Dawson has reassigned the Compton case to Johnson and Jones. AND, you are really going to love this one. Again, according to rumor you and Sam have just been gallivanting around the country, screwing each others brains out, not checking in, no reports and accomplishing nothing. How do you like them apples?"

"Willy, how did you hear this? Who started the rumor?"

"I really shouldn't say, but you have got to promise me you didn't hear any of this from me. Okay?"

"Yes of course."

"Apparently it started in the locker room with Johnson after he supposedly met with Dawson. But it has run rampant through the department."

"Okay Willy, here's the deal. I am going to pretend you and I never had this conversation. I need to call Sam, but I want the three us to go to that upstairs room at Mrs. Compton's. Can we do that?"

"Man, I don't know, if I ever get caught there again and especially now with you and Sam, it is my job for sure."

"That's fair. I don't want to put your job in jeopardy. Tell me, how did you get in, did you pick the lock?"

"Yes, and it was an easy lock to pick. Sam could do it with no problems, so can you as a matter of fact."

"Thank you so much Willy. You and I never, and I mean never had this conversation. I need to give Sam a call. Since I have not heard from Dawson directly, we are still on this case. Gotta go. Later." And I hung up.

Before I called Sam I made copies of all the receipts. I had a feeling trouble was brewing and I wanted us to be prepared. The complete report was on my laptop and I could always make more copies if necessary. But I needed copies of the receipts.

I called Sam, "Top of the mornin to ya. What are you up to?"

"We just finished breakfast and I am helping Sylvia clean up the kitchen, figured she needed a break even though she balked profusely. What are you doing?"

"Well, you better sit down for this one. There is a rumor going around the department that our case has been reassigned to Johnson and Jones, again! And I quote: you and I have just been gallivanting around the country, screwing each others brains out, not checking in, no reports and accomplishing nothing. How's that for starters?"

"Who'd you hear that from?"

"Doesn't matter, I promised the conversation never happened and you have to do the same. We have to pretend we know nothing about this and go on with business as usual. So, I want to go over and check out that upstairs room. You want to go with me?"

"Shit. Let me think. It's 9:15 now. Okay, if we go now it shouldn't take too long. I promised the girls I would watch their last softball game. Sara plays at 1:00 and Sandy plays at 2:15, same field. Are you ready to go if I come over and get you?"

"Of course not, but I will be, won't take me long. See ya in a few?"

I jumped in the shower, threw on some jeans and sweat shirt, towel dried my hair and gave it a lick and a promise with the blow dryer, put it in a single braid and pinned it up, brushed my teeth and skipped the makeup. I quickly made the bed and went in and poured some more coffee. Wow, I was getting good at this, 15 minutes. Sam would be here in a few minutes. I opened all the drapes and saw it was a little overcast outside, but then it would burn off by noon anyway, just in time for the girl's games. Uh Oh! I was starting to think like a parent. This must be a good sign. I went out side and walked out into the yard. Wow! Did this yard ever need attention. I knew what I would be doing the rest of the week end. Spook was lying on the patio until he heard Sam's car pull into the driveway and he jumped up and ran towards the car, hair standing straight up until Sam got out of the car and the tailing wagging began.

Sam gave me a big hug, "I sure missed you last night. I was cold all night."

"I missed you too. Let me put Spook in the house and grab my stuff. We can talk in the car. I'll just be a minute."

I strapped my weapon to my ankle, put my badge in one pocket and cell phone in the other. "Sam, this is my plan, see what you think about it. If we drive in we can look in the window of the side door to the garage and see if there is a car in the garage other than Mrs. Compton. If there isn't, I have my lock kit and we can get in. If there is another car we will just knock on the door to the house and leave. Or do you have a better idea?"

"Not really, we'll see how it goes. Do you want to go to the girl's games this afternoon?"

"I would love to, but I think I will stay home and catch up on the yard. It is going to be a beautiful afternoon and it is in dire need of attention. What are we going to do about Dawson? He is such a liar. We went through all the processes for this trip. We filed the agenda and he approved, you left messages when we went to Chicago and when our plans changed to come home instead of going to Portland. Our report and receipts are complete and ready to turn in on Monday, what more is there?"

"Bee, I have no idea. I have never run across a guy like him. I think we should just proceed as usual until we hear different from him. In fact, why don't I take the reports in and put them on his desk so he has them first thing Monday morning. I can do that on my way back home."

"Good idea, I am not looking forward to Monday morning. Here we are. Let's see what we have."

CHAPTER 57

Sam pulled into the driveway and around to the back of the house and circled towards the garage. Crime scene tape was still across the back door of the house and it appeared to be very quiet. Sam parked as close to the garage as possible. Sam walked around to the end of the garage to look in the door window. He signaled that there wasn't a car in there so I walked over to him taking my lock pick kit out of my pocket. Sam reached for the door knob and it opened, we went in and went up the stairs quietly with our weapons drawn and backs against the wall. We were on opposite sides of the door and Sam knocked. No one answered, he knocked again and still nothing. Sam tried the door and it was locked. I used the lock pick and we were in, in just a couple seconds. Weapons still drawn we searched and found it to be empty. We started looking around for a sign of something that could tell who this person was. We found everything to be exactly as Willy had described. I went to the closet and was checking the hanging clothes, and the sweaters and sweatshirts on the top shelf. I moved them a little and then spotted a black case, I pulled it down and discovered it was a gun case

"Sam, come over here and check this out. Isn't this a gun and shells that match the one ballistics' has?"

"Yes it is, take a shell and let's get out of here. We have been here long enough."

I took one of the shells and put it in my pocket and put the gun case back on the shelf. We took one last look around and agreed there wasn't anything else that would be of use to us. We locked the door and went down the stairs.

Just as Sam opened the door, he stopped and immediately put his arms up in the surrender position. I backed against the wall and grabbed my ankle weapon.

"Whoa, there guy, easy now. I don't want any problems here."

"What you doin here?"

"I just went up stairs and knocked on the door and no one answered so I came back down, and here we are. Now why don't you put your weapon down and let's talk about this. What's your name? I am Sam Davis."

"Why you snoopin around here? Didn't you see the yellow tape around? That means no trespassing?"

"Yes I did, that is why I was checking to see if anyone was upstairs. No one answered my knock so I came back down. You live here?"

"Don't matter if I do or don't. I'm watchin out for the place."

"Okay, just put your gun down and let's talk." Sam started to relax his arms and the guy fired a shot into Sam's chest. He fell back into the garage.

I extended my arms in front with my weapon and stepped around the corner and yelled, "Drop it! Police!" He shot and the bullet went on the inside of my shoulder sending my weapon into the garage and me to the floor. I hit my head on the concrete when I went down and was knocked out. When I came too Sam was lying motionless beside me with blood all over the front of him.

I grabbed my cell out of my pocket and called the precinct. When dispatch answered I was shaking and yelling, "This Sergeant Weathers, two officers down at Mrs. Compton's on Victoria Place. Send an ambulance immediately, Sam's been shot. Hurry!"

"Brenda, are you okay? What is Sam's status?"

"I'm alright. Sam is down and hurt bad. Hurry."

"Sam. Stay with me baby. Oh My God, Sam, I am so sorry. We shouldn't have come out here. I had no idea he would show up. Sam, stay with me." I pulled his shirt open and there was blood everywhere. I couldn't see where he was bleeding from. I cradled Sam in my arms and started rocking, "Sam, don't leave me now. We have just started our lives, we have a whole future together. God, don't take him, he has three kids, they can't lose him after losing their mother, please God, not now." I sat there on the garage floor rocking Sam, sobbing, praying, pleading to Sam to stay with me. I hadn't even noticed I was bleeding from my right shoulder, there was no pain and I hadn't noticed the blood yet. I was so concentrating on Sam. I kept rubbing his face and talking to him but he was not responding to me. "Sam, Sam, talk to me, please say something. You can't leave me, I won't let you. You made a vow to me. You can't leave your kids, they need you. God, Sam I need you." I heard the sirens in the distance and all I could do was rock Sam and cry to him, "They're here baby, you are going to be all right now, the doctors will take care of you and you are going to be just fine. Hang in there Baby, you are almost home free. I won't leave you, I am with you all the way."

I was still sitting on the floor rocking Sam when the paramedics ran through the garage door. They were opening bags, getting his blood pressure, checking his pupils, checking his pulse, put an oxygen mask over his face, ripping his shirt open, inserted an IV. Everything was happening so fast I didn't hear they had asked me a question. "Sergeant, you are shot. Get someone over here, the Sergeant's been shot."

One of the paramedics turned to me and looked at my shoulder and said, "We've got a gusher here. Get me a clamp, I've got to shut this off." And that was the last thing I remember.

CHAPTER 58

When I woke, everything was hazy and blurred and I couldn't focus on the images standing next to me. Then I heard my mother, "Brenda, it's Mom and Dad here and Candy. You are going to be all right, the doctor said your surgery went real well. You'll be home in a couple days and I will stay with you until you are all well. Now you get some rest dear, the doctor said we can only stay for a few minutes."

"What happened? What time is it? Daddy where am I?" And I started looking around and crying and not understanding where I was or why I was here. "Daddy?"

He took my hand and started rubbing it, "Baby, it's all right. You are going to be okay. You got shot in the shoulder and had to have surgery and it went very well. You need to rest right now and we will be back in a little while. Candy is here, too."

"Hey, Sis, We are here for you, all of us. You get some rest and we will be back, okay?"

"Sam, where is Sam?"

No one was answering me, I looked from Dad to Mom to Candy, they all exchanged looks and then back at me, but no one was saying anything.

"Where is Sam? Someone tell me where is Sam!"

"Baby, Sam had surgery too. He is going to be just fine, it is just going to take a few days. Now you get some rest, sweetheart. We'll be back soon."

"No! I want to see Sam. Take me to him, Daddy, please." I tried to get up and hadn't noticed I had an oxygen tube in my nose, two IV's going---one with a clear liquid and one that was obviously blood---a catheter and lord knows what else. I laid my head back down started sobbing. It was coming back to me what had happened. I was sobbing uncontrollably remembering what had happened at Mrs. Compton's.

They were lying to me, Sam was dead, I knew it. I remembered all the blood on the front of him and he wasn't moving, he wouldn't talk to me, I knew he was dead and no one would tell me.

I was sobbing and crying out, "No not Sam, NO!NO!NO! Not Sam."

Dad cradle my head in his arm, "Shhh, Baby, Sam is going to be all right."

I vaguely remembered a nurse coming in and put something in my IV and soon I was out.

The next time I woke the doctor and nurse were standing by my bed talking in a very low tone. When I moved they both turned to me, "You're awake. Brenda, I am Doctor Sawyer, and this is your nurse for the day, Kathy. You have a pretty bad shoulder wound there and we had to put stitches in the back of your head. We got the bullet out and have sent it over to ballistics. Do you remember what happened?"

"What time is it? Where is Sam?"

"It is 7:30 Sunday morning. Sam is in ICU and is doing fine. How is your pain, on a scale of one to ten where is your pain now?"

"I need to see Sam. Will you take me to him?"

"Brenda, we can't, Sam is at the Medical University. They are taking care of him there. Now let's take care of you. What is your pain level, one to ten?"

"I don't know it hurts, an eight and I really have a headache."

"We need to keep your pain down lower than that." He turned to the nurse and she went to the cupboard and got something she put in my IV. "Do you feel like eating something? You can have some jell-o, broth, soft boiled egg, and tea any of that sound good to you?"

"No, I just need to talk to Sam. Is he alive?"

"Yes, I can assure you Sam is alive, they are taking good care of him. When you feel like eating you tell the nurse and she will bring you whatever you want. Do you remember what happened?"

"Sam and I went over to the Compton house to check out the upstairs apartment over the garage. We were just leaving, Sam opened

193

the side downstairs door and a guy shot him, when I stepped into the doorway he shot me. I must have been knocked out, because when I came too the guy was gone. I called the precinct to send an ambulance. That's all I remember until I woke up here. Were my parents here?"

"Yes they are, your Dad is waiting out side. I'll send him in. I'll see you this evening."

I was just about to doze off when Dad came in. "Hey there, you feeling better this morning?"

"I guess okay. Where's Mom and Candy?"

"They're at your house. Spook is watching out for them. He sure is a cool dog. Candy told us the neighbors are moving and they gave him to you. He will be a great body guard, we weren't sure if he was going to let us in last night."

I noticed a lounge chair in the corner of my room and a blanket in it. "Did you stay here all night?"

"Yah, I did. That chair is a pretty comfy bed."

"You shouldn't have, Dad. Have you seen Sam?"

"No, they transferred him last night to the Medical University. Willy was here last night for quite awhile. He seems pretty upset about all this. He's the one that called us."

"When did you get here?"

"We got the call about 11:00 yesterday morning and caught the first flight out."

CHAPTER 59

I was getting drowsier and Dad noticed I wasn't tracking too well, "I am going to go home and check on Mom and Candy. You need to rest for awhile. We'll be back later. I love you Baby and you do what the nurses tell you to do." He smiled and winked at me and left the room.

I don't know long I had been asleep, but when I woke up Willy was sitting in the chair in the corner. When I opened my eyes he got up and came to the side of my bed. "Hey there sleepy head. How ya feelin?"

"Okay, I guess. Have you seen Sam? How is he?"

"They wouldn't let me in to see him. I guess Sam's parents and his sister got in last night. He's in pretty rough shape, Brenda, but you know Sam he's a tough one. He'll be just fine."

I grabbed Willy's hand, "How bad is it Willy? You have to tell me. I have a right to know."

"He's in very critical condition. They've done all they can for him right now. The first seventy two hours are the most crucial." Willy leaned in close and said, "Brenda, he is going to make it. He has to." His eyes watered and he turned away from me.

"Where did he get shot?"

"In the chest and lower right side, it tore him up pretty good.'

"Oh My God! Sam's going to die isn't he?" I started crying and couldn't stop.

"Brenda, you have to stop, this isn't helping you. We have to be there for Sam when he gets better. We have to believe he is going to get better. He has to."

The nurse came in and started fiddling with my IVs, changing bags and checking the oxygen for whatever. "Brenda would you like something to eat?"

"I'm not hungry."

"Brenda, you have to eat in order to get well so you can go see Sam," Willy said.

"Okay, I'll have a soft boiled egg and a piece of toast."

"That a girl. I'll phone the cafeteria and someone will bring it up in a few minutes." The nurse said and walked out of the room.

"Have you talked to Dawson?"

"No, I am staying clear of him. But I know he knows about this. He'll probably be out to see you. Just be careful what you say and if you can keep someone in the room with you. Okay? I really need to get going, I promised my wife I would get the lawn mowed today. If I don't I'll be calling a hay baler to come and I'll be looking for another place to live." And we both laughed.

"I doubt you will have to look for another home, your wife is too sweet. She'll just make you pay in other ways. If you hear anything about Sam would you please let me know?"

"You got it. See ya later."

It wasn't long until the nurse brought in two eggs and toast. I tried to sit up and realized it was not going to be easy and it hurt like hell. I let out an ouch. Kathy turned around, "Just a minute there, let me help you. First things first. Let's get your bed up a little more, and then you can swing your legs around over the edge of the bed."

She brought my bed upright then took my left arm and pulled me up and swung my legs around. "Whoa." I suddenly felt very dizzy.

"A little dizzy there? Just take it easy, it'll pass in a minute."

I reached up and felt my hair, it was hanging down long and no longer in a braid as I had started out the day, well I guess the day before. "How much hair did I loose back there?" I asked the nurse.

"Not very much, just a little strip on the right side of your head. If you had hit your head on your braid you may not have had to have stitches. There are thirteen tiny stitches, with as much hair as you have, my Dear, you won't even miss it. Wish I had your hair, it is beautiful."

"Have you heard how Sam is doing?"

"No, I haven't, but I can make a call to the University if you'd like?"

"Would you please?"

"Are you okay now to sit there? Dizziness go away?"

"Yes it has, I'm fine."

The nurse went out of the room and I tried to eat the, now cold eggs. I put one on the toast and mashed it around and took a bite. Then I tried the other piece of toast with jam on it, it wasn't too bad so I ate it.

I heard a little knock on my door and Mom, Dad and Candy came in. "My, my, look who's sitting up. How you feeling?" Dad said.

"Better I guess. Someone else can sure have this shoulder and headache. How are you guys doing and Spook?"

"We are all just fine, Baby, and Spook is a jewel. He tried to sleep with Dad and I and decided there wasn't enough room, so he ended up with Candy." Mom answered.

Candy chimed in, "He is a bed hog. I woke up staring into his eyes, his nose no more than an inch from mine." We all laughed.

"Has anyone heard about Sam?"

"No we haven't, but no news has got to be good news." Dad said.

"Mom, will you go down to the front desk and bring my bag of clothes up here?"

"Of course Dear, but you aren't going any where in those clothes. I'm sure they cut most of them off of you."

"I know, there are a couple things I need out of there."

"Candy, how's Tim doing without you? You should be home tending to your new husband."

"He's just fine. In fact he insisted I come here."

"Don't you have to go back to work? What is today, Sunday? What time is it?"

"Yes it is Sunday about 2:30. I already called in for personal leave. My boss is really a neat woman and told me to stay as long as I need too."

Nurse Kathy came in, "I called for you. Sam is holding his own, there hasn't been any change. He is listed in critical but stable condition."

"Thank you. I'm through with this, would you help me lie back?"

"Of course." She moved the food tray out of the way and got me back into bed. I winched with pain as I laid back. "Let me get you something for the pain." At this point I only had one IV going so that is where the pain med went. I hate needles so this was a good thing.

Mom came back in with a plastic bag of all my stuff. I found it hard to go through the bag with only my left hand so Mom helped me. I wanted the bullet I had put in my pocket, it needed to go to ballistics. We went through everything in the bag and I dumped it out and I couldn't find the ring, my engagement ring. "Its not here, Mom you have to go back to the desk and asked about my ring. I was wearing a ring and it's not here. My badge or weapon aren't here either." I said in a panicked mode.

"Okay, it's okay, I am sure all of that was put in a safe. I will go back down and check on them."

When Mom left the room, Dad and Candy came over to the side of my bed. "Sis, can you tell me what happened?"

"Oh, Daddy, this is all so messed up. I should have never called Sam to go with me. We had been gone for a week and he was going to spend the day with his kids, the girls had soft ball games, and he missed them because of me. And because of me he may be dying ………….."

Dad interrupted me, "Brenda, I will not let you take the blame on this. You know these are the risks of the business and so does Sam. This is your job and blame is not an equation here. Now just tell me what happened."

"Willy had already gone over to the apartment a few days earlier to check it out, but I had to see it for myself. Sam reluctantly went with me, he wanted to spend the day with his kids. I thought it would only take a little while. The outside garage door was unlocked, but the door upstairs was locked so I used my lock kit and we got in. We found everything to be exactly as Willy had described, nothing we could pin to this guy. I did find the gun case that had a hand gun and box of shells we believe to be the one that was fired on Mrs. Compton. I took one of the shells and put it in my pocket and we left. When we got downstairs and Sam opened the door someone was standing outside with a gun. Sam tried to talk him in to putting the gun down but he shot him anyway. I yelled out to 'drop your weapon, Police' and when I stepped into the doorway he shot me. I think I got off one shot, I don't know if I hit him or not. I went down and I guess I was knocked out when I hit my head on the concrete. When I came to, Sam was lying beside me and bleeding. I found Sam's cell phone and called the precinct for assistance and the rest is history. I'm actually surprised there hasn't been an officer here to report on this. Willy was here, but only as a friend and didn't ask any questions."

"There has been an officer here, but the doctor wouldn't let them in. Told him he would have to come back later. He'll probably be back this afternoon."

"Dad, you know Dawson is going to blame me for this. Do you know who the officer was?"

"No, I don't. But, Brenda, you get that out of your head right now. You won't be held responsible for this."

"You don't know Dawson. He'll turn it on me."

Mom came in with the rest of my stuff, "They told me we had to take the gun home, you can't keep it here."

She handed me the plastic bag and I started going through it. I handed Dad my gun, "Would you check to see if it has been fired? You can take it home and my badge, and would you bring my phone charger when you come back?" Then I remembered my cell phone was in Sam's car. "Candy, I am going to need some clothes to go home. A shirt or something to go over my arm. Actually, I have a pair of black sweats that are big, I think I can put the sweatshirt over the top of this arm."

"Sure, I'll look around, we'll figure something out. Has the doctor told you when you can go home?"

"No, he'll be in this evening and I hope I can go home tomorrow. I can recuperate at home as well as here. Besides, you need to get home."

"Don't you worry about me, you just take care of yourself."

CHAPTER 60

I finally got to the bottom of the bag and found my engagement ring. I took it out of the bag and put it on my finger, "I have something to tell you. Sam asked me to marry him and I accepted, we got engaged the Friday night we left for Florida. I was going to take the ring off and we were going to keep it a secret for awhile and not put our jobs in jeopardy. But you know, I don't give a shit about our jobs." And I started crying.

They were all excited about the news, admiring the ring and consoling me at the same time. "You are a brat, Brenda. You were already engaged when I was talking to you on the phone and you didn't tell me. How rude. I thought we shared everything." We were all laughing and hugging, very carefully, when Officer Matt Scott came in.

"Hey Brenda, how ya doin?"

"Better, Matt. I guess you are here to fill out a report?"

"Yes I am. Willy took the week end off to do some catch up before his wife throws him out, so you are stuck with me."

"Can't think of anyone I would rather be stuck with." I turned to Mom, Dad and Candy, "Why don't you guys go on home for awhile, I'm in good hands with Matt." I introduced everyone to Matt and they left confirming they would be back for evening visiting hours.

Matt stayed over an hour asking questions, going over and over the event and asking the same questions again and again. When Matt was through with the report and confident it was complete he stood up to leave and his eyes spotted my ring. "Ah Ha! Is there something I don't know about?"

"Yah, I guess there is. Sam and I are engaged. We got engaged the night we left for Florida. So, this will only rile Dawson even more, ya think?"

"Screw Dawson. I think he is getting worse instead of better. The department is walking on egg shells around him. I don't know what it is going to take to bring him down. But something's got to give here pretty soon. Don't you worry about this, let's just get through all this and get Sam well, okay?"

I started crying again and sobbing, "I am so sorry about all this, I wish Sam had not gone with me."

"I am only going to say this once, Brenda, don't you for one second think this is your fault. Sam wouldn't hear of it. And if you go into Dawson's office with that attitude, he will nail your ass to the wall. Risk is the nature of our jobs and we all know it. You need to rethink this and get on a different page and be prepared. You are going to be just fine, you are excellent at your work and so is Sam, and he is going to pull through. Okay?" Matt gently held me, "It is all going to be all right. You lay back and get some rest now. We'll be in touch."

"Matt, where is Sam's car? Is it still at Mrs. Compton's? It needs to be moved to his house and I need my cell phone out of it."

"We'll get that taken care of and I'll get your cell back up here to you. Now get some rest. See ya later."

I laid back and was dozing when my food tray was left on the table. Nurse Kathy came in and injected more pain meds in my IV. I didn't even bother to look at the food under the stainless lid, instead fell sound asleep.

CHAPTER 61

The next couple days were like a roller coaster ride. My room had turned into an array of beautiful bouquets of flowers looking like a funeral parlor. X-rays, physical therapy, all my tubes and IV removed, visitors in and out, Matt in for more questions, most of the department had stopped by, everyone but Captain Dawson. Sam was improving slightly, but I still had not been able to see him and it was driving me crazy. Sam's parents and Monica had picked up the car and took it back to Sam's place. I still didn't have my cell phone and had not spoken with Sam's parents or Monica yet.

I had been in the hospital three and a half days and the doctor had finally consented for me to go home the next morning. The list of instructions he gave me and appointments I needed to schedule were amazing. Physical therapy three times a week, exercises for my shoulder I had to do in-between. I put the list down, laid back, turned on the television and immediately fell asleep.

A knock on my door woke me as Paul Davis and Monica came in. I was not only shocked to see them, but I was speechless. I had no idea what to say them. Monica broke the silence, "Hi Brenda, this is Sam's Dad, Paul. How are you doing?"

"Nice to meet you Mr. Davis. I'm doing fine, much better thank you. How is Sam?"

"We just came from the hospital. He's doing a little better, he has at least made it through the first seventy two hours; that was the first hump he had to over come. He's tough, unless there is some kind of complication, he will be just fine. He has a long road to go but things are looking up compared to a day or two ago," Monica answered.

"I am so sorry. Sam didn't really want to go with me to that apartment, he wanted to spend the week end with his kids. But he didn't want me to go alone and he knew I would. I am sorry and I don't blame you if you if you hate me for this."

Paul walked over to the edge of my bed, "Brenda, I am sorry we have not had an opportunity to meet before, but Sam has talked so much about you, that Rita and I feel we already know you. And I know Sam would not tolerate for one second you taking blame for this. There are risks you take in this business, this just happened to be one of the more dangerous situations and ended with very serious repercussions."

I started crying and Monica took my left hand and was rubbing it, "Brenda, please don't cry. No one hates you or blames you for this, and above all, Sam is terrified for you and feels completely helpless lying there in the hospital. He told me to tell you he loves you very much and to be very careful." Monica was still rubbing my hand and suddenly stopped and held my hand up to look at the sparkling diamond ring. "My, my, isn't this just one beautiful hunk of rock? Is that a trinket from a box of Cracker Jacks?" And she laughed.

"I wish Sam were here, this is something we wanted to tell you together. Sam asked me to marry him the night we left for Florida and I obviously accepted. We had decided we would keep it quiet for awhile, not to risk our jobs, and to finish up this case. But, I changed the plan. I suppose it wasn't fair not to have waited for Sam so we could share the news together."

Monica smiled at me and gave me a careful hug, "Sam told me he was going to ask, and I am thrilled you said yes. Sam has been in love with you from the first moment he laid eyes on you. We couldn't be happier."

Paul stepped up, took my hand and glanced at the ring and gave me a hug, "I can speak for Rita that we are thrilled for both of you. Even though we haven't met before now, you have lived in our hearts through Sam for a very long time. Whatever makes Sam happy, makes us happy and I can see you two will be very happy together. We welcome you to our family."

Tears were streaming down my cheeks and I was smiling at the same time. "How are the kids doing with all this? And Sylvia? This has got to be devastating to them."

"Actually, the kids are doing okay. They got to go in and see their Dad today. This was reassuring to them to see him and talk to him. Rita took them back to the house or she would've come. She did send her well wishes to you."

"Thank you, I am looking forward to meeting her."

"Before I forget, here is your cell phone, we found it in the car when we took it back to Sam's. Here's Sam's number in ICU, the nurse said you could call him and talk for a couple minutes. That will make you both happy." Monica said as she handed me my phone.

The door opened with a tiny knock as my parents and Candy came in. I made all the introductions and soon Dad and Paul were off in their own conversation as were Mom, Candy and Monica. I observed the bonding of the two families, happy tears continued to flow and sad at the same time because Sam wasn't here to share in all this.

CHAPTER 62

Captain Dawson came in and the room all of a sudden became totally silent. Although no one had met the Captain, they all sensed who he was. I made the appropriate introductions and Dawson was polite with inquiries to Sam's condition. Everyone started with their excuses to leave, everyone except Dad, and he was making no signs to leaving. This made me happy and nervous at the same time.

After everyone had left, except Dad, Dawson sat on the end of my bed, "So how are you doing, Brenda?"

"I am doing just fine. In fact the doctor has released me to go home in the morning."

"That is good news, glad to hear it. Sam however, isn't quite so lucky. He's going to be laid up for quite sometime, if he recovers at all."

"I believe Sam is going to recover, he is tough and has too much to live for to ever give up. He has three kids and he won't leave them."

"I sure hope you are right. In the meantime, I have reassigned your case to Johnson and Jones. You are going to be out of commission for awhile and we need to get this wrapped up."

"Please don't do that, Captain. We are so close to the end and I want to get this guy. I can finish this case, just give me Willy or Matt or both and we'll get him. I just need the rest of the week and I promise I will be back on Monday in full capacity. Please, I have to do this for Sam, as well."

"The decision has already been made, Brenda. You are in no condition to continue with this case, mentally or physically."

"Excuse me, Sir, with all due respect, I believe you are under estimating the Sergeant." Dad said stepping closer to my bed and Dawson.

"Umm, with all due respect, Sir, this is a department issue. I don't believe that has room for emotional or bias opinions."

Oh my God! Here it comes. My Dad and the Captain in a disagreeing exchange of sarcasms.

"You are right, it is a department issue. And you are correct that it also has no room for bias opinions. So why don't you just put your bias opinion in the round file. You know Brenda can handle this, and you also know if Sam were in this room we would not be having this conversation. So why don't you just resend you reassignment and let Brenda close this case?"

"Mr. Weathers, you are treading in department business that is none of your business, with all due respect. I do not have the extra personnel to go out with Brenda and cover for her, because she is not up to full capacity."

I could see this conversation was going absolutely no where, "Dad, I......"

Dad raised his hand to me, "All right Captain, if you don't have the extra personnel, then I will come out of retirement and I will step in and work with Brenda until this case is closed. I will do this free of charge and I will sign a release to relieve the department of any liabilities. This would be no difference than if you were to bring in the FBI or some other organization to cover this case. I think this would be in your best interest, if you know what I mean."

"Do I read an underlying threat here, Mr. Weathers?"

"You can read whatever you want to, Captain. But I think we have a very clear understanding of the issue at hand and I have made you an offer you can't refuse."

"I will have to clear this with the Sheriff. I will get back to, Brenda. Glad to see you are better and able to go home. Oh, by the way, I would like to have your report from last week as soon as possible."

"Thank you Captain. Sam's and my report is complete including our expense receipts. I will see to it the report gets to your office. Dad, can you take care of that for me?"

"You bet I can, I would be more than happy to."

The captain stood up, smiled at both Dad and I with the most obvious fake smile I have ever seen, "I'll be in touch." And he left the room.

We both held our breath for a couple of seconds and then burst into laughter. "Oh my God, Dad. I can't believe you stood up to him like that."

"Well, partner, one does what one has to do. We'll get this wrapped up, you can count on that."

"I can't believe this. A father and daughter detective team. I would have never thought of this in a million years. I am so honored to work with you, Daddy, and I am speechless that you pulled this off."

"It isn't affirmative yet."

"Oh, yah, you can go to the bank on this one. You have Dawson eating out of the palm of your hand right now."

"I am going to go and let you rest, you have had quite the afternoon. Besides, Mom and Candy are waiting somewhere around here for me. We'll be back this evening. Glad you can go home in the morning, we'll get our game plan going then." He leaned over and gave me a kiss. "We love you very much and are so proud of you. You are one hell of a detective, Sergeant, and I am proud to be working with you." I saw tears well up in his eyes as he turned to walk out of the room. "Later, Baby."

Before Dad left I told him where the report was with copies of the all the receipts. He assured me it would all be on Dawson's desk first thing in the morning.

Wow, this was quite an afternoon. I laid there in disbelief and tried to digest all that had happened. I plugged my cell phone into the charger, I knew it was deader than a door nail and I wanted to make some calls. The first call I wanted to make was to Sam. I couldn't find a phone in the room, so I rang for the nurse. She explained they had not put a phone in my room so as not to disturb my rest. She would get one for me.

When Sam's nurse answered the phone and I told her who I was she said he was anxious to talk to me and would take the phone to him. I hardly recognized his voice he sounded so weak. I started crying and could barely talk, "Sam, I love you. How are you doing? I am so sorry this happened, I should've let you stay home with the kids."

"Hey there, Bee, now don't do this, it is not your fault and I won't let you blame yourself. Enough of that, okay? How are you doing Baby?"

"I am fine. I am being let out of jail in the morning. On my way home I am coming by to see you. I can't believe this has happened to us. Guess we aren't as invincible as we thought. But we aren't destructible, either." And I laughed. "I have so much to tell you, but the nurse said I could only talk for a couple minutes. I love you, Sam. I will see you in the morning."

"I love you too. Be careful." And he hung up. He sounded so weak and I knew he had to be in a lot of pain. Even though Sam didn't sound like himself, I felt so much better after talking to him.

I laid back and dozed off.

CHAPTER 63

When I woke I decided to take a walk. I put on my robe and hospital socks and went down the hall. I knew the rules that patients were not to visit other patients, but I didn't think I knew any patients here so I just walked. I made the loop around the nurse's station a couple times and took a chance on the elevator. I went down one floor to the third and walked to where Mrs. Compton had been. I was standing in front of the room Mrs. Compton had been in and a nurse stopped, "Can I help you?"

"I was taking a walk and wanted to see if a friend had gone home. Mrs. Compton, Miss Ellie was in this room last week. Doctor Cutter was going to move her to a re-habilitation center and I was just curious."

"Miss Ellie had a little set back, she was supposed to go to the center on Saturday, there wasn't a bed available so she will be going in the morning."

"I am Sergeant Brenda Weathers, I have been working her case, may I go in and see her for a minute?"

"I'm sorry I didn't recognize you, what happened?"

"It was just a minor accident."

"How is she? Can you bring me up to date with what's going on?"

"There actually wasn't much change until Doctor Cutter told her he was moving her and she went into a, let's say a fit and started thrashing around which elevated her blood pressure. It really surprised us because she had been rather docile. A little agitated at times, but for the most part pretty calm."

"May I go in? I won't stay long?"

"Let me go in and see how she is doing."

When she came out the nurse said she was resting and her vitals were normal for her. So I went in.

"Miss Ellie, it's Brenda Weathers. Remember me, I am the one who found you when you got shot? Can I talk to you for a couple minutes? All I want you to do is squeeze my hand if you understand." I didn't get any response.

"Miss Ellie , Sam and I went to see Susanne and your grandchildren. We met them all, they are delightful children. I think Susanne is in real trouble with her husband and I think she needs you. We met with Daryl in Chicago, too, didn't get to meet his wife, though." She squeezed my hand.

"You do hear me don't you?" She squeezed my hand again.

"Miss Ellie, would you open your eyes and talk to me?" Nothing, she made no move or response to my question. "Miss Ellie, I know you know who I am, and I know you know more than you are letting on. I need you to open your eyes so I can help you. I have been to your house and I know someone is living in an apartment over the garage. Can you tell me who he is? I need your help. Please, Miss Ellie, you have to help me. Please open your eyes and talk to me." And she did. Her eyes fluttered and she looked me square in the eyes and closed them again.

"Okay, have it your way. Just listen to me. I believe this person living above your garage is Todd Thompson. Who is he? What is your connection to him?" She pulled her hand from mine. "You're afraid of him aren't you?" I put my hand over hers again, "You are afraid, aren't you?" She moved her fingers.

"Miss Ellie, I can't help you if you won't talk to me. I am going back to my room. I will be back later. I hope you will talk to me then."

The nurse came in just as I was standing up to leave, "You need to leave now." She leaned down to Miss Ellie, "Are you feeling better, Miss Ellie? Maybe you will have a good appetite later."

"How is her appetite? Does someone have to feed her or does she eat by herself?"

"She doesn't eat much. Someone has to feed her. We've tried everything to get her to eat, mainly soft foods. Lots of jell-o, broth, cottage cheese, puddings or something like that. She often either holds her lips tight or pushes it out with her tongue. She is a tough one."

"Would you happen to have some vanilla and chocolate pudding and key lime pie yogurt for me to try and feed to Miss Ellie later? I am going back to my room. But I want to come back and continue our conversation and try the puddings."

I went back up to my room feeling frustrated with Miss Ellie. I know now she had been faking her semi coma and had just gone into being stubborn. I had to break that cycle and find out why. I still wanted interviews with a couple of her friends and the Reverend. Reverend Stearns was still a thorn in the back of my mind, there was the dinner table set for two the day Miss Ellie was shot, and then there was Todd. I felt given all the information I now had, the trip to see Susanne and Daryl had been a total waste of time. Had they been cooperative and forthcoming with their information we could have avoided that whole weeks trip. Personally, I would never regret the time spent with Sam, but professionally it was a waste of time and money.

I put another call into Sam, his nurse said he was resting and she wouldn't wake him. She told me his condition hadn't changed. I laid back and sobbed, Sam had to pull out of this, he just had too.

CHAPTER 64

Mom, Dad and Candy came in and brought clothes for the next morning's departure. I told them about my visit with Miss Ellie and my intentions for the interviews. We visited for awhile but I really wasn't in any mood for chit-chat. My mind kept wandering back to Sam and all the what ifs. Then I remembered I had not checked my messages on my cell phone and there were fourteen. Most of the messages were from friends, some from the department and two from Mr. No Name and those two I listened too. I put the phone on speaker, "Now look what you made me do. You Bitch, I told you to back off. This is all your fault." The second call, "If you had minded your own business this wouldn't have happened. Now your friend may die and it is all your fault. Live with that, Bitch."

"Brenda, did you by chance save any of the other messages?" Dad asked.

"Yes, I have all of them. I need to turn my phone in and see what kind of trace we can get if any. Dad, I have a plan for in the morning, first stop is to see Sam, I called to talk to him but he was sleeping, there is still no change. Then I have a couple of interviews, one with Reverend Stearns and the other with a neighbor of Miss Ellie's."

"Brenda, you are just getting out from a four day stay in the hospital, surgery to repair a gunshot wound and crack on your head. Don't you think you ought to take it a bit easy for a day or two?"

"Dad, I do not have a day or two. We are too close to getting this guy. I am not slowing up now. I am moving forward with or without the Captain's blessing. I have to do this for Sam, for us." I started sobbing uncontrollably. Mom and Candy tried to console me but it only seemed to make it worse. A nurse came in to give me a shot, I told her I didn't want a shot and when she insisted it would help calm me down, I screamed at her, "I do not want your God Damned shot, you got that?" She stepped back and shot a look at Dad, he nodded for her to leave and signaled it would be okay.

"Okay, now let me tell you something. You get control of yourself, get your head back on your shoulders and out of your ass. You have gone through one hell of a lot here in the last couple of weeks or so, now is not the time to fall apart. Do you hear me? Now get it together." Dad turned away and walked to the window and just stood there.

Candy put her arms around me, "It's okay, Sis, Dad is worried and scared all at the same time."

"He's right, Candy, now is not the time to fall apart. I'll be all right. I'll be just fine. I am going to get this guy. Now why don't you take Dad and Mom and go home and take care of Spook. I'll be ready to go in the morning. You want to pick me up and take me to see Sam?"

"I would love to. I'll be here by ten. Get a good nights rest, tomorrow is another day."

I tried to watch the news and couldn't get interested. I went to the nurses' station and asked for some paper and a pencil. I had to make out my plans. I didn't have my brief case with me so I couldn't make any calls and I didn't have phone numbers. It took me only one second to figure out I couldn't write, my right arm was strapped to my body. Then it occurred to me I was not going to be able to drive. Damn it. I really did need Dad to assist me. I made a list of calls I wanted to make, with my left hand. I had to see Nellie Goodman and the Reverend for starters. I couldn't get my head around the connection of Todd Thompson. I thought Sam and I had given every possible consideration, but no one we had questioned, so far, could or would admit to any knowledge of this man.

I decided I would sneak down to Miss Ellie's room and try another visit. By now it was nine o'clock and the nurses should be busy settling patients in for the night. I put on my robe and slippers, the halls were empty, I took the elevator to the next floor down and went in to Miss Ellie's room.

On the night stand were the three puddings and a spoon I had asked for. I leaned over her and touched her shoulder, "Miss Ellie, Sergeant Weathers here, I came to visit. How are you this evening?" She didn't move and with her back to me I couldn't see her face. I walked to the other side of the bed, her eyes were closed.

I took her hand, "Miss Ellie, would you look at me? I need to ask you some questions. If you understand me, squeeze my hand." Nothing. "Has Todd been in to see you?" No response. "Do you know where Todd could be?"

Again, nothing. "Miss Ellie, please, we need to talk to Todd, we need to know where he is and I think you know." She moved her hand from mine. "Miss Ellie, you have been playing games now long enough, it is time for you to wake up so you can go back home. If you don't you will be going to a nursing home." She opened her eyes and stared at me. I took her hand again, "Good Girl, do you know where you are?" She squeezed my fingers. "Do you know why you are here?" Again she squeezed. "Good, do you know Todd Thompson?" She closed her eyes and moved her hand from mine. "Miss Ellie, please do not shut me out, I am here to help you." I reached over and got a spoon with Key Lime Pie yogurt and put it to her mouth, "Open your mouth Miss Ellie, I have some pudding for you." When she got a taste of the tartness, she opened her eyes again, "Yuk!" I was so startled I dropped the spoon and the rest of the pudding went on her nightgown. "Oh, Miss Ellie, I am so sorry I am afraid I have made a mess of your gown. Let me get a wash clothe and clean it up."

As I was cleaning off the pudding, the nurse came in the room, "What are you doing? You can't be in here." She obviously recognized I was a patient, few visitors show up in their bathrobes and slipper and a hospital band on their wrist.

"I was giving Miss Ellie some pudding and dropped some on her nightgown, I was just cleaning it up."

"Why are you in her room? Patients are not supposed to go in other patient rooms."

"I know, I am Sergeant Weathers and I have been working on Miss Ellie's case."

"I don't care who you are, it is too late, you have to go back to your own room now."

"Please, just give me five more minutes then I will."

She looked at her watch, "Five minutes that is all." And she stormed out of the room.

Miss Ellie's eyes were closed again. "Miss Ellie, you talked to me. Can you tell me why you are so afraid? Is someone threatening you?"

She opened her eyes and just stared at me. "Please talk to me."

"I can't. Now go. Just go and leave me alone." She rolled away from me and closed her eyes.

"Miss Ellie, I can't do that, I have to get to the bottom of all this and you are the only one who knows what happened. I can protect you, but I have to know who I am protecting you from." She wouldn't budge and the nurse came in and told me it was time to leave.

CHAPTER 65

My cell phone was ringing as I walked back into my room. It was Monica, "Brenda, we are at the hospital. Sam has an infection and is running a high fever. They have taken him back into surgery."

"Oh my God! Monica, what happened, what is the surgery for?"

"The doctor suspects when they removed part of the intestine and reattached it, there is a possibility it developed a slight leak. They have to go back in and stitch it back together. At least that is what they are thinking right now. The doctor ordered all kinds of tests, ex-rays, ultra sound and CT scan or something like that. They all confirmed something was in there that had not shown before. The test showed a cloudy image that could either be bruising or fluid and with the spiked fever they are going with the fluid."

"Monica, what are his chances of surviving the surgery? He is so weak, this can't be good."

"Brenda, Sam is a strong man, he is a healthy man, we have to believe he is going to make it through this. And so do you. I don't want to hear you talk this way, I can't believe anything other than Sam is going to make it. Do you hear me?"

"Monica, I am so sorry, of course he is going to make it. It's just that I haven't been able to see him, I have only talked to him once very briefly on the phone and I am scared shitless. Will you please call me as soon as he gets out of surgery? I don't care what time it is. Please?"

"Of course I will. Brenda, I am sorry I snapped at you. We have to be positive, okay?"

"Yes, I will be waiting for your call."

I immediately dialed my house and when Candy answered I was sobbing and she could hardly understand me, "Brenda, you have to stop crying so I can understand you."

After I explained everything Monica had told me and had settled down somewhat I asked, "Candy will you come over and take me up to the University Hospital? I need to be there."

"Brenda, do you know what time it is? They won't let you out of the hospital to go see Sam."

"I don't plan to ask anyone. I plan to put my clothes on and walk out like a normal person."

"Are you nuts? You can't do that. Now think about this. You can't see Sam in surgery, then he will go into recovery and then back in to ICU. He isn't even going to know if you are there or not. Wait until the morning and you will be able to see him. They won't let you in to see him tonight, Brenda."

"I just feel the need to be there, Candy. Please come get me. If you don't, I will take a cab."

"You don't have any money for a cab, my dear. But I'll come over and sit with you until Monica calls."

"Don't bother if you won't take me." And I hung up.

I turned on the T.V. and flipped through the channels trying to find something of interest, but nothing struck me as very interesting at all. I laid on my bed staring at the screen and found myself in deep thought about Miss Ellie. She is terrified of someone and I believed it to be Todd. But why? What was the connection?

Much to my surprise in walked Candy with a deck of cards, note pad and cribbage board. "Now, I am going to kick your ass and take some of that sassiness out of you." She said laughingly as she pulled the tray over the bed and climbed on the end of bed sitting Indian style. "Call it, gin or cribbage."

"I really don't feel like playing cards, Candy."

"Fine, then gin it is. Do you want to cut for deal or you just want me to deal?"

"Just deal." Soon I was totally distracted and concentrating on kicking Candy's ass since she was such a cocky little shit and very competitive. She hated to lose and usually made everyone's life miserable if she did.

We played five lines for the first game and she just barely beat me. So we played another five lines and I beat her badly. That naturally called for the tie breaker, another five lines. We were about half way through the game when my phone rang. I glanced at the clock and it was 1:15.

"Monica, how did it go?"

"Sam is out of surgery and in recovery for the next hour or so. The doctor's speculation was right, there was a tiny leak and he was able to repair it. And he found another area he had missed the first time and was able to repair it as well. He said there was so much blood during the first surgery he had missed it. He felt everything went real well and Sam should start to recover more rapidly now. He's still in pretty rough shape and it is going to take some time, but he feels more confident now after seeing how the rest of the injuries are starting to heel."

"Oh Monica, thank you so much for calling. I get out of here in the morning and I am going to stop by and see him on my way home."

"That would be wonderful, I am sure by then he will be a more alert. We are going home now, not going to wait for him to come out of the recovery room. We'll talk to you in the morning. Now you get some sleep and we are going to do the same. Night."

"Night Monica and thanks again for the call."

"I gather everything went well with Sam's surgery?" Candy asked.

"It appears it did. The doctor thinks he should recover more rapidly now, because he not only had this repair but a minor one the doctor had missed the first time. I hate it when they miss something." Then I laughed.

"That is great news. Now I am going back to your place and go to bed. We'll finish this game another day. You get some sleep and I'll see you in the morning at ten." Candy leaned over and kissed me on the cheek and gave me a careful hug.

CHAPTER 66

I woke up at 6:30 and tried to get in the shower. It didn't take long to see I could not do this alone without getting my shoulder harness wet. What was even worse I couldn't figure out how to get out of the damn thing. I buzzed for the nurse, when she came in and saw the predicament I had gotten myself she started laughing.

"This isn't a laughing matter. I want to take a shower and shampoo my hair. I have only had sponge baths and haven't been able to shampoo my hair in four days. I am going home today and I would like to get out of here early if at all possible."

"Let me see if I can find an aide to help you. We will be getting patients up here in a little bit and starting the morning duties, so we are going to be very busy. I'll see what I can do."

So, there I sat. Stark ass naked with my robe wrapped around me, waiting for someone to come help me. I waited for a half an hour and not liking it. My patience level was at zero.

The aid finally came in and after a comedy of errors and a painful process we accomplished my mission. My shoulder was throbbing but I was trying to tough it out. I relented and asked for a pain shot. I knew the shot would make me drowsy, I laid on the bed and fell asleep.

I was awakened with the breakfast tray, it was now eight, only an hour and a half had passed. I called Candy, "Can you come early to braid my hair? I am hoping to get checked out of here early."

"I'll get there as soon as I can. Dad has the car, he and Mom left about seven to get your report in and then stopping by the grocery store and shopping. I'll come on over as soon as they get back. Have you heard anything on Sam?"

"No, not yet. I am going to call up there and ask his nurse. Thanks Candy, I'll see ya when you get here."

I called the hospital and got the report from Sam's nurse, "He had a restful night. He has a slight fever, but nothing to be alarmed about. I am going to wake him up in a few minutes and see if I can get him to eat something. Other than that he's about the same, improving some." I thanked her and hung up.

Now, it was the waiting game. My patience level moving right to minus zero.

Candy showed up, braided my hair, I was finally checked out and in the car on my way to see Sam. It was 11:15 and I was a wreck; nervous, scared and anxious with every emotion described in Webster's.

CHAPTER 67

Sam's parents and Monica were at the hospital when we got there. Monica was in seeing Sam so we sat down to visit since I couldn't go in yet.

We talked about everything possible, how the children were doing and surprisingly they were coping quite well. Paul and Rita, and Sylvia were keeping things as normal as they could and keeping the kids well informed. The three kids had only been in to see Sam twice, hopefully that was going to change if he continued to improve.

Monica came out and she was smiling, "Sam is awake and talking. His first words to me is how you are doing Brenda. I think he is anxious to see you."

My eyes filled with tears but Monica put her arm around me, "He is better, Brenda, so buckle up and get in there. You can only stay for a few minutes, but he needs to see you as you need to see him."

I don't know what I expected when I saw Sam, but I could hardly contain myself. I thought I was going to faint. He was hooked up to every machine possible, IV's and tubes everywhere. His face was swollen and a bandage around the top of his head, apparently he had a huge split in the back of his head when he went down in the garage. But through it all, Sam gave me a big smile when I got to the side of his bed. I took his hand and leaned down to kiss him, and the tears started flowing.

"Hey Bee, don't cry, I'm going to be okay. I love you Baby, how are you doing? You look pretty damn good to me, a real sight for sore eyes."

"Sam, I love you, too. Are you in much pain? That was really a stupid question, of course you are in pain. I am going to get this guy, Sam. He is not going to get away with this."

"Bee, you are going to have to turn this over to someone else, you can't do this alone. Please, let it go. You are in no condition to move forward with this. Let Dawson reassign the case."

"Sam, don't you worry about work now. You just concentrate on getting well and getting home to your kids. They need you and I need you."

I leaned over and kissed him as the nurse came over and put her hand on my shoulder, "I'm sorry, you are going to have to go now, Sam has had a busy morning and we need to check vitals and he needs some rest."

"Okay, I've got to go, Baby, I will be back later today. I love you, very much."

"I love you, too. Let it go, Bee, just let it go, please." He squeezed my hand and then closed his eyes.

When I got into the waiting area Paul, Rita and Monica had already left. I sat down in a chair and put my head in my hands and started sobbing. "He looks awful, Candy. I don't know what I expected, but not this."

Candy put her arm around me and just held me and let me cry it out.

As we drove home it was amazing how Candy had taken on the 'big sister' role. Dishing out orders what I could do and couldn't do. How she and Mom had everything all planned out so all I had to do was lay around and go to physical therapy and doctor appointments. Dad had already done all the yard work, so that wouldn't be of concern for me. Candy assured me they had everything under control. I just let her rant about the plans. I knew there was no need to start any arguments now.

Spook was the first to greet me as we pulled in the driveway. I sat on the edge of the deck and petted Spook, he was so excited to see me. Dad had done a wonderful job on the yard. It was immaculate, mowed, edged, flower beds cleaned out and some plants in my pots around the deck. Mom had lunch ready. They were pleased with themselves and all their accomplishments. As I stepped inside I could see Mom and Candy had been busy cleaning house, it too was spit polished and shined and fresh flowers on the table. We still had a car full of flowers from the hospital, some were plants that would add to the deck pots.

"Oh my God. You guys have been busy. Everything looks absolutely wonderful. I can't thank you enough, you guys are all amazing, thank you." I gave each a hug and of course they assured me, "it was nothing, we didn't have anything else to do."

After lunch I took a pain pill and laid down for a bit, Spook on my bed right beside me. I was immediately asleep.

CHAPTER 68

I woke to voices in the other room and Spook's nose. I brushed my teeth and went out to join the rest and was surprised to see Penny and Bob King.

Bob got up from the chair and walked towards me, "Oh my God, Bob. Look at you. You got your new leg." I threw my left arm around him and gave him a big hug. He was beaming like a little kid, as was Penny.

"Well, if you aren't a sight. How ya doin? Penny has called the hospitals everyday checking on you two. Glad to see you are home."

"Thank you both, I'm doing good, tougher than shit. It'll take more than a bullet to keep me down. Sam on the other hand got hit pretty bad. He had another surgery last night. I saw him for a few minutes on my way home, he looks pretty bad, Bob. It is going to be a long haul for him."

"Sam will be just fine. He is tougher than shit, too. Please give him our love and we'll get over to see him when he can have visitors."

"So, I see you took my advice, Miss Brenda." Penny said as she walked towards me and took hold of my left hand. "Pretty piece of rock there my dear. Congratulations. We had already heard the news, it traveled like wild fire. So if you had plans to keep it a secret you can kiss that plan good bye."

"Ya, I know. That was the original plan, but I changed it. Repercussions are probably not going to be pretty. But what the hell. Life just doesn't always seem to turn out pretty, even on a good day. How is everything going with you two?"

Bob chimed in, "Actually everything is coming along great. Penny's folks brought the kids home last weekend, so they can finish school here. I am behaving like a responsible husband and dad. Life is good.

I am getting used to Stick," he patted his prosthesis, "we are becoming real good friends."

Penny put her arm around Bob, "Yes, life is good. It is great to have everyone back home. Honey, we need to go, we left the kids at home, and by now they have probably cleaned out the refrigerator." We all laughed.

After Penny and Bob left, Mom immediately started fluffing pillows on the sofa for me. "Come lie down now for awhile."

"Mom. I just got up from lying down, please don't fuss over me. I'm okay. I have been doing nothing but lying down for the last four days. I think I will just stay up for awhile."

Dad and I sat at the table with my computer and briefcase of files. I gave him all the reports to bring him totally up to date with complete details, including the incidents I had purposely held back from him. He read quietly, expressionless and laid the papers down. Dad took my hand, "I had no idea you have gone through all this. Why didn't you tell me?"

"I didn't want to worry you. I thought Sam and I would break this case right away. We were so close. I still think we are almost there."

"Let's go back from the beginning and go over every single detail."

"Okay, can we go out on the deck, I want some fresh air?"

We sat outside for a couple hours and went over and over the case. Dad jotted down some notes and would go back and ask me questions. I felt like I was being interrogated. I stood up, "I think I have had enough for awhile."

The next three days were a rat race. I had so many calls from friends, checking on me and to see how Sam was doing. Several calls I let go to voice mail and would call them back later.

I was going to physical therapy, going to the doctor, visiting Sam at least twice a day and in between all that Dad insisted we go over everything in the reports again and again. "There has got to be such a simple answer to all this that we are missing. It is right there, I know it is." Dad would say almost ritualistic.

We had a great time, the evenings were like our old family days. Play cards games, laughed and told old stories. Sam was getting better everyday, in fact they were planning to move him out of ICU and into a private room on Monday.

Dad took Mom and Candy to the airport early Sunday morning. To be quite frank, I was relieved to have them go. My house was getting rather small with four people. I appreciated everything they did, and it was truly good to be all together again, but it was time for them to go home. Candy had a husband and job to get back to and Mom needed to check on Grama and Grampa.

CHAPTER 69

I got up early Monday morning, put on the coffee and got toast ready for when Dad got up. I was sitting at the table making out my agenda for the day as he walked in. He had already taken Spook for a walk. "Wow, you are certainly up bright and early."

"Ya, Spook came in and nudged me until I got up to let him out. How'd you sleep?"

"I really slept pretty good for a change. Didn't have anyone to wake me for a sleeping pill or pain pill. I fixed us coffee and toast."

While we had breakfast I laid out my plan to Dad, we would first go see Sam. I wanted to set up an appointment with the Reverend and the afternoon with Nellie Goodman. It was too early to call now, but with Dad driving I could make my calls later.

We got ready and were out of the house by 7:30.

At the hospital Sam was sitting up a bit and looking better. He didn't look great, but much improved. "Good morning Baby, you look better. Are you feeling better?"

"Hey there, Bee, how's my girl?" Then he saw Dad. I had forgotten they had never met. "I see you've got yourself a chauffeur."

"I do, Sam, I would like you to meet my Dad, Gordon. Dad this is Sam."

"It is a pleasure to meet you, Sir, I have heard a lot about you and your police career. Sounds like you were quite the respected officer."

"It's a pleasure to meet you too, Sam, and the name is Gordon, please. And I likewise have heard plenty about you."

"Bee, would you step out for a couple minutes? I need to speak to your Dad."

"I'm not sure I should trust you two alone. I have a feeling you are about to gang up on me." I leaned over and gave Sam a gentle kiss and went out into the waiting area.

"Mr. Weathers, I am afraid I have handled things very badly. However, considering what's done is already done, I would like to ask your permission to marry your daughter?"

"Sam, it is my pleasure to give you my permission to marry Brenda. Phyllis and I would be thrilled to have you as our son-in-law. We couldn't be happier for the two of you. You have our blessings."

"Thank you. I promise you I will protect her the best that anyone can ever protect Brenda."

Dad and Sam were both laughing when I came back in, "Is the coast clear? May I come back in?"

"You sure can, I just asked your Dad for permission to marry you. We have both your parent's blessings. So what do you think of them apples?"

"I think them apples are just fine, but we've got to get you well first. Are they going to move you to a private room today?"

"That's the rumor. We'll see."

The nurse came in and told us we had to leave.

"Okay, Baby, we'll see you later. I love you."

"I Love you too. Hey Gordon. You know you have your hands full with this one, don't you? You're gonna have to keep her reeled in. And Good Luck."

"Ya, I sure do know that. But I have my bag of tricks I pull out every once in awhile. She just thinks she's in control."

We all laughed, I kissed Sam good bye, Dad touched Sam's hand (no hand shake) and we left.

Out in the hall I looked at Dad, "A bag of tricks, huh? How long have you been packing them around?"

"All of your life, my dear, all of your life."

"Really?" I gave him a light punch in the shoulder and laughed.

PART IV

REVEREND PAUL STEARNS

CHAPTER 70

In the car I put a call in to the Reverend. Mrs. Stearns answered the phone, "Mrs. Stearns, this is Sergeant Weathers, may I speak with the Reverend?"

"Just a moment, I'll get him."

"Sergeant, what a pleasant surprise. What can I do for you?"

"I was hoping to be able to drop by for a short visit. There have been a couple events I would like to talk over with you regarding Mrs. Compton."

"Of course, I'd be delighted. When did you want to come by?"

"Is there a slight chance I could stop by in about thirty minutes or so? I promise I won't keep you long?"

"No problem, I don't have any appointments until this afternoon. I'm looking forward to seeing you again, Sergeant."

"Thank you, Reverend, I'll see you in a little while."

"So, Dad, I guess you get to meet the Reverend Paul Stearns. It will be interesting to see your take on him."

"What's so interesting about him? There's something troubling you."

"You're right, there is something, but I can't put my finger on it. To me, he just isn't the typical 'good guy Reverend'. He feels sleazy to me. In fact Mrs. Goodman is a member of his church, or used to be, related the same feeling to me. Which reminds me, I want to meet with her this afternoon, if she isn't socially engaged? I need to call her before we get to the Reverend's."

Mrs. Goodman answered very quickly and sounded a little out of breath. "Mrs. Goodman? This is Brenda Weathers."

"Oh, hello there dear. How are you? I was wondering if you would call. What can I do for you?"

"Did I catch you at a bad time?"

"Oh, my, no. I am just puttering around the house."

"Is there a possibility I could meet with you this afternoon for tea? That is if you don't have a previous engagement?"

"Well, let me check my calendar. Oh my, I have a luncheon at 11:30 at the Country Club, and then we are playing bridge for a couple hours or so. But you know, my dear, I will be home between 3:30 and 4:00. I would love to see you about 4:00. You know I don't drink tea at that hour of the day; it keeps me awake at nights. I like to have a brandy or even a scotch or two if that is okay with you?"

"That will be just fine Mrs. Goodman, I will be happy to join you. I'll see you at 4:00."

"Please, dear, call me Nellie. Mrs. Goodman was my mother-in-law, rest her soul, she wasn't a real nice person. I'm looking forward to seeing you at 4:00."

"Okay Nellie, 4:00 it is."

"Oh my. Am I in for a treat this afternoon. I can hardly wait. I think I will have you drop me off and I will call you to come get me when we are done. Then we can grab a quick bite before we go to the hospital. Is that okay with you?"

"That's okay with me, but you know Mom and Candy cooked a bunch of stuff for us. The refrigerator is crammed full of food."

"Ya, I know, but Mrs. Goodman's is on the way to the hospital and it will be faster to pick something up. Guess I better be paying attention to where we are. Turn left after this light at the next one. Then we go about four blocks to the church and turn right just before the church and go to the parking lot in the back."

As we turned into the parking lot I said, "Dad, feel free to jump in and ask any questions you feel are relevant. But don't indicate in any way that Sam and I were shot. I am going to address this as a minor accident with my shoulder."

"You got it. This will be interesting to meet this guy from everything you've said about him. Let's hit it Partner." We bumped knuckles and Dad gave me a wink as we got out of the car.

The Reverend was on the phone when we went in to his office, but quickly said he would call back later. He stood up and reached across the desk to shake my hand, "Good to see you again Sergeant. Oh my, did you have an accident?"

"Just a minor mishap. I'd like you to meet my Dad, Gordon Weathers. Dad this is Reverend Paul Stearns. Dad is my chauffeur for a few days until I get rid of this thing and is my assistant until we get this case closed for Mrs. Compton."

"Hmm, what happened to your partner, Detective Davis?"

"Sam is on leave dealing with some personal issues. Dad has come out of retirement to be my partner to finish up this case. So, having said all that, can we get to the business at hand?"

"I don't know how else I can help you, but I will try. What can I do?"

"I guess my first question to you is, if you have been in to see Mrs. Compton lately. We were out of town for several days and I have been out of touch with her. How is she doing?"

"Well, the last time I was in to see Miss Ellie, I didn't see there had been much of a change. I tried to talk to her, but I didn't get any responses. I don't really know what her issues are now."

"When was that last visit?"

"Oh, I don't know, maybe a week ago. I don't remember exactly when I was there. I have been pretty busy here lately."

"You are pretty close to her personally as well as through the church, aren't you?"

"Well, I'm not sure what you mean by personally, but Miss Ellie is a very active member of our church. She is on many committees and attends most of the social events here. I have been the Pastor here for many years, so I am personally involved with a lot of families of the church."

"Would you consider yourself a closer friend to Mrs. Compton than most of your church members?"

"Sergeant, I'm not sure I like your inference here. My wife and I have a lot of close friends within and out of the church. So where are you going with this?" The Reverend was starting to get a little irritated.

"Reverend, I merely want to understand your closeness with Mrs. Compton. If you have any ideas who could have made this attack on her. It is evident robbery was not the motive. Who or why did someone enter her home in the middle of the day and shoot her?"

"I wish I could help you, but I have no idea who that could be or why. Miss Ellie is loved by everyone who knows her. This is equally a puzzle to everyone."

"Sam and I made a trip to visit with both Suzanne and Daryl. Although Daryl displayed some concern and caring for his mother, he seems to be way too busy to put forth any effort or time for her. Suzanne on the other hand made no pretense to the fact she could care less whether her mother lives or dies. She also has her own set of problems with her husband. So that leaves us with the only person that has any connection what so ever, at this point and that is, Todd Thompson. What do you know about him?"

He looked at his watch, "I don't know anything about Todd Thompson. I have no idea who this person is. I don't want to be rude, but I do have another appointment in a few minutes. Is there anything else I can do for you?"

"Oh, I thought you were free until this afternoon, my mistake."

"Something else came up just before you got here."

"Reverend, I find it hard to believe you know nothing about Mr. Thompson. He has been living in the apartment over the garage at Mrs. Compton's for some time. How long has he been living there?"

"I don't know who is living there. Miss Ellie said it was a family friend. She has only mentioned it one time and did not tell me his name and I didn't ask."

"As a friend and her Pastor, weren't you just a little bit curious about this person and possibly concerned about her safety having some guy living in her garage when she lives alone?"

"You need to understand, Miss Ellie is a very private person. There are some areas of her life she does not discuss. Her children is one of them and obviously this tenant happens to be another. I don't know what else I can tell you, Sergeant?"

"Reverend, when you made home visits to Mrs. Compton, did she appear to be nervous or anything that would indicate an issue with this guy living there? Do you know how long Mr. Thompson has been living there?" Dad asked.

"No, I do not know how long he has been living there, I have already said that. Like I said, I don't even know his name. And as far as Miss Ellie being nervous about a visit, she often has a social event she is about to attend, so is anxious for me to leave. Like the day she was shot, she was expecting someone for dinner."

"So, you were there the day she was shot? You never mentioned that before." I interrupted.

"You never asked, and I was there early in the afternoon for only a few minutes. I saw no importance in my visit at all. I really need to cut this meeting off, I have an appointment and I do need to get going." The Reverend stood up and walked to the door.

"Thank you for your time, Reverend. We will be in touch. If you think of anything I would appreciate a call." I gave him another business card.

"It was nice meeting you, Reverend. I'm sure we'll be meeting again soon." Dad said. "You have a great day.

CHAPTER 71

In the car I looked at Dad, "He is lying through his teeth. He knows one hell of a lot more than he is telling. Besides, when I had called for the appointment, he said he had plenty of time, he didn't have any appointments until this afternoon. But all of a sudden he had an appointment he had to get to."

"No question there. I think we ought to get out of the parking lot and see if we can follow him. I have a feeling his next appointment could be Todd Thompson."

"I agree, we just need to keep a car in between us so he doesn't recognize my car."

"Sis, you forget this was my business too, and I haven't forgotten how to tail someone."

"I'm sorry, you're right. I did forget."

We drove for quite awhile keeping a safe distance from the Reverend and discussing the visit at the same time. "You know, I still haven't heard from the Captain. Don't you think that is a little weird? I would've thought he'd have called by now to remark about my report and either tell me I was off the case and it was reassigned or give his consent to you working with me. What do you think?"

"I think you have a very incompetent Captain. I think he is backed into a corner and doesn't know which way to turn, therefore just standing still. If he doesn't make any firm decisions then he can't be faulted if anything goes wrong, because he did not make his statement of his intentions. On the other hand if it all turns out well then he can take the glory because he didn't make a final decision and we are the only ones privileged to his alternative suggestions. He is truly a 'scum bag'. I don't know how he has kept his position."

We stayed a reasonable distance from the Reverend. A couple miles later he made a turn into a gas station. He got gas, went across the parking lot and into a barber shop and got a hair cut. Then into the grocery store and came out with two bags, got in his car and headed back to the parsonage.

"He didn't have an appointment. He just wanted to get rid of us, we were getting on his nerves and too close to a subject he did not want to discuss."

"You are so right, Sis. Let's go home and have some lunch, I'm starved. I forget what it is like to work without eating. Guess I am out of training."

I laughed, "Okay, take us home and I will feed you. Maybe I will lie down for a little while before I meet with Mrs. Goodman."

"Sounds good."

I went through the refrigerator when we got to the house, Dad was right, it was full of all kinds of food. I heated up a couple bowls of soup and made one and a half roast beef sandwiches. We talked more about the Reverend while we ate and tried to figure out every possible angle to connect Todd Thompson to Mrs. Compton. We had lots of possibilities, but with out Mrs. Compton to answer any of the questions, we only had possibilities.

I called Sam and he was moved to a private room. "Hey Baby, you sure sound better. I am so anxious to see you. It has been so difficult and scary. I have so much to tell you now that you are feeling better." Sam had so many injuries and so many complications, it was amazing he was progressing so well. He had a long recovery a head of him, but it was finally looking more positive.

"I am better, Bee, and I am anxious to see you too. It makes me so nervous having you out there unsupervised. Please be careful. You have no idea what is out there, just like what we walked into. Bee, I wish you would let someone else take this over. I am worried about you and your determination."

"Don't worry about me. Dad is keeping a close watch on me. In fact he is with me every minute. We'll see you this evening. Now you rest. I love you."

"I love you too. See you later."

I called the hospital to see if Mrs. Compton had been moved. She had and of course as requested by me and Doctor Cutter, her location was not revealed. My only chance of getting that information was to leave a message for Doctor Cutter to call me. I left a message, again, for the Doctor to return my call. I also called his office and left the same message. Then I went in and laid down for awhile.

CHAPTER 72

Dad woke me at 3:15 for the appointment with Mrs. Goodman. I got up and got in the shower, I decided a change of clothes was in order and maybe look somewhat cute for Sam that evening. I had finally mastered the sling on my shoulder and was taking fewer and fewer pain pills.

As we were pulling into Mrs. Goodman's driveway, my cell phone rang. "This is Sergeant Weathers."

"Sergeant, this is Doctor Cutter. I had two, actually three messages to call you. I apologize for not being in touch earlier. What can I do for you?"

"Thank you for returning my call, Doctor. There are a couple issues I wanted to discuss with you. I found out this afternoon Mrs. Compton was moved, can you tell me her location?"

"Yes, it took some doings, but I have her in a private foster home. My hopes with other people around she will come out of her state of mind and condition."

"That brings me to my other issue. I don't know if you knew I was in the hospital for four days and I made a couple visits to her room. I can confirm that Miss Ellie has been faking her condition. I did get her to talk to me, as brief as it was, she did talk. I can assure you she is terrified of someone and I believe that person is Todd Thompson. I have yet to make the connection with Miss Ellie, but Mr. Thompson is living in an apartment over her garage."

"Really? I know we have discussed a while back regarding her faking the semi-coma, but I'm curious how you got her to talk?"

"Well, it was a trick. She was pretending to be asleep and ignoring me during my last visit. So, I put some Key Lime pie yogurt on a spoon and put it in her mouth. She spit it out and yelled, 'Yuk'. When I pressed her about who she was afraid of and please tell me, she opened her eyes and stared at me and said, 'No I can't. Now go. Leave me alone.' Then she turned over, closed her eyes. The nurse made me leave the room. I was discharged from the hospital the next morning and haven't had a chance to locate Miss Ellie. I need to see her again. This whole case has taken a real wild turn of events, Doctor."

"Very interesting, Sergeant. You certainly have accomplished more with Miss Ellie than either myself or the staff have. I guess at this point the only thing I can say is good luck and please keep me informed. I won't be seeing Miss Ellie unless there is some complication. I have requested that someone bring her to my office in a week. There is no reason at this point she can't be transported for an office visit."

"Doctor, can you tell me where she is?"

"She is at the Del Mar Re Adult Living Residence on Upper Hill Drive. I don't know the exact address off the top of my head. I really need to go, please keep in touch."

"Thank you Doctor and I will certainly keep in touch." We hung up.

"Well, Dad, I guess you got the gist of that conversation. Now I've got to figure out a time to go see Miss Ellie. Right now I better get in there and see Mrs. Goodman. I'll call you when to come back and get me, okay?"

"I'll be at the house, think I will take Spook for a walk, but my cell will be on."

"See ya in a few."

CHAPTER 73

Mrs. Goodman opened the door before I even got on the front porch. It was a beautiful old farm styled home with furniture on the wrap around porch and the landscaping was perfectly manicured. I expected the interior would be equally immaculate and I wasn't disappointed.

"Welcome, you must be Sergeant Brenda Weathers?"

"Yes, I am. Thank you for seeing me Mrs. Goodman."

"Please come in. And do call me Nellie, Dear. May I pour you a cocktail? I am having a scotch, but I can get you anything you want. I have wine, vodka, gin, bourbon or most anything else."

"I'll have a vodka and water over ice. Make it light, please."

"Of course, Dear, I'll be right back."

I was admiring the elegant furnishings and walked over to the wall with what appeared to be family portraits. I should have known better than to do that, because when Nellie came back in the room and sat my drink down, "Oh, I see you have spotted my prize possessions. My family. This is Harold and I when we were married and this one when we celebrated our twenty fifth anniversary and this one is our fiftieth anniversary. These are our four children and various stages of their lives and families. They are all of such great pride to us, all the way down to the newest little addition, my great-great-grandson. I am truly so fortunate and blessed to be surrounded and loved by all of them."

"How long has Harold been gone, Nellie."

"Oh, my Dear, it seems like just yesterday. I still miss him terribly. Let's see, it's been over twenty years now. You see Harold and I married when I was just sixteen and he was nineteen. He was killed in a most unfortunate automobile accident just three years after our fiftieth wedding anniversary."

"I am so sorry, Nellie. It must have been very hard for you to live alone all these years."

"Yes it is at times. But I have been so blessed with my family and friends it hasn't been too bad. I guess the hardest part has been not knowing who had hit Harold and left the accident for him to die. You see, ironically, Harold was going to town to pick up a few groceries and a prescriptions for me when someone came speeding out of the driveway of the Compton's and hit Harold broadside. The car flipped over and hit a big rock on the other side of the road and rolled over the rock and into the field. He was there several hours before anyone found him. He was still alive, barely, but the injuries were so serious and with his age, at the time, was just too much for him to survive. Please, let's sit. May I call you Brenda?"

"Please do. Did they ever find out who hit Harold?"

"No, they didn't. Blake and Miss Ellie weren't home at the time, so they had no idea who had been to their house. There was quite an investigation, but nothing ever turned up. To this day they have not a clue, and of course they gave up the search and investigation many years ago."

"But you have remained friends with Blake and Miss Ellie all these years. Was that hard for you?"

"Miss Ellie is such a sweet lady, it would be hard not to like her and be a friend. She was very helpful to me during that time. Harold and I could never get very close to Blake. He was always so busy, traveled a lot and just not very social. It wasn't until after Daryl was born that he started staying home more and he became obsessed with that boy. Susanne was ten when Daryl was born and was immediately shoved aside."

"I thought Blake had a law firm in town. Why did he travel so much?"

"Well, it was rumored that he had ladies on the side. But he claimed he had out of town business. It was a curious subject to Harold and me that he would travel to Reno, Las Vegas, Portland, San Francisco and I don't where all he was. Miss Ellie never questioned him. I'm sure she knew, but she would never let on. There was only a couple times that she confided in me that Susanne had become such a naughty little girl and Blake ignored her. She complained a few times about his travels, but then would shrug it off. I think Susanne was just seeking attention after Daryl was born. Blake and Miss Ellie seemed to devote most of their time and attention to that boy and Susanne was pushed aside. Blake was extremely hard on that child, it is no wonder she grew up being naughty."

"Nellie, did you know there was a man living in the apartment over the garage at Miss Ellie's?"

"No, not really. I knew there was someone that called on her quite frequently. I asked her about that one day, because I had dropped by a couple times to pick her up for bridge. Someone was there and she said she would drive herself, she wouldn't let me in and seemed a little nervous. But when I asked her about it later, she would say it was a repairman of sorts. But I didn't know anyone was living in her garage. Who is it?"

"Has Miss Ellie ever talked about a Todd Thompson?"

"No, I have never heard that name. Is that who is living there?"

"I'm not sure. What about the Reverend Paul Stearns, what do you know about him? I understand he has been pastor at your church for a number of years?"

"Oh, my Dear. Not my church. I quit going there several years ago. I think he is a scoundrel. There was a committee many years ago that tried to get rid of him, but when it came down to a vote of the membership we lost. I gave up my membership as did many others. I can't believe he is still there. Miss Ellie and I never discuss the church or the Reverend. She had made it very clear one time that he was someone she wished not to discuss. And we never have again."

"Why did the committee want to get rid of him? What did he do?"

"Well, it was rumored that he was patronizing many of the single women in the church. It was rumored that he convinced, or tried to convince, many of the widowed members to include in their Wills a large contribution to the church. He is just sleazy. He gives me the creeps. May I fix you another cocktail, Dear? I am going to fix another one for myself."

"Just a short one, make it weak, please."

"What is the Reverend's wife like?"

"She is really a meek and mousey sort of person. She hardly ever enters in a conversation, she just stands back and smiles and lets Paul lead with whatever."

"Did they ever have children?"

"Well, my Dear, that is the funny thing. At one time we all thought she was pregnant, but she never appeared when she should have been showing. Then all of a sudden she was back to being slim and trim and there was never again any mention of a child. So who knows what happened. The gossip was soon a thing of the past."

I glanced at my watch and saw it was now 5:00 and I thought it was time I break up the conversation. Nellie was so full of information I wasn't sure I wanted to leave.

"Nellie, I am confused. Did Mrs. Stearns have a baby? Did she give it up for adoption? Did she have an abortion? What happened to the baby?"

"You know, Dear, no one was ever sure about that. No one ever knew for sure what happened. And like I said, the rumors and gossip soon just faded away. I have no idea what happened. But I can tell you, Mrs. Stearns became more reclusive and the Reverend became far more vocal and active. So I don't know what to tell you I know, I removed myself from that membership and went to another church and I love it there. I'm not a real active member, on committees or that sort of thing, but I am very comfortable with the worship and the closeness to God, that is all I really need. I have enough activity outside of the church, quite frankly I don't care to get anymore involved than I already am. Very selfish of me."

"Oh, Nellie, I don't think you are the least bit selfish. You have a heart as big as all out doors. I would be privileged to have you as a friend as you are to Miss Ellie. You are truly a jewel."

"Oh my Dear, you are way too kind. You know I didn't even ask you what happened to your shoulder. Are you going to be okay?"

"Oh yes, I am going to be just fine. It was just a minor accident. How about if I come back and have a visit with you another time? This has been so much fun learning about your family and you have been more than helpful. Can we get together again real soon?"

"Oh my Dear, I would love that."

I called Dad to come get me. Nellie and I walked around in her yard and I admired her flower gardens.

"You have such a beautifully manicured yard. Do you work out here yourself or do you have a gardener?"

"Oh, my Dear, I putter around here some, but Jeff is such a good man and takes such good care of everything, I wouldn't dare get in his way. But I do like to get out here once in awhile. I used to do it all myself, the flower beds anyway, and Harold used to do all the rest. All the mowing, edging and pruning. Then Harold decided he wanted a gardener, actually, I think Harold just didn't like all the garden work. So I worked with Jeff and slowly I have given most of that up. Jeff has been with me for many years, he is truly a sweetheart."

"Well, you two certainly do a beautiful job. Nellie, here comes my Dad. I will be in touch with you real soon and we'll do this again. I have thoroughly enjoyed getting to know your family. I admire you and your families' relationship, I think it is truly wonderful."

"Thank you so much for coming by. I have enjoyed our visit immensely and hope we can do this again real soon. You take care."

We said our goodbyes and I promised I would come back another day for cocktail hour. Tea was totally out of the question.

CHAPTER 74

When Dad pulled up in front of Nellie's home and I got in the car, I leaned back against the seat. I felt a little bit of a buzz from the two drinks Nellie had mixed for me. I chuckled and thought they were not mixed light as I had asked her.

"So what are you chuckling about?"

"That Nellie is quite the character. She mixed me two vodka waters that I had asked to be mixed on the short and light side. I don't think she knows how to mix either short or light. I certainly got an education this afternoon. I think I am more confused than ever."

"How's that?"

"First off, she certainly painted a pretty grim picture of the Reverend. There was a committee to get rid of him several years ago, but they were unsuccessful. She doesn't know anything about Todd Thompson. She knew there was a family friend staying at Miss Ellie's house but said Miss Ellie never mentioned his name. So, I think I want to go see Miss Ellie tomorrow. At this point she is the only one that can answer any of the questions. She is a tough ole bird."

"So far you are the only one that she has spoken too, so she knows she can't fool you anymore. You know there is always the 'false trick tactics' to get a confession. Maybe we need to make up a story about Todd to hopefully get her to tell you who he really is. Sometimes it works and sometimes it doesn't. With a little luck, you can get it to work."

"We sure don't have anything to lose. Let's work on that this evening after we visit with Sam. In the meantime, we better feed you. There is an Out Back restaurant not too far from here. How about a nice juicy steak? I know you never get those at home. Mom's a really good cook, but 'well done' is the only way she cooks anything. How long has it been since you've had a really good steak?"

"Can't remember. Your Mom can do wonders with hamburger, fixes a mean pot roast, her recipes with chicken are endless, but a steak, that isn't even an option. Your idea is awesome."

We were seated and I ordered another vodka water with a lime and Dad ordered a beer. Our drinks had just been delivered when I heard someone say my name, "Brenda? Is that you."

I looked up and standing by our table was Alexis and Jim Taylor. "Alexis and Jim, what a surprise. Good to see you."

"You won't believe this, but Jim misplaced your phone numbers and both you and Sam are unlisted. I was so mad at him. How are you? I see you had an accident, are you okay?" She looked at Dad, "And Sam, how is he?"

"I would like you to meet my Dad, Gordon Weathers. Dad this is Alexis and Jim Taylor. Sam and I met them when we were in Chicago and ironically they live pretty close to me. We were so sorry to have to cancel our last dinner date with you, but our plans changed and we had to get back. How have you been?"

"Oh, we are just fine. Jim is back to his usual busy schedule, or lack there of, but I finally dragged him away this evening for an early dinner. It was a struggle, but I succeeded. Would you mind if we joined you and we can catch up?"

"Alexis, that is pretty presumptuous of you that they are dining alone and want company." Jim said.

I looked at Dad and he winked. "We'd love to have you join us and we are dining alone. It's nice to meet friends of Brenda and Sam's."

"Great. Where is Sam and how is he?" Jim asked as he slid in next to Dad and Alexis, next to me.

CHAPTER 75

The four of us ordered dinner and talked mostly about Jim and Alexis with Alexis doing most of the talking. They asked about my shoulder and I explained I had a minor accident and would be fine. I also told them Sam was on personal leave when Jim inquired. I certainly didn't want to go in to the details of the shooting. We had finished our dinner and the table was cleared and Jim and Dad decided they wanted dessert and we all ordered coffee.

Just before dessert was brought, I caught a glimpse of four men walking by our table. They stopped, "Well, Sergeant and Mr. Weathers, what a pleasant surprise to see you again so soon. I see you are in the keeping of good company."

"Good evening Reverend Stearns. I see you must know Alexis and Jim Taylor?"

"Of course, good to see you Mr. and Mrs. Taylor. It has been awhile. You are both looking well." He gave us a fake smile, or so I thought it was certainly not genuine.

"We are very well, Reverend." Jim said with an equally fake smile. To my surprise Alexis said nothing, just stared at the Reverend.

"Please don't let us interrupt your dinner. It was nice to see all of you." And the four men walked away.

"Mr. and Mrs. Taylor. How nice." Alexis said sarcastically. "Doesn't appear as though he has changed much. Still the sleazy scum bag he always was."

"So you know him?" Dad asked.

"Oh Ya, much better than we would like," Jim said and continued, "we used to be members of his church. I was on a committee several years ago that tried to get rid of him. We had quite the investigation going, nothing really criminal, but lots of moral issues. There were so many rumors going around about him having affairs with the older single women and getting them to re-do their Will and leave a sizeable amount to the church. Then there were some, for whatever information he had on these women, he would use it to get larger tithes.

It was getting way out of hand and he was out of control. The committee confronted him with the information and of course he denied all of it and started his own campaign to save his job. And apparently he did a real good job on that, because when it came to the final vote of the membership we lost. It was really close, but we still lost. So the end results was that a lot of the members left the church and went somewhere else."

"Interesting, I heard that same story just about an hour ago. I was visiting with Nellie Goodman. Do you know her?"

"We sure do. She was one of the instigators. Stearns was trying to put the squeeze on her to change her Will and made a few passes at her. When she complained to the board it was discovered she wasn't the only one. She was just feisty enough to get the ball rolling. Tell me, Brenda, how do you know Nellie and how is she? I'm surprised she is still alive, she's got to be getting up there."

"She is doing fine and I have to assume she is close to ninety if not a bit older. Mrs. Goodman is just someone I needed to talk to regarding a case we are working on. I assume then you must know Mrs. Compton?"

"Oh yes, Miss Ellie, she is another spry one. We heard a month or so ago that someone broke into her house to rob her and she got injured and was hospitalized, but we never heard any more. How do you know Miss Ellie? Ah, is that the case you are working on? You must have been there to see her son. I believe he has a law firm in Chicago."

"Yes it is. So what can you tell me about Miss Ellie?"

"So that's why you and Sam were in Chicago. You were meeting with Daryl, Miss Ellie's son. He is another sleazy scum bag. Miss Ellie sure didn't have good luck raising those two, Susanne and Daryl. But then I understand it was more because of Mr. Compton than it was Miss Ellie. We never met her husband, but it was rumored that he was quite the rounder. There was an accident and quite the investigation. I don't remember all of the story, but something to do with a speeding car coming out of their driveway that hit another car and didn't stop".

"Wasn't that Mrs. Goodman's husband that was killed? Or am I mixing this up with something else?" Alexis said.

"Ya, you may be right. I don't think they ever found the driver or the car. I don't know if Mr. Compton was part of the investigation or not, but it wasn't too long after that he died from a heart attack. Remember this is just a rumor to us, we weren't around when all of this happened. But I guess it was pretty ugly."

"Do you know anyone in the church or who left the church that was around during that time that I could talk to?" I asked.

"Oh man, most of those people are probably already dead or in a nursing home with Alzheimer or dementia of some kind. Off hand I can't think of anyone."

"Have you ever heard anyone mention a Todd Thompson in connection with Miss Ellie?"

"No. But there were lots of jokes that Mr. Compton probably had more kids out in the world than he knew about. I think he was considered a really scum bag lawyer. But like I said, these were just remarks made during our investigation several years ago. Nothing you could take to the bank based on what I've said. You'd have to ask someone that was around at that time. I'll think on it, if I come up with anyone, I'll be sure to call you, Brenda."

"That would great, let me give you another card. Dad, I think we ought to get going. I am so glad we ran in to you two. Let's keep in touch."

"Of course. The horse racing is on, you and Sam need to go with us some Saturday or Sunday. We prefer to go in the afternoon rather than Friday night, then we go out for dinner. You guys want to go with us one day this weekend?" Alexis chimed in.

"I'm afraid that won't work for us for a while. Sam is on personal leave for awhile, we'll just have to plan on this later. But we will be looking forward to going with you. We really need to get going. Give me a call if you come up with anyone I can contact."

"Sure will, tell Sam we said hello."

"You got it, see ya later."

CHAPTER 76

"Wow! How interesting was that? I wonder if Todd Thompson is Blake Compton's son or maybe Paul Stearns's. If he is Blake's son, then where does Stearns fit in unless for blackmail, but why? And if he is Stearns son, then what does Miss Ellie have to do with it? Unless, Paul and Miss Ellie were involved many years ago, then Todd belongs to both of them. But..........that doesn't make sense that Todd would try and harm his own mother. Guess we need to make another visit to Stearns tomorrow. I really want to pay a visit to Miss Ellie in the morning and see what I can fish out of her. Then it is back to the Reverend and see how he reacts to the information we have from both Nellie Goodman and Jim and Alexis. I would sure like to have one more person that was involved in the church way back when."

"That was some pretty juicy stuff, all right. Lots of scenarios for sure. We'll have to be careful how we approach that subject with the Reverend. I can see him in an explosive rage."

"Ya, so can I. Well we are here, let's go see Sam. I don't think I want to mention any of this to him quite yet. We can talk about seeing Alexis and Jim, but I think Sam is still too fragile for the rest. You know I still haven't heard from the Captain. I've spoken with Willy a number of times, I've kept him pretty much up to date on what is happening. His hands are pretty much tied as far as giving me any assistance. He did say they are keeping somewhat of a surveillance on the Compton house, but nothing is happening. So Todd must be holing up someplace and Lord only knows where."

When we got to Sam's room he looked amazingly better. The bandage was gone from around his head, all of the machines were gone, he just had the IV still going.

"Wow, do you ever look good. How are you feeling Baby?" I leaned over and kissed him. I started to stand up and Sam grabbed me and gave me another and bigger kiss.

"Now that was better," Sam said and laughed. "That felt good. Sorry Gordon, I've been waiting for that one."

"No problem. Glad to see you feeling better."

"So what have you two been up to? You keeping a close eye on my girl here?"

"Oh Ya, she can't drive yet so the keys are in my pocket. Takes me back to the days when she would get grounded for some thing or another, I carried the keys in my pocket then, too."

"I took Dad to the Out Back for dinner tonight. Poor guy never gets a big juicy steak at home. Just ain't in Mom's line of cooking."

"Now, now, don't pick on your Mother. She is a very good cook, just so happens steak isn't one of them."

"Anyway, you will never guess who we ran in to. Jim and Alexis Taylor and of course Alexis invited themselves to join us."

"What have they been up too?"

"I guess the usual, according to Alexis. Jim always works, she probably shops till she drops. But they do want us to join them for the horse races. I told them you were on personal leave so it would be awhile. They did tell me to say hello. Gosh, I am so glad to see you looking so good, Sam. What a difference a day makes. What is the doctor saying about your condition?"

"He said everything is coming along. I think he is going to remove the drain tubes in the morning. I've been up twice already today for a couple walks around the nurse's station. I know I am ready for some real food. This blended soft shit is for the birds. Now tell me how is the case coming along?"

"Oh about the same, not much going on. How bout if I bring you a couple books or magazines? That will help pass some of the time. I know day time television sure won't cut it for you."

"Gordon, how is the case coming along? I see I'm not getting anything out of Bee. I know you two aren't just sitting around playing tidily winks."

"Come on, Honey, don't drag Dad into this. He has been my chauffeur, I am not driving, I'm being a good girl. We went to see the Reverend and got the same ole nothing from him. I had cocktails with Nellie Goodman, remember, she is Miss Ellie's neighbor down the road. I got a tour of her family photo wall and a little scuttle butt about the Reverend. Apparently, there was a committee that tried to get rid of him several years ago, but when it came down to the final vote of the church membership they lost. So a lot of the members moved on to different churches. AND, ironically, Alexis and Jim were members of that church and Jim was on the committee and pretty much confirmed Nellie's story. That is it in a nut shell."

"What do you hear from the Captain?"

"Quite frankly, I haven't heard a word from him since he came to the hospital to see me. He told me he was reassigning the case, he and Dad had a few exchange of pleasantries, Dad told him he would come out of retirement and be my assistant, sign a release and work for nothing. And that is the last I have heard from him. I've talked with Willy several times, he said they have had a minimal amount of surveillance on Miss Ellie's house, but Todd has been nowhere. Willy says there's not much being said around the department, seems to be pretty quiet, and he has not seen Jones or Johnson around."

"For some reason, I think you are holding back."

"Sweetie, you don't need to be fretting about this. There is nothing you can do. We are handling things. Now let's drop this subject."

"Bee, I know how you are. You go at things like you are killing snakes and that terrifies me."

"Sam, don't get yourself all worked up. I am with her all the time and we are not in any danger. Just calm down. Brenda is right, there is nothing you can do. We are okay." Dad pleaded to Sam.

"I have to trust you are keeping my Baby safe. Because she doesn't have the common sense to do it herself."

"She's my baby too, Sam. Don't worry, I've got a short leash on her."

"Okay, you two. I am still in the room. Let's talk about something else, okay? You haven't even asked how my physical therapy is coming along. It's not always about you." I laughed and Sam scowled at me.

"Then tell me, show me your progress, sorry."

"Sweetie, don't be angry at us. I can assure you we are being careful and not in any danger. So far we are only asking questions. That's all. So will you please relax?"

"Do you know how impossible that is with you out there and this Todd is still running loose? He's already been in your house and made I don't know how many threatening phone calls to you. And you want me to relax?"

"Well, that is just how it has to be. You are in no position to do anything else. If we are going to fight about this when I come to visit, then I'm not coming back. It's up to you." I turned my back and walked to the window.

Dad leaned over and spoke softly to Sam, "She's right. There is nothing you can do here. You have to trust us to do the right thing. You seem to forget I was in this field of business about as many years as you are old. Sam, you have to let it go. Your hands are tied, so to speak."

"I know, but do you know hard this is? The love of my life is out there and we've already had one very close call. I can't bear the thoughts of another."

"Sam, you have to trust me. I am as vested in this girl as you are. She is my daughter, I won't let anything happen. Let it go."

"Hey Baby, we are going to go. It's been a long day for you. We'll be back in the morning and I'll bring a couple books and some magazines. Now will you settle down and get some rest. Turn the television on and watch something, there has got to be a program to distract you. I love you. We'll see you in the morning."

"I'm sorry I was such a butt. I'll be better in the morning, I promise.

Bring me that new James Patterson book you got before our trip, have you had a chance to read it yet? Maybe you could pick up a flyer on the race track that tells about the horses that have been running. I'll study it and figure it all out so we can be the big winners when we're able to go with Jim and Alexis."

"You do that, I don't think I have ever won at the races. It would be a first. Night Baby, you sleep tight and rest well. See ya in the morning."

"Sam, it's going to be okay. You rest now. Tomorrow it is." Dad and Sam bumped knuckles and we left.

CHAPTER 77

Dad and I rode home pretty much in silence. I was exhausted and was anxious to just go to bed. I hated fighting with Sam, if that's what you'd call it. He was totally off of the case and I was determined to solve it. There just seemed to be a few small puzzle pieces missing and I felt we were on the right track. I had to get through to Miss Ellie and get her to open up to me. I wasn't quite sure how I was going to approach the Reverend considering the information I had. Maybe I could try the 'false trick tactic' on him as well.

It was strange not to have Spook greet me when we got to the house. Since Karyn and Daniel had the sold the house and closing was just around the corner, they had come back to let the kids finish school and get everything packed. But it appeared he was going to be a permanent resident in a few days. I went straight to my bedroom and put on my bathrobe. I went to the kitchen and poured a half glass of wine and got a beer for Dad.

I sat down on the sofa, put my feet on the coffee table and took a deep breath. "God, I feel sorry for Sam. It has got to be so frustrating for him. But I can't stop now, I won't. I am going after this guy and get him if it is the last thing I do."

"Sis, it is frustrating for Sam, but he'll be okay. He just has to work through it all and he will. Here's a suggestion for you. Do you suppose Miss Ellie's son would've drawn up her Will? If so it might be worth a call to have him check how current it is and if the Reverend got to Miss Ellie as well as the others. Not sure what that would prove, if anything, other than confirm everyone else's opinion of him. What do you think?"

"I've been thinking about calling him, not about the Will, but to bring him up to date on Miss Ellie's condition. But the real purpose is to see if I could get any thing out of him about Todd. See if he knew his mother had a tenant over the garage. That is a good idea, though. Gives me another reason for the call. I will give him a call first thing in the morning. Sure can't hurt."

We visited for a little while and Dad decided he'd give Mom a call. I started working on my daily report on the case. When I finished I asked Dad to proof it and make any changes. I was tired and going to bed.

The next morning when I woke, I put a call in for Daryl Compton. With the two hour difference, I tried his home first. His wife answered and told me he had already left for work. I tried his cell phone and it immediately went into voice mail, I left a message. Then I called his office, and as I expected, his secretary reported he was not yet in. I left another message of urgency for him to return my call before his first client, if at all possible. I was sure I would have to make several calls to Daryl if history repeated itself.

I got in the shower and dressed for the day. Dad was up and dressed as well. We had coffee and cereal and I impatiently waited for Daryl's call. We were about to leave for the hospital when my cell phone rang. It was Daryl.

"Daryl, this is Sergeant Weathers. Thank you so much for returning my call so promptly."

"You said it was urgent. What's up? Something wrong with Mother?"

"Well, yes and no. I mean she isn't any worse, but she has worked herself into some kind of self inflicted amnesia of sorts and refuses to talk. I know she can, because I caught her off guard and by surprise. I will continue to work on that with her. She has been moved from the hospital to a re-hab center to get her strength built back up. I have two other reasons for calling."

"I'm glad she is doing better. I was calling the hospital most every day and then they said she was released, but she wasn't home. No one seemed to know where she was released to. Obviously, you do."

"Daryl, I do. But that's not the point right now. I know I have asked

260

more than once, but I have to ask you again. You need to think back in your life. Do you ever remember your Mom or Dad mentioning anything about Todd Thompson?"

"Geez, what is it with this guy. I have never heard of him. Why is he so important to you?"

"Because he has been living in an apartment over the garage at your Mom's house. I believe he is the one that shot her. We need to find him, he is dangerous and that is the reason no one but your Mom's doctor and I know where she is at this point. We are trying to keep her safe."

"I wish I could help you, that just isn't a name I've ever heard my parents mention. You said you had another question. I have a client waiting so we are going to have to make this fast."

"Did you write up a Will for your Mother? And how current is it?"

"What does my Mother's Will have to do with any of this?" He was starting to get irritated now.

"Daryl, it is believed that the Reverend from her church has tried to convince some of the single elderly ladies to leave a large sum of money in the event of their death. Is this something Miss Ellie would have had you do for her? And do you keep a copy of her Will?"

"Yes, I have a copy of her Will and she has never requested that I make that sort of change. If she had another attorney write an addendum to the existing Will, by law, it has to be added to the original. I have seen nothing of the sort."

"Does Miss Ellie have a safe in the house or a safety deposit box at the bank where she would keep her Will?"

"As far as I know all of Mother's legal documents and valuables are in a safe at the house. But I don't think I will be sharing that information with you."

"That's fine. But there may be some point in time you will have to fly out West for us to gain entry to that safe, if it comes to that. Daryl, doesn't it concern you at all, that some stranger is living over Miss Ellie's garage?"

"Sergeant, you need to understand my mother is a very independent woman and has made it very clear, many years ago, she did not want her children or anyone else telling her how to live or what to do. And I have done just that. Now unless you have anything else to discuss, I have a client waiting."

"Nope, that's it Daryl. Thanks for your help."

"Well, that was certainly a waste of time. I got about as much information out of him as talking to a damned post. I cannot believe those two kids of Miss Ellie's"

"You know, maybe Miss Ellie has just pushed them away over the years. That happens when people get older, sometimes. Both of my parents did that a little bit with us kids. When my sister died, they mellowed some, and it was better, but only to a point. Then when Mom died, Dad completely folded and was helpless, but he only lived less than a year after Mom. I think he gave up and didn't care any more."

"I barely remember them. You hardly ever talk about them, Dad."

"Since I was ten years younger than my brother, pretty much an unplanned child, they lived on the farm in Missouri with my brother. We didn't see too much of them. Seemed like Mom and I were so busy with Grama and Grampa that we didn't have the time. That's not true. We just didn't take the time. We weren't a very close family."

"What about your brother, Uncle Tom? Do you ever hear from him?"

"Oh, we exchange phone calls a couple times a year. He has never been out here to our place and it's been maybe five years since we have been back. Probably should do that one of these days."

"Ya, you might want to do that before you have to go back for a funeral." Dad agreed.

CHAPTER 78

"So Sergeant, what is on our agenda for the day. I'm sure you have a plan all lined up for us." Dad asked.

"I do. Let's go see Sam for a few minutes. While we are in that area I want to go over and see Miss Ellie. I'd like for you to meet her, but I don't know if I can get her to talk to me with you present. Let's play that one by ear. Then I want to have a surprise visit with the Reverend. See how he reacts to the new information I have."

"You need to be very careful with your approach to the Reverend. I'm not sure I trust him at all."

"Okay, let's get on with our day Partner."

Sam was sitting up and watching television when we got to his room. "Good morning there Baby. Did you sleep good? I brought the book and I will stop later to pick up some racing magazines. How ya doin this morning?"

"I'm doing better and yes I did sleep pretty good. You know how that goes, they wake you up to give you a sleeping pill. I'm sorry I was such a butt last night, Bee and you too Gordon. I have too much time on my hands and I know how this lady operates. She's scary." He laughed and squeezed my hand.

"No problem, Sam, I've got her back. She doesn't venture far without me." Dad chimed in.

"Talk about a shadow, the only place Dad doesn't follow me is the bathroom." We all laughed and the air was lightened. Sam appeared to be more relaxed.

We visited for a while and told Sam of our plans for the day. He was concerned, as was Dad and I, about the visit with the Reverend again. But we assured him we would be cautious. I was anxious to go see Miss Ellie, so we didn't stay long. Besides the nurse was going to get

Sam up and do some walking and maybe try a little physical therapy in the afternoon.

"I promise we will fill you in this evening on our day. I really want to get over to see Miss Ellie so we need to get going. I love you Baby. You be a good boy and do everything the nurses say, okay?"

"Ya, right. You two be very careful. I love you too."

When I walked into Miss Ellie's room she was sitting in a chair and looking out the window. This was the first time I had seen her out of bed and was happy for the change.

"Miss Ellie, Brenda Weathers here. Do you remember me?"

She continued to stare out the window without acknowledgement to my presence.

"How about I pull up a chair and we have a little chat. Will that be okay with you?" I turned her chair around so she was facing me. She just stared at me. "I am going to shut your door so we can have a private conversation and no one will hear us."

I shut the door and sat in a chair in front of her. I took hold of both her hands, "Miss Ellie, you have had quite a shock to your system. I want to help you work through this. I need you to tell me who Todd Thompson is, can you do that?" She looked at the door, then back at me, but didn't say anything. "Why is Todd living over your garage?" She just stared. "Please, I want to help you. I know you are afraid of him and have every right to be. How do you know him? I need to know this. Please talk to me."

Tears welded up in her eyes, "I can't. I can't talk about anything. You need to go."

"I can't go. I have to know about Todd. He is not a nice person and is dangerous. I have to protect you, but you have to tell me about him. Please."

"Blake will be very angry if I tell you."

"We won't tell Blake, he is away. But you can tell me."

"Todd is Blake's son. He used to travel and play around and got this woman pregnant?"

"I see, do you remember how old Todd is now?"

"Yes, he is about fifty, I think."

"When did you learn Todd was Blake's son?"

She started to cry and just sat there and shook her head. "It's okay, take your time." I put my arm around her and she stiffened up. "Miss Ellie, I am your friend, you don't need to be afraid of me."

"I know, what was the question?"

"I asked you when you learned about Todd."

"About a year before Blake had his heart attack and died. It is so confusing and such a complicated story. I don't even know where to start."

"Just start where ever you want too, we have all kinds of time.

"Well, it seems Blake had many women on the side. I didn't know about it for many years, but I began to think something was wrong with our marriage because I didn't have children. We had been married several years when Susanne came along. Blake had wanted a boy so he didn't treat her very good. He was hard on her and we were constantly fighting about it, so he started to travel a lot for the law firm. Then Daryl came along ten years later and Blake was elated with his son and treated Susanne even worse, but he did stop traveling and stayed home. He was obsessed with his son and took him every where and they became great pals." She paused as though she was trying to remember something.

"Miss Ellie, can I get you some water or juice? You are doing great."

"I would like a glass of water, please." I got it for her and she continued. "Harold and Nellie had moved in down the road and we had become friends. At least Nellie and I were friends, Blake and Harold never seemed to hit if off too good, so we didn't socialize as a couple too much. Blake wasn't ever really a very social person, anyway, so I thought nothing about it. I was busy with the children and the church and trying to keep peace in the house, keeping peace was my biggest challenge."

"I'm sure it was. But I know you did the best you could. Do you remember me telling you that I met Daryl and Susanne and her two children?"

"Yes I do. But Susanne has three children. Jane, her oldest daughter doesn't live with her and Clinton, just Tommy and Joey. Daryl and Melinda never had children. Too busy with their careers."

"Did you ever find out who Todd's mother is?"

She paused for a very long time. "Yes, I did. But I really don't want to discuss it."

"Why not?"

"Because Blake made me promise never to discuss the subject. I promised this on his dying bed."

"Okay, maybe we can come back to this later. Do you remember when Harold Goodman was killed? Did you know anything about that?"

"You know, I am really getting tired and I think I would like to lay down for awhile. Would you mind?"

"Of course not Miss Ellie. May I come back this afternoon after you have had lunch and a little rest?"

"I don't know if there is anything else I can tell you."

"Oh, I think there is a lot you can tell me. Let me help you back into bed. You can get some rest."

I helped her into bed and was about to leave, and she took hold of my hand, "Why are you so interested in Todd? And why are you so interested in me?"

"Because I care about you and your safety and because I think Todd is a very dangerous man. You get some rest and I will see you later this afternoon." I smiled at her and kissed her on the forehead.

She smiled back, "Thank you. You are a good woman."

CHAPTER 79

Dad had been sitting in the lobby of the re-hab center all that time. When I joined him he seemed as though he had been asleep. "Sorry, I took so long, but when Miss Ellie started talking, I didn't want to interrupt her. I am coming back this afternoon to see what else I can get out of her."

"She must be doing much better then."

"Oh ya, she is one stubborn woman, but she sure opened up to me once she got started. And I want to keep her going. We may have to post pone the Reverend till later. Let's go home and get some lunch."

"Sounds good to me."

"Todd is Blake's son. You know we talked about various combinations of connections to Miss Ellie, but I don't think I really expected to hear that for a fact. She's known about Todd for about twenty years and has kept it to herself ever since Blake died. I am really curious if Todd has been in contact with her during this time. I know she is terrified of him now, but I don't know anything about the last twenty years, yet. This has been quite the morning."

Spook was in the driveway when we got home and excited to see us. I threw a ball out in the yard for him. Dad went in the house and I stayed out and played with Spook for awhile. We chased each other and I threw a Frisbee for him and then the ball. It felt so good to be outside playing with Spook, but I also felt good about my break through with Miss Ellie. I was really anxious to see her later in the afternoon. I was on a high.

My cell phone rang, "Sergeant Weathers."

"Brenda, this is Willy. You have a minute? I've got to talk to you."

"Of course, I always have time for you. What's up?"

"The Captain. He's on the rampage again. He says we are now pushing two weeks without anything having been done about the

Compton Case and is moving again to assign Jones and Johnson to the case. Have you done anything at all on this?"

"Willy, I am all over this. I have a report up to date, as of yesterday anyway. I met with Mrs. Compton today and had a great break through. I'm going back this afternoon and get more information. This has turned into a real story and I think we are not far from an arrest of Todd Thompson."

"That's the other issue, he sent those two to the hospital to question Mrs. Compton and she has been moved. No one would tell them where she's been moved. The Captain made a call to the hospital and they wouldn't tell him either and that really pissed him off. You obviously know where she is. The Captain hasn't called you yet?"

"Yes I do know where she is. Her Doctor and I are the only ones that do. No the Captain hasn't called me. Maybe I better get my report to the office. Man, I don't want to go in that office. I'll send Dad over with it. Dad can handle the Captain better than I can."

"I think you better get that report in ASAP. He is on a roll, again. So how is Sam doing?"

"He is doing much better, they moved him out of ICU and into a private room. He's been up and walking around and should be starting physical therapy soon, maybe this afternoon."

"That's great news. How are you doing?"

"I'm just fine. I have Dad as my chauffeur and baby sitter, so all is well here." And I laughed.

"You need a baby sitter from what I hear. Let me know how things are progressing and if there is anything I can do. I better get going, just wanted to keep you abreast of the happenings."

"Thank you Willy. You are a doll. I will call you when I have enough information for an arrest."

"Great. Talk to you soon. Get that report in. Later."

I went in the house and Dad was watching the noon news. I started slamming things around in the kitchen trying to decide what to fix for lunch. All I had to do was open the refrigerator and the answer was there. Mom and Candy had left enough food to feed an army.

"Brenda, what is wrong with you? You are making so much noise in there I can't even hear the T.V."

"Just another call from Willy. The Captain is on the rampage again and thinks I am not doing anything with the case and assigning it AGAIN to Jones and Johnson."

"Oh for Christ sake. Give me that God Damned report and I will take it over there right now. Print if off."

"Let me fix lunch. Then you can take me back up to see Miss Ellie, while I am there you can take the report in."

"I'll take it now while you are fixing lunch. With a little luck I can have a word with your Captain."

"Dad, don't make it any worse than it already is. I don't need him to have anymore ammunition than he thinks he already has."

"Just give me the report. I will be right back. Don't worry, I know how to handle his kind."

I printed the report and put it in an envelope addressed to Captain Neil Dawson. "Please, just leave it at the front desk."

"No problem, I can do that. I'll be back by the time you have lunch ready." And out the door he went.

CHAPTER 80

I fixed lunch and had it waiting for Dad to return. I reached in the drawer for a note pad to jot down some questions for Miss Ellie. There they were. My cigarettes. I hadn't had one since before the accident and quite frankly hadn't even thought of one. What the hell, now is a perfect time to have one. I'll just sit outside, make some notes for Miss Ellie and have a smoke. I waited outside for over an hour and a half before Dad returned. It should have only taken him a little over thirty minutes in the worst of traffic.

"What took you so long, Dad. Did you get lost?"

"Nope, just delayed a bit. Lunch ready. I'm starved." And he walked straight into the house.

"Okay, Dad, what happened at the precinct? You must have had a run in with Dawson. Come on, tell me what happened."

"It wasn't much. We had a very short meeting of the minds. It was short and sweet after I reminded him I was NOT one of his staff. That's all. He sure has an ego problem. I don't know how he got where he has with his attitude. Has he always been like this?"

"I don't know what he was like when he was out in the field. He was promoted after Captain Clark retired. I think there was a lot of resentment among some of the officers that thought the assignment should've gone to someone else within the precinct. He's pretty much been an ass hole from the beginning, though."

"I sure didn't put up with that attitude in any of my departments."

"I know, Dad, and that's what makes you a much better man than he ever will be. You are my idol."

"Well, thank you, sweetheart. Now let's eat."

While we ate Dad started his inquisition about Sam and my plans. If we had set a date, what my plans would be after marriage, if I would continue my career or be a stay at home mom. The stay at home statement hit me like a ton of bricks, that thought had never occurred to me. In fact the engagement was still so new I wasn't used to that, let alone thinking about marriage. But when he asked me if I had given thought of having my own children, I thought I was going to fall out of the chair.

"You know, Dad, Sam and I have not talked about any of those topics. I think we are still getting used to being engaged. The rest will come, but I don't think wedding bells will be ringing real soon. We have lots of hurdles to get over before any of that happens."

"You know you are not getting any younger, and if children are in your future you better start thinking about it."

"I know, I know. But I have been single for ten years since Brian and I divorced. I have gotten so used to my independence, coming and going as I please and having no one to account to, or someone to be accountable to me for that matter of fact. I'm trying to work through it all, really I am. Right now I just want to have Sam well and I want to get this case closed. Speaking of which, I am going to make a quick call to Sam's house, I keep missing Paul and Rita and Monica at the hospital. And then I want to get back up to Miss Ellie."

Sylvia answered the phone and said Rita and Paul were at the hospital. Monica had gone home for while. She assured me everything was going fine at the house and the kids had been to see Sam a couple times and were feeling better about the situation.

I relayed the conversation to Dad on the way to Miss Ellie's and suggested maybe he could go visit with Sam and his family and then come back to get me.

CHAPTER 81

I opened the door to Miss Ellie's room, "Hey, Miss Ellie, how about if we take a little ride outside in the garden area? It is such a beautiful day, I think an outside adventure would be good for you. The flowers are blooming and it's gorgeous out there. What do you think?"

"Oh, I don't know. I'm not dressed properly for outside."

"You are just fine. I'll get a wheel chair and we'll put a blanket around you and over your legs. You haven't been outside for quite a long time. I'm going to find a nurse and get a wheel chair, okay?"

"That would be nice, thank you."

The nurse and I got her all bundled up and made our way down the hall and outside. I pushed her around and we admired the flowers, she named almost every variety that was around the walkways and in the garden. I was impressed that she was so sharp after all this time. This was another confirmation for me that Miss Ellie had been faking her semi-coma, she was good and she was stubborn. I had to chuckle to myself at how clever she was.

"How's this? Look out there, isn't that just a breath taking view?"

"Yes it is. I miss my home. When am I going to be able to go home?"

"Miss Ellie, I can't answer that, Doctor Cutter will have to tell you that. But I do know you are here for your protection as well. I have to ask you more questions about Todd. We need to pick him up and anything you can tell me, will help speed up that process. Okay?"

"I'll try." She smiled at me and took my hand, "this is going to be very hard for me. I have never, ever discussed this with anyone after Blake passed away. He made me promise."

"I know, but I am sure Blake would not want you to live in danger and he knows what kind of man Todd is. I am sure he would want you to tell me whatever it is that would protect you. Don't you think?"

"I'm not sure."

"Well, let's give it a try. Do you remember when Harold was killed in that horrible accident by your driveway? What can you tell me about that?"

Miss Ellie's eyes welded up with tears as she began, "Todd had made several visits to Blake asking for money in return for not exposing Blake as his father. I didn't know this for many years, until Todd's demands became more often and dollar amounts were increasing. Blake finally told me he had met this woman while he was on a case in Las Vegas. She was married to a minister and was considering a divorce. She said he was dishonest, convinced the older single women into large donations to the church to pave their way to heaven. And she suspected he was having affairs with many of them. Blake said they met several times and he felt sorry for her, she was so sweet and innocent. He began to comfort her and one thing led to another. He said he just about had the divorce papers ready to serve when she came to him and said she was pregnant. She knew Blake was the father, because she and her husband had not had a sexual relationship in a very long time. Of course she dropped the divorce. She had the baby and they gave it up for adoption. From that time on I guess she just became docile and a meek little person to her husband." She took a long breathe and stared out at the view.

"When did you find out who she was?"

"Oh, many years later. Blake occasionally went to church with me, but not too often. He would go if the children were in a program but that was about it. We had gone through a couple pastors and then got this guy that just swooned the board and they hired him and gave him a ten year contract without doing a thorough previous check on him. The Reverend Paul Stearns was the new pastor. He naturally was accepted with open arms and swooned the membership as well. The only one that refused to ever attend church again was Blake, and I didn't understand why. But Blake often made decisions that I never understood. One day, the Reverend called Blake and wanted to meet for coffee.

Even though Blake initially refused, he ended up going. I didn't know for a good many years that the Reverend had told Blake he knew about him and Mary and the baby they shared. He said the child had recently located Mary and wanted a relationship and of course they refused, at least the Reverend refused. Then the Reverend started demanding money from Blake to keep the story quiet and Todd was demanding money from the Reverend and Mary to keep it quiet. And later the Reverend started on Blake. It became a real mess. Brenda this is so hard. I don't know if I can go on."

"It's okay, take your time."

"Blake and I had gone to the senior center for lunch and cards that day, but we didn't stay for cards, I wasn't feeling well, so we came home. When we got home Todd was there and demanding more money. He and Blake got in a horrible argument, Blake gave him some cash and told him to never return to this house again. When Todd left he was angry and drove out very fast. That is when he hit Harold and kept going. Blake and I didn't know about the accident because I had gone to the bedroom to lie down and Blake was in his office. When the police came to the house they questioned Blake because the tire tracks indicated the car had come from our driveway, but he told him we had been to the senior center so we weren't home and he couldn't help them. And it went down hill from there. The pressure became too much for Blake and he started drinking a lot and then started having heart problems and eventually had a massive heart attack. He swore me to secrecy to protect me, he said it had all died down and would soon be forgotten and I needed to let it go. It took me a long time to get over all that and my depression, everyone just thought I was mourning Blake's death. Part of that was true, but I think most of it was the guilt of knowing what had happened to poor Harold and we never reported it."

"That was quite a burden to carry all of these years, Miss Ellie. When did Todd move in to the apartment over the garage?"

"Two months ago. He came to the house one day and said he needed a place to stay. When I told him he couldn't stay here, he said I had no choice and he was moving in and would be of no bother to me. He stayed away from me most of the time, but he came in the day he shot me and demanded more money and when I refused he threatened me. He had a gun, but I don't think he meant to fire it, he was angry and was pointing the gun at me and yelling obscenities and it just went off. That's pretty much the whole story. I am so ashamed and I feel so bad for Nellie. She has suffered so much. I tried to be friends with her, but it was so hard to look her in the face, I just couldn't do it."

"Miss Ellie, I am so sorry for you. I can't imagine how difficult this was on you. You and Nellie are both victims in all of this. I am going to put an APB out on Todd Thompson, and when he is picked up he will be charged with the murder of Harold. You need to understand that I have no choice in revealing Harold's accident. Todd will be charged for the murder and leaving the scene and other charges as well. Do you understand this Miss Ellie? This is going to open up a lot of old wounds."

"I know, maybe it is time to cleanse the soul. But poor Nellie, I can't bear to think what this is going to do to her. What will happen to me? I have kept this information to myself all these years, won't I be charged with something?"

"I don't know. Why don't I call Daryl and tell him, he is an attorney and I am sure he will come out here and represent you. Would that be all right with you?"

She started crying, "I can't let my children know, Daryl thinks his father was a saint and Susanne will only hate him more."

"Let me call Daryl, he needs to come out here now. You two can decide what to do about Susanne, okay? We need to get you inside and let you rest before dinner. You have been more helpful than you will ever know. I am sure everything is going to be okay, after awhile.

By the way, the day you were shot, your dining room table was set for dinner for two. Who were you expecting?"

She smiled at me and then gazed off, "Oh, a gentleman friend from the church. Leonard is a very nice man and stops by occasionally for dinner, we are just friends. He lost his wife a couple years ago and is very lonely. We play cards at the senior center and have gone to the movies a few times, just enjoying each other. I' sure that will go away when he finds out what kind of a person I am."

"Miss Ellie, you did what you thought was right for Blake and Nellie, that does not make you a bad person. Now let's get you inside."

I took her back to her room and got her into bed. "I will be seeing you real soon. Don't you worry about a thing, that is my job." I leaned down and kissed her on the forehead.

I called Dad and asked him to come get me and he said he was on his way. "How is Sam doing?"

"He's had a pretty rough day, so I didn't stay too long. I got your report turned in and made a few phone calls of my own and was reading a book in the car you were going to take into Sam. I'll be there in a couple."

CHAPTER 82

I told Dad in a brief summary about Miss Ellie's story. He was as amazed about it all as was I. The palms of my hands were sweaty and I was anxious to get to the Reverend's. Things were starting to get really dicey.

"I'm not sure how far I want to interrogate the Reverend, because I think he can lead us to Todd if I play my cards right. Given all this information we now have, do you have any suggestions?"

"You have to let him know that you know the whole story about Todd and the connection he has with the Compton's. Then you have to find out if he knows where Todd is. I guess we just play it by ear and very guarded."

When we pulled around to the back of the church, I recognized the Reverend's car so I knew he was probably in his office. Before we got out of the car I jotted down the license number, make and model of Stearns' car. Dad parked the car and we bumped knuckles, "Go getum Sergeant."

I opened the door to the office without knocking, "Hello, Paul. It seems we have a few things to talk about."

"Excuse me Sergeant, but I don't have anything to talk to you about. So if you would please leave, I have work to do."

"That's not going to happen, so sit down and hear me out. I have spent the last two days with Mrs. Compton and she had an abundance of information about Todd. Let me tell you what I know: Todd Thompson is the one that shot Miss Ellie, he is the one that shot Sam and I, he has been blackmailing Miss Ellie for a number of years and Mr. Compton prior to that. I know he is Blake's son and your wife's. I know he is responsible, some twenty plus years ago, for the accident that killed Harold Goodman. I know he was blackmailing you and I know you were blackmailing Blake for silence. Is there anything else I should know about Mr. Thompson, or does that pretty much cover it, Paul?"

"You are out of your mind, I don't have any idea who you are talking about. I want you to leave right now before I call the police." He got up and started for the door.

"Sit down and I am the police. This will go much easier on you if you co-operate and tell me what you know. If not I can charge you as an accomplice and harboring a fugitive. Todd is a fugitive and I believe you know where he is hiding out. So why don't you make it easy on both of us and tell me where he is."

"Sergeant, you have unloaded a whole bunch of stuff on me about someone I don't know. You are making absurd accusation towards my wife that are unbelievable. Mary and I do not have children nor have we ever. I can't help you, I am sorry."

"I believe you are lying, Paul. You know all of this to be true. Why are you hiding Todd, you have to know what a dangerous person he is. I know he has blackmailed you and your wife about Blake and Mary and him being adopted. How long has this been going on?"

"Believe me, I don't know what you are talking about. I think Miss Ellie has become delusional, she is old and has had a traumatic experience. I don't know where she got this story. I really don't. I need to go to the pharmacy and pick up a heart medication for my wife. They close in fifteen minutes and I really need to get there. If you want to wait, I'll be right back. But I do need to go."

"We'll be back, Paul. Do not leave town or I will have an APB put out on you and you will go to jail. Do you understand what I am saying?"

"Yes I do. But you are making a big mistake, Sergeant. I am not involved in this charade in any way shape or form. Please excuse me, I really need to get going."

When we got in the car, Dad said, "You are so smart. You know he is going straight to Todd. Why did you let him go?"

"Because we are going to follow him. So, pull out of the parking lot and go around the corner and stay a car or two behind him."

"Brenda, you need to remember, I know how to tail a suspect. I think I can handle this."

"You're right Dad, I did forget. I am just so anxious to get this Todd off the streets."

I called in for SWAT that we would be following a person of interest that hopefully was leading us to Todd Thompson. There had already been a warrant for his arrest out there, but so far he had successfully stayed in hiding.

We were sitting in the car around the corner and hidden from the view of the Reverend. He pulled out and headed for the main part of town. At first I thought maybe he was going to the shopping center where we had followed him before, but instead he made a left turn. We followed for a couple miles and I called SWAT that we were following Paul Stearns. I gave the license number, make and model of the vehicle and our present location.

CHAPTER 83

We were getting into the slums of San Diego when the Reverend turned into the Sleep Over Inn. He parked his car and walked into a room. From the street we couldn't see the room number. I ducked down in the seat and Dad drove through the parking lot to the end of the motel and back out on the side street. "Room number twelve. I am going to call and ask for Todd Thompson's room and see what happens. I doubt he is registered under his own name, if that is who Stearns is meeting." Dad parked on the main street, a little ways from the entrance to the motel.

He dialed the telephone number written under the Sleep Over Inn sign. "Yes, I would like to have Todd Thompson's room please." ----- ---------"That would be room number twelve."----------------"Oh, yes, Tom Dotson? Yes Ma'am, I was looking at another name here on my paper. Yes, it is Tom Dotson, my mistake."

Dad looked at me and mouthed 'clever' and gave me a thumbs-up. "No, thanks anyway, I'll call back later." When he hung up he said, "How clever is that, just reversed his name."

I called SWAT and gave them our location and said I needed them here code three.

"Stearns just went in the office. Duck!" We both ducked down in the seat for a couple seconds, Dad took a peak between the steering wheel and the dash, "Stearns is out on the street looking up and down. He knows someone is out here and maybe he knows we followed him. Stay down. He's going back to the room. I think we need to go in while Thompson is still in the room."

Dad started the car and pulled forward enough to close the gap with the car in front and to give him a better look at room twelve. "Stearns just came out and is getting in his car. Stay down until I see which way he goes." Dad positioned himself in a way he could see out of the side rear mirrors in case Stearns went out the back way and around like we did, or if he came out the main drive.

I could hear in the distance the sirens and at the same time Dad saw Stearns pull out from the street behind us and go back the same direction we had come at a pretty high speed.

Dad started the car and pulled around to the front of the room. We jumped out of the car and as I was pounding on the door I was yelling, "Police, open up." We both had our weapons drawn and standing to the side of the door. Then I heard a car squeal out of the parking lot towards the rear of the motel. I didn't see the car as it rounded the end of the motel nor did I see which direction it went as he hit the street. At the same time four patrol cars pulled into the front entry and got out with drawn weapons.

I opened the motel room and it was empty. "Damn it, he got away." I ran to the office. "I need the make, model and license of the car registered to room twelve, Tom Dotson." I flashed my badge and the clerk started looking through registry cards and when she pulled one out, I grabbed it and ran back out to the police cars.

"This is the suspect's vehicle description, Todd Thompson, alias Tom Dotson. He just pulled out of the parking lot as you pulled in, I didn't see which direction he went. I have an APB for pickup on Reverend Paul Stearns. He is headed North on Van Ness, I believe the destination is the Trinity Lutheran Church on Henrici Drive, North East Rancho Bernardo."

I called the precinct to have officers go to the Compton's and do a search of the apartment and stake it out in case Thompson showed up there.

Police cars squealed out of the parking lot of the Inn and headed back the way Dad and I had come. I put the red light on top of my car and turned on the siren and we headed out just as fast. We were behind the squad cars in the left lane keeping up as best we could. Stearns had a head start on us so our intention was to go to the church in the hopes that was his destination. Cars scattered to the right side of the highway as we breezed by. It was amazing to watch Dad drive in unfamiliar territory, yet keep up as well as he did to the much faster patrol cars. The return trip was much faster than when we followed Stearns in the beginning.

As we pulled in the parking lot of the church, four patrol cars were already there and had stormed the house. Stearns was sitting at his desk with his hands clasped behind his head. When I walked in the office, one of the officers said, "Sergeant, I believe this is the man you are looking for."

"This is one of them. Todd Thompson is still out there."

"Well, this one's yours'."

"Thank you. Paul Stearns you are under arrest for harboring a fugitive and at least three counts of blackmail. You have the right to remain silent. Anything you say can and will be held against you in a court of law. If you can not afford an attorney one will be appointed for you. You have had your Miranda Rights read to you, do you have anything to say at this time?"

"I would like to speak to my attorney." Paul said.

"Book him and take him in." I said. As I turned to step out of the way, I saw Mrs. Stearns standing in the door way, her hands over her mouth and tears streaming down her cheeks. "Mrs. Stearns, can I call someone for you? How about if we go in the other room and you sit down and I'll get you some water."

She just stood there as though she was paralyzed. "Mrs. Stearns, let's sit down for minute. Can I get you a glass of water? Do you need any medication?"

Mrs. Stearns was robot like as I turned her around to take her in their living room to sit down. I got her a glass of water and again asked, "Is there any medications you need?"

"Medication? What for?"

"Paul said he was picking up some prescription for your heart."

"You must be mistaken, I don't have a heart problem."

"Maybe I am. Can I call someone to come over and stay with you? Is there anyone you would like here right now?"

"I don't know, I can't think. Why did you take Paul away? What has he done?"

"Mrs. Stearns, do you know Todd Thompson? What can you tell me about him?"

"Todd? He is the baby I gave up for adoption over fifty years ago. He found me, when he was about twenty, we were still living in Las Vegas where Paul was a minister. He started blackmailing us to give him money or he would ruin Paul's ministry. When the opportunity came up for this church we both jumped on it and thought it would be an escape from Todd and he would never find us. Then twenty plus years ago he found us and it started all over again. Only this time he had found out Blake Compton was his father. Then he blackmailed Blake, too."

"Do you have any idea where he could be now?"

"No, not at all. He didn't come around here much. Paul wouldn't allow it."

"We need to call someone for you to go stay with until Todd is picked up. He is very dangerous and you are not safe alone here. How about someone in the church?"

"I can't think, this is all happening so fast. Let's see. My sister lives not too far from here, I'll call and see if she will come get me. I really don't want to stay here."

"You call her, if she can come I will have an officer stay here until you are ready to leave."

"I just don't understand what has happened to Paul. Are you sure he did everything you said he did?"

"Don't you worry about that now, Mrs. Stearns, you just call your sister."

CHAPTER 84

We left Mrs. Stearns with an officer until her sister came to get her. I was anxious to get to the precinct and talk to the Reverend. For some reason, duh, I was having difficulty relating to Mr. Stearns as the Reverend, he no longer fit the title.

"Well, we got half of the scheming team, but the dangerous half is still out there." I said to Dad when we were in the car.

"Great job, Sis, you are a real pro. Now it is up to the rest to find him. Maybe with a little luck Stearns will give you information where Todd can be found."

"I'm not counting on it, but it sure would be a bonus. I need to call Sam, I don't think we are going to make it to see him tonight. I have to call Daryl Compton, too, he needs to get out here for his Mother. I would be surprised, at her age there will be a charge for withholding information. But it is possible. I better call him first before it gets any later. It is nine in Chicago."

I first tried Daryl's cell and it went straight to his voicemail. I left an urgent message to return my call ASAP. Then I called his residence. Unfortunately, he didn't answer there either so I left another urgent message.

"Damn, doesn't this guy ever answer a phone? He probably has caller ID and purposely doesn't answer."

Sam answered, not sounding very chipper. "Hi Baby, how ya doin?"

"I'm okay. Just laying here waiting for your beautiful face to show up. Where are you?"

"Dad and I have had a very exciting afternoon, we are on the way to the precinct right now. Dad said you had a rough morning, what's up with that?"

"I don't know, my fever went up again and the doctor couldn't tell me why, so I am on another kind of antibiotic. But enough about me, what kind of excitement did you two have? Did you catch Thompson?"

"No, not Thompson, but the Reverend Stearns is behind bars as we speak, or will be soon. I got so much information from Miss Ellie earlier, we went over to Stearns but he of course denied it all. We left his office in hopes he would lead us to Thompson and he did. By the time SWAT got there he got away from us, so we went back to Stearns and arrested him on a number of charges being harboring a fugitive, at least three charges for blackmail and there will be more. We are on our way to question Stearns now. I doubt that we will be able to come visit this evening, Baby, I'm afraid it will be too late."

"What kind of information did you get out of Miss Ellie to get an arrest of Stearns? That came right out of nowhere."

"Sam, can I all you back, Daryl Compton is calling in right now?"

"Sure, Mom and Dad just came in anyway. Later."

"Yes, Daryl, thank you for calling. I hope you are where you can talk, because I think you need to be sitting down."

"Sergeant? What's going on? And, no I am really not at a very good spot for any conversation, my wife and I are out with clients."

"Would you rather call me back later this evening when you get home?"

"Just tell me what the hell is going on?"

"Okay, you asked for it." I told him the complete chain of events since Sam and I had left his office, the week prior, as briefly as possible to make sense of it all. I told him it appeared he and Susanne had a step brother, not that I thought he would be too excited about it.

"Oh my God. Poor Mother, and she has kept this quiet all these years. How is she holding up under all this?"

"Actually, I think she is rather relieved to have it all out. She has been terrified of Todd and his threats for a very long time, Daryl. So, I guess I would say she is doing quite well considering all she's been through. I have not been back over to see her since the arrest of Stearns.

I won't see her until tomorrow in the morning sometime, it is getting too late. The other reason I needed to call you, is that your mother is probably going to need legal council. She did withhold information for twenty plus years regarding the death of Harold Goodman. I can't say for sure, that is out of my hands. But I think you need to get out here and see her ASAP. She needs her family and she needs your legal advice, and if you have her Will, I would bring it along."

"Sergeant, I don't think I can get away right now. I will have to check out my schedule. I have some court trials coming up."

"Mr. Compton, with all due respect. Your mother needs you and Susanne right now, AND the last time I was in your office you have at least twelve attorneys. I would think if you don't have anyone competent enough to take over for you, then you did a very poor job with your hiring. You do what you have to do. I am so sorry to have bothered you. I will call Susanne myself, you won't have to bother. Go enjoy your clients." I didn't wait for any kind of feed back, I just hung up.

Dad looked at me, "Whoa, do I detect a bit of hostility towards Mr. Compton?"

"He is such a piece of shit, I don't know why I even wasted my time calling him and I am sure I will get much of the same results when I call his sister. If Candy and I ever treat you and Mom this way, take us out and shoot us."

I placed a call to Susanne, and much to my surprise, when the Nanny, Maria answered, she immediately called Susanne to the phone. "Sergeant Weathers, what a surprise. Is everything okay with Mother?"

"Yes, Susanne, she is doing quite well. Miss Ellie has been moved to a private foster home. There has been quite a number of events that has affected Miss Ellie tremendously and I am afraid is going to impact yours' and Daryl's lives as well. At least I think so. You might want to sit down for this."

Susanne was totally silent during my conversation, I thought maybe she had hung up and I asked, "Are you still there?"

When I was through, Susanne's response came as a total shock to me, "That bastard, how could he have done this to Mother? I never trusted him, I just never knew why."

"I thought you said you didn't know Todd Thompson?"

"I don't, I'm talking about Dad. How he could have done this. I wish he were alive to take the brunt of all this and not Mother. I guess I had better come back there and help her through all this. Did you call Daryl?"

"Yes I did. And quite frankly, I don't know what he is going to do. I called him just before calling you. Susanne, I really need to get going right now. But will you call me when you know what your plans are? I will be happy to meet your plane if at all possible, okay?"

"Let me see what I can do and when I can get out there I will call you. Thank you so much for calling. Bye for now."

CHAPTER 84

Dad had pulled into the precinct just as I was hanging up from Susanne, "Well there might be hope for at least one of Miss Ellie's children. Let's get in there and interrogate this asshole and get some answers."

Willy was in the office when we walked in, "Good job, Sergeant. I believe your man is in there. What led you to the Reverend?"

"Just a gut feeling, I never did really like him and didn't trust him from the beginning. Miss Ellie actually led me to the Reverend. I have a real problem addressing him as the Reverend. For some reason he just doesn't fit the title."

I walked into the room and Paul Stearns was sitting in a chair at the table. The anger and sarcasms he displayed was amazing, he had no conscience and immediately started in on me about how wrong I was.

"Excuse me; have you called your attorney?"

"I don't need one; there has been a terrible misunderstanding. I am a man of God; I couldn't have done these terrible things you are accusing me of."

"Mr. Stearns, this is going to go much faster for both of us if you will come clean. Miss Ellie has told me everything, and your wife has confirmed the relationship with Todd Thompson. I need you to tell me where he is before anyone else gets hurt."

"Mary doesn't know what she is talking about. She has a bad heart and is on lots of medication as well as Alzheimer's. She couldn't possibly know what she was saying."

"Paul, this game is over. Tell me where Todd is."

"I don't know a Todd, so I can't tell you where is."

"We followed you to the motel when you went to meet Todd. Then we followed you back to your office. I'm not stupid. Now let's get this over with."

"I have nothing to say." Stearns sat back in his chair, crossed his arms and stared at me.

"Have it your way." I raised my hand and two officers came in the room. "Take him to his cell. I am done with this piece of shit." And I walked out.

Captain Dawson was standing outside his office as I came out, "Good job Sergeant. Would you come into my office?"

"Sure." I nodded to Dad to go in with me.

"So, I see you have been busy. The Reverend was quite the surprise."

"Quite frankly, Sir, this whole thing has been quite the surprise. Not that Todd Thompson is any surprise, but the connection he has certainly is. He's still out there and is very dangerous; there is still work to do."

"We put out an APB on Thompson. We've got good guys out there that are looking for him. They're watching the Compton house and he'll show his face someplace. They always do. You should go home for the night, not much else to do for now."

"Thank you Sir, I think we will do just that."

"How is Sam?"

"He has good days and bad days. We visited this morning, but I didn't make it this evening. Been a little busy." I smiled at the Captain.

"I expect there will be an up to date report on my desk tomorrow?"

"There most certainly will be. Is that all?"

"For now, and again good job."

"Thank you." And we started out of the office.

"By the way, thank you Mr. Weathers for keeping an eye on our girl."

"No problem at all, it has been a pleasure working with Sergeant Weathers, you are damn lucky to have her." Then we walked out.

CHAPTER 85

As we were driving home I called Sam. I hoped he wouldn't be asleep, but at that point I guess I really didn't care, I needed to share the events of the day. When he answered he sounded a bit groggy, but I could hear the T.V. in the background, he needed to wake up to turn it off anyway.

"Hi Baby, sorry if I woke you. How are you doing?"

"I'm fine. What happened today?"

"Well, we booked and charged Stearns with three counts of blackmail and harboring a fugitive. Baby, he is in jail. We still don't have Thompson but we have an APB out on him, it is only a matter of time. And believe this or not the Captain even told me I had done a good job which was amazing in itself."

"Good girl, I am so proud of you. So what information did you have to put you on his trail? Guess you don't need me after all."

"Oh stop that, of course I need you. In more ways than one. What kind of talk is that?"

"Just kidding."

"So tell me, how are you really doing? What are the doctors saying?"

"Not much, just trying to get this infection under control. They have taken so much blood from me I am going to need a transfusion. I still have the drain tubes in, other than that I guess things are improving some. I feel pretty good until I move and I seem to get tangled up in one tube or another. Just part of the process, Baby, just part of the process. How about you, how's the shoulder and physical therapy?"

"Shoulder is fine. I have been rather busy and physical therapy has gone by the wayside. I see the doctor on Monday; hopefully he can get me out of this harness. It is more of a pain in the ass than the shoulder itself. So tell me about this infection they can't get rid of, where is it and what is causing the reoccurrence?"

"I really don't know for sure. As I understand it, the infection is from the gunshot itself, some is the complication of the surgeries in putting me back together and handling all of the internal organs. An infection was bound to happen, but trying to identify exactly the kind of bacteria is another issue. And now the doctor says I have a low grade pneumonia from lack of activity. So now the plan is to get me up and moving around again. Do you realize I have been in here almost two weeks? I am really getting pretty tired of all of this, probing and poking around and not coming up with any solutions. I'm just about done with all this shit and ready to go home."

"I am so sorry. I wish there was something I could do for you. I will be up there first thing in the morning and spend some time with you. I know I have been really lax in seeing you, but maybe that can change now a little bit."

"Bee, you have been busy, you have a case that needs your full attention. I am not being a baby and whining because you are not here holding my hand, I have just had enough of this."

"Maybe that is a sign you are getting better. So Sweetie, you get a good nights rest and I will see you in the morning and maybe we can go for a walk around the hall, okay? And maybe you can give some helpful hints on how to move forward on this case. I think there are some blanks that need to be filled in. So get your thinking cap on and I will see you in the morning. I love you Baby, sleep tight."

"Yah, I love you too and you sleep tight. Night."

"Wow, Sam is in a real state of depression and I can't say I blame him. This has really been an ordeal for him, two gun shots, two surgeries, one infection after another and now maybe pneumonia. I'd like to spend a little time with Sam in the morning, you want to join us Dad?"

"That's up to you; maybe you need to spend time alone?"

"Actually, I think it would be good for Sam if we brought him up to date on the case and get his take on all of it. Give Sam a break from thinking about himself for awhile."

When we got home, Spook was there to greet us. Spook was giving me such a sense of security and something to look forward to coming home. We got out of the car and Spook's welcome was heart warming.

I fixed a quick dinner and Dad watched the news with Spook on the sofa beside him. "I am going to get this report done after dinner. Why don't you just call it a night. It has been a very busy day, Dad. You know? I think it is time you went home to Mom. I can handle things now, this harness should come off tomorrow afternoon and I will be able to drive. My mobility isn't completely back, but getting there. What do you think?"

"Yuh know Sis? I think my job is pretty much done here. The rest is up to the apprehension of Thompson and who knows how long that will take or even where he is by now. I know you have been working minimally," and he smiled, "exercising your shoulder, but that will come around. So you are probably right, maybe it is time I went home. Let's see what happens after your doctor's appointment tomorrow, okay?"

"You got it. Dad I have so enjoyed having you here with me. I admire your expertise and I have so much respect for you. Who would have ever thought we would have ended up working together? I can't even tell you what a privilege it has been for me."

"It has been for me too, Sis. And you are right, who would've ever thunk it?"

We ate our dinner and Dad went to bed. I cleaned up the kitchen and started on my report. I actually had only a little bit to bring it up to date, but I went back through to proof it and really just recapture what had actually happened in the last couple days. So many turn of events and so many surprises, I was in awe of it all myself. I made an extra copy of the report so I could show Sam.

My thoughts wandered back to Mrs. Goodman and how she was going to react to the news of how Harold had been killed. The fact that the Compton's both had known and had withheld the information had to be devastating to her. This got my curiosity going why the case had never been solved and closed so rapidly. I decided I was going into the case files and see what I could find out, probably nothing, but I had to satisfy my own curiosity.

CHAPTER 86

While I tidied up after breakfast and got dressed for the day, Dad took the report to the precinct then we would be off to see Sam. I put a call in to Willy. I had been so preoccupied by my own activities over the last couple days, I had no idea what his work schedule was, so I was really surprised when he answered after the second ring.

"Hey Willy, how's it going?"

"Good, you had quite the end to your day, yesterday. Good job, I might add. Have you talked to Sam yet about it?"

"Thank you Willy. Dad and I are going to the hospital in a little while and I am taking a copy of the report for him to read. I did call him last night, but I thought it would be good for him to read it. Still need that big guy, I just hope something comes of the APB on Thompson real soon and no one else gets hurt in the meantime."

"When did you put an APB out on Thompson? I haven't seen a thing on it yet."

"You are kidding aren't you Willy?"

"No I am not. Did you put out the bulletin?"

"No I did not. Dawson told me last night in his office he had. In fact Dad was with me when he said it."

"Brenda, this is weird, why would he not have put an APB out on Thompson, especially after having told you he had?"

"I can't answer that question, Willy. I am at a loss for words right now. Willy, would you do me a favor? I need the CLOSED FILE on the accident that killed Harold Goodman about twenty years ago. The story is that a vehicle was speeding out of the driveway from the Compton house and hit Mr. Goodman as he was driving by. They never found the vehicle or the driver so they closed the case. I don't know the exact date but it shouldn't be hard to find. Harold Goodman, Victoria Place and Reese Road. Can you do this?"

"Why would you want that file? What's going on here?"

"I don't know yet, just curiosity right now. Will you give me a call when you have the file? And I think at this point you need to be careful and not let anyone know what you are looking for, okay?"

"I'll see what I can do. It might take me a while I am not at the precinct right now. I'll call you."

"Thanks Willy, you know where I will be the rest of the morning."

"Got it."

I had just hung up when Dad pulled in the driveway. "Ah, I see you are all ready, been waiting long?"

"Actually, I haven't, I just got off the phone with Willy? Dad when we were in the Captains office last night, what did he say about putting an APB out on Thompson?"

"He said he put out an APB on Thompson, they had guys watching the Compton house and they would get him. Something like Thompson would show his face, they always do. Why do you ask?"

"I just talked to Willy and he said he hasn't seen the APB yet. Doesn't that strike you a little weird? Why would he say he had already done something that he hadn't, and still hasn't? This is a dangerous man out there that should be behind bars, and he isn't even looking for him. Something is wrong here, terribly wrong."

"I agree, so what are you thinking? You have something going on in your head."

"Man, I don't know. I asked Willy to go into the archives of closed case files and get the file on Harold Goodman."

"What do you expect to gain from that, Sis?"

"I'm not sure. Just curious I guess. According to Nellie, Harold's case was closed pretty quickly. And we already know Thompson was the one that killed Harold. I just need to see that report."

"How long has the Captain been in this department?"

"I don't know for sure, but I think twenty three years or so. He's only been Captain a little over two years, before that he had been on one special force or another, so our paths didn't really ever cross. I have never worked a case with him. I know there was a lot of anger when he made Captain; a lot of the officers were wanting someone else. He's never really been liked and certainly hasn't been a team player. So what are you thinking?"

"Probably the same thing you are thinking. That Dawson was an officer on the Goodman case?"

"He sure could have been and if he was that would really thicken the pot. Let's get up to the hospital and see Sam."

CHAPTER 87

Sam was sitting up reading the newspaper when we walked in his room. "Hey, there's my star, Sergeant Brenda Lou Weathers. You sure pulled that one out of your ass didn't you?"

"I knew what I was doing the whole time." I was strutting and laughing at the same time. "Now, we need to get Thompson and I will be a happy camper. Which leads me to another Dawson issue? But first how are you doing? Your color looks better today."

"Actually, I feel much better. My temperature is down to almost normal which means the infection must be clearing up. The doctor removed the drain tubes last night and that feels a whole lot better. A couple nurses got me up and I got a real shower, I thought I had died and gone to heaven. I even got to take a short walk this morning. First time in two weeks that I feel like I might really make it."

"That's good to hear Sam. But I knew you would make it, you're tough and you have too much going for you to check out now." Dad said. "Besides you got to get out of here and take charge of this girl. I am too old to follow her around, she's wearing me out." And he laughed.

"I hear ya, she is a go getter. Smarter than I am and that is a challenge here. She is too practical and methodical. I just fly by the seat of my pants most of the time and most of the time I land on my feet, but sometimes I just end up out there in cyber space and have to work my way back to reality."

"So what's the issue going on with Dawson now? I'm sure it's no surprise, but go ahead."

"Well.......after the arrest of Stearns, Dawson asked Dad and I to step into his office, he commended me for a 'job well done', he said he had an APB out for Thompson and we may as well go home and get a good nights sleep. He said they were watching Mrs. Compton's house, they had good guys out there watching for Thompson and that he would eventually show his face they always do and they would get him. So we left. When I talked to Willy this morning he said he hasn't seen the APB. Doesn't that seem rather weird to you?"

"It sure does. So what are you thinking about this? What are you going to do about it?"

"Right now, I don't know. I have asked Willy to pull out the closed file on Harold Goodman, when he was killed and see what I can find out why that case was closed so quickly."

"So you think Dawson might have been an officer on that case? Then what?"

"I'm not sure, just a gut feeling."

"Your gut feelings usually turn out to be something, so don't waltz over them. So Gordon, you thinking about going home and getting some rest?"

"Brenda and I talked about that last night. If she can get out of that harness this afternoon, and she is able to drive, then I think it is time for me to go. This has really been an exciting case and I never expected the chase or the arrest. Sure took me way back in years. I am so proud of Brenda; she is one hell of a detective and handles everyone so professionally. It has been a real pleasure working with her. I'd do it again in a heart beat. Well, maybe not, I think I am getting too old to keep up with her."

Sam laughed, "I know exactly what you mean. I don't know where she gets her energy, but she runs circles around me."

"All right you two, enough picking on me. I brought you a copy of my last report, thought you might want to read it. I do need to go over and see Mrs. Goodman and tell her that Thompson was the one that hit and killed her husband. This is going to be a tough one considering it's been about so many years ago and is going to bring it all back to her. Plus, her very good friend withheld that information for her. She has got to feel totally betrayed. I know she is going to be ecstatic about the arrest of Stearns. I am considering calling one of Nellie's children to be there when I break all of this to her. And I want to see Miss

Ellie. Believe this or not, Susanne is supposedly making arrangements to come out to see her Mother. She was quite appalled by her father's involvement in all of this. Daryl ,on the other hand isn't sure if he has the time to come out here. That, was no big surprise."

"I wish I could be with you for all of this. You are one strong 'chick' you can pull it off."

My cell phone ran and it was Alexis. They had just read the morning paper and were shocked and thrilled at the same time about the arrest of Paul Stearns. They of course wanted more details that at that point I couldn't reveal. They commended me for a job well done and asked about Sam and when we could get together. I told them we would get together soon, but I had to cut the call short, I needed to get going. I promised to call them back.

CHAPTER 88

As Dad and I were walking out of the hospital I said, "While we are so close to Miss Ellie I would really like to stop by and see her. Would you like to go in with me? I would like for you to meet her. Ordinarily, I would say that she is pretty feisty, but I think she is in pretty much a remorseful and ashamed state of mind right now. It is going to take a while for her to get over all this if she ever does. This has been one hell of a burden for her to carry for all these years. Anyway she's got to be relieved that Stearns was arrested."

When we walked in Miss Ellie's room, she was sitting in a chair in her bathrobe and staring out the window. "Miss Ellie? It's Brenda Weathers and I would like for you to meet my Dad, Gordon Weathers."

She turned around and I could see she had been crying, her eyes were red and swollen. "Nice to meet you Mr. Weathers. I'm afraid I am not very good company. I am so ashamed; so many people have been hurt by Todd."

"Miss Ellie, you didn't do any of this, none of this is your fault. You have to remember this was all caused by your husband, Todd and Paul Stearns. Do you know that Paul Stearns was arrested last night and is in jail?"

"No I didn't. I guess that is good news. Did he tell you where Todd is?"

"His claim is he doesn't know Todd and is holding firm to that. But we'll get his story, he can't hold out forever."

"I called Susanne yesterday and she is coming out, maybe tomorrow. She is really mad at her Dad. I guess I can't blame her, so am I. I called Daryl, too, and he said he will be out in a few days. He's pretty busy."

"Maybe when Susanne gets here you can go home. You seem to be doing real well right now. How are you feeling?"

"I feel just fine, just embarrassed and ashamed by all of this. I had hoped I would die before all of this came out. And now I have to tell Nellie the truth about Harold's death."

"Miss Ellie, I will tell her for you. I have been over to her house and she is quite a delightful lady. I need to ask you a question, though. Do you remember anything about the accident when Harold was killed? Do you remember anything that was strange or odd about why the case was closed so quickly?"

"It was all very strange and odd, but you see Blake handled all that. He had several meetings with the officers and then there was nothing more said about it and I was told to never bring it up again. And I didn't. I just figured out myself what happened and I was right. After Blake died everything went back to normal after a while. I never saw or heard from Todd until a few months ago when he needed a place to stay and demanded money. I was so afraid of him and his threats that I didn't dare tell anyone."

"Well, I hope this will soon all be over for you. We will get Todd and when he is behind bars you will safe. Miss Ellie, we need to go, I have a doctor's appointment this afternoon, and I hope to get this harness off. I'll be back to see you again real soon. In the meantime, please do not blame yourself for any of this. It was not your fault. Okay?"

"I know, but it is still hard. Please come back again soon, I feel better after I have talked to you. I have no one else I can talk to. It was nice meeting you Mr. Weathers, you have a pretty special daughter here. I wish my daughter was like Brenda."

"Thank you, yes we think she is pretty special too. She's a good friend to have, you remember that. Brenda is here for you. It has been my pleasure to meet you as well. You take care now."

Just as we got in the car my cell phone rang. "Hey, Brenda. I got the report for you and you are not going to believe this. I thought I would bring it over. Are you home?"

"We are on our way home, we've been at the hospital visiting Sam. Why don't you come by for lunch and show me what you have?"

Vicki Eide

"I'm on my way."

I got busy getting lunch ready and Dad took Spook for a walk. When Willy got to my house we immediately spread the papers out on the table. "Look at this, Dawson and Johnson both were on the Goodman case. That could very easily explain why Dawson wanted you off this case, Brenda. He knows how good you are, how thorough you are and I bet he was afraid you would eventually put this together. He has set you up through this whole thing hoping he could make his accusations stick and this would all go away. I want you to take your cell phone in and have all of those anonymous calls you received traced. You did save them didn't you?"

"Yes, I did. I will go out and get another cell phone so I can keep my number. Do you think Dawson could have been the one making those calls? Maybe we shouldn't say anything about this for awhile." We went through the file with a fine tooth comb and couldn't really find out much wrong with it, except it was too short and just ended abruptly. "I wonder if Blake Compton paid Dawson to keep this under wraps, but Johnson was on the case too. This will be very difficult to trace this many years later. But I wouldn't put it past him."

"Brenda, anything is possible with Dawson. This explains his behavior from the get-go with this case. Plus, he has had Johnson under his thumb for years, he had to do something to keep him hushed. Getting the phone calls traced will certainly be a start. Take it in as soon as you can Brenda. Let's go over that report again, Gordon, would you join us, three sets of eyes are better than two?"

"Sure, I'll take a look. Well, the first thing I see is that these are copies, reports are always filed in their original form and the page numbers are gone. Looks like they could've been whitened out. See that tiny little dot up there, looks like to me the white out didn't get it all. This report has been altered. That is my opinion." Dad said and stepped back. Willy and I looked at each other and simultaneously said, "Oh my God!"

"I was looking at the contents and didn't even see the obvious. Dad, you are our 'hero'."

We ate lunch and continued to talk it all over and agreed my phone calls traced was next. Depending on the results, which we were so positive what they would be, we would put every thing together and then go directly to the Sheriff and by-pass the Chief.

"So many pieces were coming together now, like when I questioned Johnson for giving out my cell number that he claimed was a woman. I now don't believe that even occurred, that was just a cover up. The fact that Dawson kept trying to put Johnson in charge was only his means of taking control and getting another quick closure.'

I looked at the clock, "Hey guys, I have an hour to get to the doctor. We better wrap this up. I will get another cell this afternoon and turn mine in for a trace. Willy, thank you so much for your help. I think we have just nailed Dawson. Dad, I can't even believe how quickly you picked up on the flaw in that report. Guess I shouldn't be so surprised, that's what experience and expertise has over us amateurs."

"You are so right, Brenda. Gordon you just saved us a whole bunch of time. Thank you so much. So I will wait to hear from you this afternoon or whenever you get the results back on those calls. I need to get going as well. See ya later."

CHAPTER 89

My doctor's appointment was everything I had hoped for. He removed my harness, checked the mobility of my shoulder, which was not exactly where he wanted it to be a this point, but ordered to continue with physical therapy more consistently than I had been. I promised to do so. Other than that everything was healing pretty well and I should have full use within a few months. He did okay me to drive as long as I had an automatic shift rather than a clutch shift. I was good there. I left his office on a high.

Our next stop was to pick up a new cell phone and turn mine in for tracing calls. By now it was 3:30. I so wanted to see Nellie Goodman, but I wasn't sure if I should call her on such short notice. I really wanted one of her children to be there. I felt she needed the support and comfort of family. I went ahead and called her.

When she answered, "Nellie, this is Brenda Weathers. How are you doing today?"

"My what a surprise Brenda. I am doing quite well, thank you for asking. What can I do for you? Are you coming by for cocktail hour?"

"Well, I would like to do that. But I was wondering if we could do this sometime when your daughter was there. Didn't you tell me you had a daughter that lives not too far from you? I would like to meet her."

"Is there something wrong? Why would you want my daughter here? Has something happened?"

"No, no, Nellie nothings wrong. I need to talk to you and I would like your daughter to be there. Nothing you need to worry about, I enjoyed our cocktail hour, I would like to see you again."

"So, did you want to come by now or some other day?"

"That is up to you Nellie, you tell me."

"Well, let me call Sally Anne and see if she is busy and come by after work and I will give you a call back. If she can't, will another day be okay?"

"Of course it will. I will give you my cell number and wait for you to call."

"You got it my dear, talk to you soon."

"I really kind of hope we can meet another day, I'm not sure I'm quite up to this today. I am dreading telling her about her husband." I said to Dad.

My phone rang and when I answered it was Susanne. "Sergeant, this is Susanne and I wanted to let you know I will be coming in tomorrow afternoon. Mother called me and I told her I was coming, but I didn't think to get her telephone number or where she is staying. I understand you and her doctor are the only two that know where she is. I guess I need that information from you?"

"Of course, Susanne. I am so glad you are coming out. She really needs you desperately right now. What time are you coming in and I will be there to pick you up?"

"That won't be necessary, Mike is coming with me. Maria is staying with the children. Mike rented a car and my plan is to go to Mother's house. After we get settled in we will go up to see her. I do want to meet with you, though."

"This is great news." I gave her the phone number and told her how to get to the facility where Miss Ellie was staying. "Susanne, I need to ask you about Clinton, what has happened there?"

"Clinton didn't make it. He had so many injuries and didn't survive the last surgery. He passed away about a week after you and the detective had been to see me."

"Susanne, I am so sorry. How are you and the kids doing?"

"I am doing okay, the kids are having a tougher time of it because they don't know the details of it all. I hope to keep that from them for awhile. They sent Clinton's body home, but we had a very small private service. Mike has been wonderful to me and the kids, which has made it much easier for us all."

"I have another call coming in, give me a call when you get here and settled in. Got to run."

The call was from Nellie, "Hello Brenda dear. I just talked to Sally Anne and she reminded me she was stopping by to bring me a few groceries. She will be here about 4:30, will that be all right for you?"

"That will be just fine, Nellie. I'll see you then."

"Shit! I guess I am going to Nellie's at 4:30."

"Let's go home, you can go over there and I will start dinner. How's that sound?" Dad asked.

"Perfect."

CHAPTER 90

It felt a little strange driving but I was doing just fine. As I drove by Miss Ellie's I slowed down and stopped in front of her driveway. My what a turn of events since that May 1st when I was so innocently admiring the beauty and the view of the Compton house. So much had happened and we still weren't done.

I was just pulling away and caught a glimpse of a light in an upstairs window. I stopped abruptly and watched, but I didn't see it again, then it appeared in a downstairs window. It was a flashlight and someone was in the house. I immediately called Willy, when he answered I told him to get here ASAP and I was calling SWAT code three.

I parked the car up the road away and repeated my path of May 1st through the trees to the back of the house. The difference this time was I had my weapon drawn and was far more prepared. I circled the back of the house and didn't see a vehicle, but it could have been in the garage.

I put my phone on vibrate, the last thing I needed was the ringing. I stayed my distance and hid in the trees where I had perfect vision of the back door from the house and the garage side door.

Willy called for my position and told me to stay put. He had parked his patrol car down the road from mine. He and Matt Scott were making their way through the trees. When he joined me he said SWAT was right behind him and we were to hold our position until they were in theirs. I hated this part, I wanted to get in there and see if this was Thompson which I was sure it was, who else could it be?

I could see SWAT making their moves through the trees and circling the house. I started moving closer as Willy and Matt followed. The back door to the house opened and someone walked out with a small box in his hands and walked across to the side garage door. He set the box down and paused a moment and looked around as if he had spotted something and then went on inside. I gave the signal to move in and we started running to the wall of the garage. Three of the SWAT team went in the garage and up the stairs, I heard the demand, "Police, come out with your hands up." Then an exchange of fire.

"Oh God! I want this guy alive." I said to Willy.

The silence was deafening and anticipation was even worse.

Only two SWAT officers came downstairs. As they walked towards me,

"Sergeant Weathers, you better call 911 for an ambulance, I believe Todd Thompson is in need of medical attention."

I turned to Willy with a big smile, extended my arms up and we hit hands as I yelled, "YES! WE GOT HIM!"

EPILOGUE

Sam was released from the hospital a few days later and was recuperating very nicely at home.

Willy and I were able to prove Captain Dawson and Stan Johnson's involvement. Dawson was sentenced to ten years for blackmail, withholding information from the Harold Goodman accident and harboring a fugitive. Johnson was sentenced to five years for withholding information on the Goodman case. Paul Stearns was sentence to fifteen years for harboring a fugitive, twenty five counts of fraud with ladies from the church and mismanaging church funds. Todd Thompson was sentenced to life without parole and charged with Harold Goodman's murder, three attempts of murder on Miss Ellie, Sam and I.

Susanne and Miss Ellie patched up their relationship and Miss Ellie invited her and the children to move in with her for as long as she lived. Mike was in the process of settling up his life in Florida and then would be joining them.

Daryl did make a short visit out to see his mother and sister and confirmed Miss Ellie's Will was in order. At least Stearns had not gotten to her. Daryl also convinced the court Miss Ellie should not be charged with withholding information, considering the whole scenario of the case, they agreed.

As for me, I took a six months leave of absence. Just kicking back taking time for me and Spook. We have been rather busy running back and forth to help Sam on occasion and getting acquainted with the kids. We only have until June 1ˢᵗ of next year to get all the plans ready for the wedding. Trying to keep it simple won't be easy.